"*Sleeping Over* is a snappy tale of love lost, gained, revamped, re-hashed, and true friendship through thick and thin . . . a remark-able chick lit novel . . . Don't let this entertaining tale pass you by."

—*Romance Reviews Today*

"Fans of relationship dramas will appreciate this fine, character-driven tale."

—*The Best Reviews*

"*Sleeping Over* will have you laughing, crying, and planning your next girls' night out. This is the first novel I have read by Stacey Bal-lis, but I guarantee it won't be the last!" —*Romance Reader at Heart*

"Ballis presents a refreshingly realistic approach to relationships and the things that test (and often break) them. Ballis's sophomore effort will please readers who want something more than fairy-tale romance."

—*Booklist*

"The characters were real, unique, and quirky, and each had their own situations to work out and emotional issues to overcome. Each woman's story drew me in and made me want to keep reading."

—*Chick Lit Books*

"This is one of the most entertaining chick lit novels I've read in a long time! In short, this engaging story delivers everything you ask from a great read: it makes you laugh, it makes you cry, it makes you *feel*. *Sleeping Over* gets my highest recommendation."

—*Romance Divas*

"Four stars. Ms. Ballis has written an excellent story of love and friendship between five life-long friends, this is one author we need to hear from again." —*The Romance Reader's Connection*

"Not your average chick-lit novel. Four Stars." —*A Romance Review*

continued . . .

PRAISE FOR
INAPPROPRIATE MEN

"An insightful and hilarious journey into the life and mind of Chicagoan Sidney Stein." —*Today's Chicago Woman*

"This is the ultimate read for women everywhere . . ." —Flare.com

"Ballis's debut is a witty tale of a thirtysomething who unexpectedly has to start the search for love all over again." —*Booklist*

"Stacey Ballis's debut novel is a funny, smart book about love, heartbreak, and all the experiences in between." —Chatelaine.com
(also named *Inappropriate Men* one of their Seven Sizzling Beach Reads for 2004)

"Without compromising the intelligence of her readers, Ballis delivers an inspiring message of female empowerment and body image acceptance in her fun, sexy debut novel."
—*Inside Lincoln Park*

"Cheekily comic . . . Sidney Stein is a heroine to cheer lustily for, because that is how she lives her life: in grand style, and refusing to settle." —*Bookpage*

"*Inappropriate Men* is wickedly funny, fresh, and real."
—*Curvy Novels*

"Without a doubt, *Inappropriate Men* is one of the best books of 2004. Stacey Ballis has a way with words. Effortlessly, she makes them exciting and pulls the reader into the life of one of the most engaging characters ever created, Sidney Stein." —*A Romance Review*

"For an insider's look at dating and relationships, with all the laughs and wit you could want, *Inappropriate Men* by Stacey Ballis is a wonderful choice for your reading pleasure."
—*Romance Reviews Today*

ROOM FOR IMPROVEMENT

STACEY BALLIS

BERKLEY BOOKS, NEW YORK

THE BERKLEY PUBLISHING GROUP
Published by the Penguin Group
Penguin Group (USA) Inc.
375 Hudson Street, New York, New York 10014, USA
Penguin Group (Canada), 90 Eglinton Avenue East, Suite 700, Toronto, Ontario M4P 2Y3, Canada
(a division of Pearson Penguin Canada Inc.)
Penguin Books Ltd., 80 Strand, London WC2R 0RL, England
Penguin Group Ireland, 25 St. Stephen's Green, Dublin 2, Ireland (a division of Penguin Books Ltd.)
Penguin Group (Australia), 250 Camberwell Road, Camberwell, Victoria 3124, Australia
(a division of Pearson Australia Group Pty. Ltd.)
Penguin Books India Pvt. Ltd., 11 Community Centre, Panchsheel Park, New Delhi—110 017, India
Penguin Group (NZ), Cnr. Airborne and Rosedale Roads, Albany, Auckland 1310, New Zealand
(a division of Pearson New Zealand Ltd.)
Penguin Books (South Africa) (Pty.) Ltd., 24 Sturdee Avenue, Rosebank, Johannesburg 2196,
South Africa

Penguin Books Ltd., Registered Offices: 80 Strand, London WC2R 0RL, England

This book is an original publication of The Berkley Publishing Group.

This is a work of fiction. Names, characters, places, and incidents either are the product of the author's imagination or are used fictitiously, and any resemblance to actual persons, living or dead, business establishments, events, or locales is entirely coincidental. The publisher does not have any control over and does not assume any responsibility for author or third-party websites or their content.

Copyright © 2006 by Stacey Ballis.
Cover design by Rita Frangie.
Cover photos: "Woman Looking at Blueprints in Room, Rear View" by Stephen Swintek / Getty Images.
"Portrait of Young Man Positioning Artwork on Wall" by Hill Street Studios / Getty Images.
Text design by Kristin del Rosario.

PRINTING HISTORY
Berkley trade paperback edition / June 2006

Library of Congress Cataloging-in-Publication Data

Ballis, Stacey.
    Room for improvement / Stacey Ballis.
        p. cm.
    ISBN 0-425-20982-2
    1. Women interior decorators—Fiction. 2. Chicago (Ill.)—Fiction. 3. Reality television
programs—Fiction. I. Title.

PS3602.A624R66 2006
813'.6—dc22
                                                        2006041780

PRINTED IN THE UNITED STATES OF AMERICA

10 9 8 7 6 5 4 3 2 1

This book is dedicated with love to my grandmother,

HARRIET "JONNIE" BALLIS

*Whose adventures in decorating have been
inspiring me my whole life.*

Now where did I put that can of spray paint?

This book is dedicated to the memory
of an extraordinary woman,

CINDY BANDLE

Who was my gentlest of readers,
who lent me her favorite writers
and took the time to read mine,
who always bought the perfect gifts,
who always winked at the right moment,
who was the consummate hostess, colleague, and friend.
I miss you very much.
Opening nights are not the same.

acknowledgments

There are always many people to thank, and very little room to thank them in. And since friends and family are about the only people who ever read these things, and you all know who you are, I'm just going to stop with the actual naming and say I love you, and if you didn't know that without reading the acknowledgments page, then you aren't paying attention. (Special welcome to my new goddaughter Charlotte "Charley" Boultinghouse, who is the most perfect pink confection ever. You may not read this book until you are twenty-one.)

The people who always get the actual name recognition are Mom and Dad, 'cause they are the coolest, and they buy the most books anyway, so they should get their names in them . . . STEPHEN AND ELIZABETH BALLIS, so there. (Actually, based on sales alone, I should try and figure out how to put their names on about every page . . .) My sister, Deborah Ballis, because she is my not-so-gentle reader and always tells me the truth, and because she would probably smack me in the forehead if I didn't put her name here. My grandmother, Jonnie Ballis, Queen of Kvelling, which she does beautifully, thanks for always facing my books! My ridiculously fabulous agent, Scott Mendel, who takes such good care of me. My editor, Christine Zika, for her faith and good humor. The entire Penguin family for letting me be a teeny tiny little fishlet in your very lovely pond. Hans and Gabe for keeping my heart rate up, and Marcel for keeping me company.

I would like to stop being flip for a moment to truly thank BBC NYC Productions and TLC for their support of my research for this book. And my entire adopted family from *While You Were Out*, with special mention for: Sara Kozak, series producer and the perfect gal pal and partner in crime; Chayse Dacoda, designer and inspiration; Nadia Geller, designer and hostess of fabulous barbecue; the most skilled carpentry team ever to don a pair of muscle shirts, Andrew Dan-Jumbo and Jason Cameron; director Chris Perera, for being so clear about your process and smart about what makes good TV, even if you can't remember the number 287; the most amazing and generous crew, whose work is tireless and spirit generous; and host Evan Farmer, who is just as sweet as he appears to be on TV.

Other miscellaneous thanks: My community of fellow writers for their support and encouragement, especially Jennifer, Laura, Sarah, Lynda, Cara, Liz, and Johanna. My family away from home at The Goodman Theatre. The good people of Veuve Cliquot for making those tasty bubbles. The PUMA company for all the cute shoes. The Swedish people who invented the little pink fish.

Now for goodness' sake, read the book already, it's much more entertaining than this. But I do hope you've stopped by the dedication pages first . . .

prologue

swap/meet

I'm on all fours, on a rug of questionable cleanliness, fumbling in the dark for my boots.

"Lila?" A sleepy voice mumbles from the bed above me.

Sigh. My name is actually Lily. He screwed it up the first time he called me. Then I called him Don. His name is Ron. In the course of one brief conversation, it became our little "thing," the alternative names. One should never have a cutesy "thing" with a relative stranger. Then again, one should also probably not sleep with a relative stranger on the first date.

"Shhh," I say. "Go back to sleep. I didn't mean to wake you, I just have to get home."

There is the rustling of sheets. The creaking of a bed frame. A shadowy figure peers over the side of the bed. Moderately handsome generic face, rumpled dark hair, broad, if somewhat sloping shoulders.

"C'mon," he says, reaching a hand out to me and smiling in the dark. "Come back to bed."

I pat his hand. The schmuck. "You're sweet, but I have a big day today, and I've got to get some rest and take care of stuff at home. I'll call you later."

"Will you be all right getting home?" He makes a weak effort to rise. Having found my boots, I stand up and lean over the bed. I push him back into the pillows and kiss him on the forehead, pretending to be fine.

"It's no big deal, I'll grab a cab. Go back to sleep, it's very late."

"Or very early." He puts a hand on the side of my face and pulls me down for a deep kiss. "Okay, get home safe, I'll talk to you later."

"Sure thing, Tiger," I reply. He's snoring before I get to the bedroom door. Fucker. He could have at least offered to come downstairs and be sure I got into a cab.

His living room, in the very pale predawn light, is a total disaster. Clothes, books, boxes—I can't believe anyone can live in such chaos. It's disgusting. I have to sit on a pile of old newspapers to pull on my boots. Very classy.

As quietly as possible, I tiptoe down the narrow hallway and into the bathroom. The fluorescent light is harsh, but I don't look too bad, considering.

My brown curls, which earlier this evening had been a fetching corona around my heart-shaped face, are now a fuzzy sort of shrubbery. I run the water, splash some onto my head, and twist my hair into a makeshift bun. A bit of moistened toilet paper removes the minor mascara smudging from under my gray-blue eyes. Looking at the less than pristine toilet in a who-knows-when-it-was-cleaned-last bachelor bathroom makes me think that I can wait until I get home to pee. I pop in a Listerine breath sheet, put on some lip balm, and turn out the light.

There's a cab passing by just as I get outside. I put two fingers in my mouth and whistle for it, a trick my Uncle Eli taught me. It stops, reverses, and I get in.

"Eleven-twenty-two Dearborn, please."

I lean back into the vinyl seat, replaying the evening in my head. A blind date. Why do I ever say yes to blind dates? They are notoriously awful. Except this one wasn't. Until it was.

About a month ago I'd met up with my best friends Hillary and Naomi after they got off of work for cocktails at Thirsty Mc-Carthy's. One martini became two, then this guy Dave that Hillary knows from her law firm showed up. The next day Hillary calls me to say that Dave wants to fix me up with a buddy of his who works at a packaging plant or something. She hopes it's okay that she gave him my number.

He calls about three weeks later. I'd practically forgotten about him. We do the whole screw-up-the-names thing in the first thirty seconds. It makes us laugh and breaks the tension. I don't ask why he took so long to actually call. We talk on the phone for almost an hour. He's smart, and funny, and when he asks me to dinner, I say yes. Hillary is very excited that I'm going out with Package Boy. Hillary is big on labels. She and Naomi even go shopping with me, since it's been ages since I needed a great first-date outfit.

Tonight, I was full of hope and possibility. Which is a really bad thing to be full of on a first date. And what is worse, things were good. Mostly. He picked me up. Reasonably good-looking, in a nebbish sort of Zach Braff kind of way. He took me to Smoke Daddy, a fun barbecue place, explaining that he tends to be a messy eater in general, but that he thought I wouldn't notice if the food was messy to begin with. Conversation was easy and light, and in spite of the occasional feeling from our conversation that he is a guy used to getting what he wants a large percentage of the time, I was having fun. So when he suggested dessert and drinks at Sugar, a hip bar that serves sweets and cocktails, I said yes. And when the chocolate martinis started flowing, so did the mutual flirting. We both got bold. We both got a little tipsy. We decided to leave the car and share a cab.

I meant to go straight home; after all, I really do have a very big day, a very important meeting. But Package Boy turned out to be a really good kisser, and then the cab took us to his house instead of mine, and before I knew it, I was actually using the just-in-case condom I always stash in my purse. And since we're being confessional, Package Boy took on a whole new meaning once the jeans came off.

I'm not usually such a slut.

In fact, until about four months ago I was happily, boringly monogamous (rhymes with monotonous) with my then-boyfriend of eight months, Josh. Then Josh decided he needed "space," and I've been avoiding the dating scene ever since.

The sex with Ron wasn't too bad for a first time, not fireworks, but competent and with potential. And it was really nice to snuggle up with someone. I tried not to wonder when the last time was that he might have washed his linens. He held me close. He kissed the top of my head. And then he whispered, "If I'd have known it was going to be this great a first date, I'd have called sooner!" He chuckles to himself and pulls me closer.

Oh. My. God. I have broken the cardinal rule of dating. Do not, under any circumstances, sleep with a guy on a first date unless you have no intention of an actual relationship. No good relationship ever blossomed out of a semidrunken first-date sex-fest. And now he thinks I'm "one of those girls." Because tonight, I was "one of those girls." And what is worse, I just slept with a guy who would not only think that I'm "one of those girls" (for real as opposed to just tonight), but who had the audacity and poor taste to point it out to me while I am naked.

I feel Ron relax against me, and suddenly he chuckles and mumbles, "Dave owes me fifty dollars," and within seconds he is breathing deeply with a slight wheeze. I am mortified. Dave owes him fifty dollars? What the hell is that? Did he make some bet with Dave that he could get me into bed on the first date? Why would I let myself sleep with this guy? I wasn't THAT drunk, just a little tipsy. And I like him. Liked him. But after the "great first date" jibe and now the fact that I was apparently the source of some wager that he's now won, I just can't relax. Maybe he didn't mean it the way it sounded. Maybe he thought he was being cute. Maybe he just meant that it was a fun date and wasn't referencing the sex per se. Maybe he was just tired and Dave owes him fifty dollars for some sports bet.

Regardless, I can't get it out of my head, and the thought of facing him in his grim and filthy apartment when he gives me the awkward "see you around sometime" speech, not guaranteeing another date, but leaving him room for a future booty-call, it is too much to even consider on a day that should be golden. Hence the four AM sneak.

The cab pulls up to my building, rousing me from my reveries. I greet the night doorman and head upstairs. My apartment, a great little two-bedroom condo I bought last year, is calm, cool, and clean. I drop my purse on the kitchen island, sit on the ottoman to pull off my boots, and shimmy out of my skirt and tights on my way to the bathroom. I pee for at least forty-six minutes, brush my teeth, pull off my sweater and bra, and get into my delicious bed, naked.

Lily's Rule #32: There is no point in spending a damned fortune on six hundred thread count sheets and then putting a nightgown between you and them.

The alarm goes off at nine, way too early for my liking, but despite the previous evening's adventures, I'm surprisingly awake. I've got an hour to shower, put on my only power suit, and get over to 1000 West Washington to have the meeting that may or may not totally change my life.

📺

"Lily Allen?" A tired-looking woman in a wrinkled, shapeless black dress looks at me expectantly. It is ten-twenty, and I've been waiting for over a half-hour.

I take a deep breath, rise from the extraordinarily uncomfortable folding chair, and follow her down a gray hallway. There's a muffled chattering coming from behind each door we pass, until we reach the last one. She knocks quietly and then opens it. A very small man with a three-day beard and unkempt hair gets up from behind the desk.

"Lily! Finally. Live and in person. How are you, darling?" The accent is central-casting entertainment-biz British. He comes over to greet me, and in spite of my being only five-feet-five-inches, and wearing low heels, I have to bend to receive the kiss on my cheek. The reek of alcohol is overwhelming.

"Mr. Brownmiller, a pleasure." I smile at him in my most winning, please-hire-me sort of way.

"Sit, darling, sit." He motions to the chair and returns behind the desk. "So, you know why you are here?"

"I hope I'm here to thank you for my new job." I have a business alter ego that I call upon in times of stress. She's a much better negotiator than I am and has far more confidence in my abilities than I do. I think of her as my inner superhero and she's in charge of all meetings.

"Of course, darling, of course, didn't they tell you over the phone? Yes, pumpkin, it's yours if you want it." He takes a deep swig out of a coffee cup that I can tell from here doesn't contain coffee and pulls a packet of nicotine gum out of his pocket.

"I'm very pleased, Mr. Brownmiller, it's a project I'm very excited about." HOLY SHIT! I actually GOT it! I hope my smile is calm, and that he can't hear my pounding heartbeat.

"Excellent, darling, excellent," he mumbles around the wad of gum. "I wanted to go over the details of the offer with you in person. And please, call me Paul. We're going to be working long hours together. Might as well be friendly." He is either winking at me or has some sort of spastic twitch in his left eye. I decide to ignore it.

"Terrific. Paul it is." The offer. For my DREAM JOB. Wait till the girls hear about it.

So here it is. I'm going to be one of two resident interior designers on what may very well be the next big thing in do-it-yourself television. They are *finally* doing an American version of *Swap/Meet*, which has been one of my TiVo BBC America staples for the past two years. The perfect combination of home improvement, personal makeover, and dating show. One single gal and one single guy swap homes for four days. Days One and Two, total decorating overhaul. The girl helps design an apartment to impress the ladies, and the guy helps design an apartment that won't scare off the fellas. Day Three is makeover day, new outfits, new hair, personal grooming tips. Day Four is the reveal . . . he invites all his single guyfriends and she invites all her single girlfriends, they meet at the new apartments to check them out, then the whole crew heads to a local club to meet each other and see if anyone clicks. At least once out of eight shows, the two contestants end up hooking up with each other, which is always the best. I can't get enough of it. Being an interior designer makes me particularly susceptible to do-it-yourself television addiction. I'm either vindicated that I could do so much better than the designers on the shows, or I get really cool ideas to borrow. Win-win.

Anyway, six weeks ago I got a call from a former client, Jane Madison, whose bedroom I turned from shabby chic into actual chic, telling me she had recommended me to her husband's golfing buddy Paul Brownmiller, who was producing some new show for Bravo. I was hesitant—after all, I've never had any ambition to be a television personality, but when I found out what the show was, there was no way to avoid getting excited. I met with four other producer types, went over my portfolio, offered references and my transcripts from Harrington College of Interior Design, did a screen test, the whole shebang. All the while trying to keep my head on my current projects: a bathroom remodel, a master bedroom redecorate, a kitchen redesign, and a closet reorganization. It seems most of my life is devoted to the re-ing of something or other. Including, if I'm being honest, myself, since I always seem to be repeating the same old mistakes with my relationships, which makes me think I should maybe reevaluate my desire to reproduce.

But whatever good sense I lack in my romantic life, I make up for it with decent business sense. The decision to hang out my own shingle after design school was slightly risky, but worth it and I've been supporting myself nicely through referrals for the

past six years. I'm going to have to think about how to manage
the business, since now I'll be needing two days a week on location when we are filming, plus shopping and production meetings. You know, since I'm going to be on TV.

I'm going to be on TV.

Holy career change, Batman!

Naomi and Hillary want to hook up to hear about my meeting, and
I tell them to just come over to my place. I stop at Sam's on my way
home to pick up some wine. They arrive together just after seven.
Hillary, all tall and angular and severe in her Armani-I'm-just-as-
badass-as-the-boys suit and sleek black bob, having been in incom-
prehensible legal negotiations all day. Naomi, wan and waifish with
her dishwater-blond pre-Raphaelite curls twisted up in a sloppy
bun, after a long afternoon doing art therapy with the patients at a
very exclusive downtown rehab facility.

They are my bestest friends. We met the first day of kinder-
garten at LaSalle Language Academy. I was building a house with
blocks. Hillary tried to take them away from me, and I cried.
Naomi hugged me and scolded Hillary, who grudgingly offered
to share them, and that was that. The Three Musketeers. Nine
years at LaSalle, suffering through French so that we could all
take the exchange program to Paris in eighth grade. Four years at
Lincoln Park High School, Hillary in the international baccalau-
reate program, Naomi and I both art majors.

We went our separate ways for college (me at Brandeis, Naomi at
Sarah Lawrence, Hillary at Cornell), but reconvened in Chicago after undergrad to pursue our careers (Hillary at U of C Law, Naomi
at DePaul for Social Work, and me at Harrington). We rented a big

apartment in Ukrainian Village and were roommates for three years. Then Hillary landed a fast-track associateship at a big law firm and moved downtown to be closer to work. Naomi and I found a smaller place in Wicker Park for a couple of years until she made two large announcements. The first being that she was gay, the second that she was in love and moving in with Toby, her secret girlfriend of six months. I found the moving out much harder to deal with than the lesbianism. But my business had been going pretty well, so I bought my first place, a large-ish studio in the West Loop.

When my folks split up two years ago, my dad decided to keep the Sarasota apartment and live there full-time and my mom sold the big house on Mohawk and moved into a small place in Deerfield to be near her brother Eli and his family. As I am an only child, and unmarried and childless at that, and since my Aunt Judy passed away fairly young of breast cancer, my mother has become a surrogate mother to my cousins and an adopted grandmother to their kids. She fills at least three afternoons a week baby-sitting, another playing tennis at Bannockburn with Uncle Eli, and the rest of her time hanging out with her suburban girlfriends. I think she was relieved to get out of the day-to-day hustle and bustle of the city.

But since she had no intention of giving up the cultural endeavors in her life, she suggested that I get a bigger apartment so that she could have a place to stay downtown when she came in for the theater or opera and offered to help boost my down payment in return for occasional housing. My studio had significantly increased in value and my business was doing well, so I sold it, took the check from Mom, and moved to the Gold Coast. When Naomi and Toby split up last year, Naomi crashed with me for a couple of months and liked being downtown so much that she rented a coach house on Elm. Being within ten minutes of each other has been a real treat.

I pour the wine; Naomi throws their coats in my little hall closet while Hillary uses the powder room.

"So," Naomi says when we are all settled on my couch. "What's the good word?"

"I got it," I say, trying not to grin too widely.

"That is so AWESOME!" says Hillary. "Congrats!"

"Oh, sweetie." Naomi reaches a hand over to squeeze mine. "I'm so proud, tell us everything."

I fill them in on the details of the deal and tell them that I will be meeting next week with the rest of the team to have our first production meeting. We'll be filming the first show in about a month, and the producers have already chosen the participants for the first four shows. We are scheduled to air twelve episodes as a summer replacement show on Wednesday nights, and if there's good response, they could pick us up for as many as thirty episodes for next season.

"That's just so cool!" Naomi may be even more excited than I am.

"Yeah, yeah, yeah. Great news," Hillary pipes in. "More importantly, how'd things end up with Ron?"

"Ron who?" I ask, coyly.

"Ron Schwartz." She looks at me expectantly. "Ron Schwartz from last night, my friend Dave's buddy."

I decide to play saucy. "Package Boy. I went home with him." Plus, I have to fess up, since Ron might tell Dave, who might tell Hillary.

"You little slut!" Hillary laughs at me. "Good for you, how was he? When are you seeing him again?"

"It was a lapse. He was fine. Took the edge off. I'm not seeing him again."

"Why not?" Naomi asks. "You liked him enough to sleep with him."

"He was nice, I think, since I was mostly drunk. But I have too much on my plate to think about a new boy right now." Way too much. And I'm too happy to think about confessing his little comments to them, not to mention that there are some sort of Vegas odds on my sluttiness, or my flight from his apartment, it just makes me feel stupid. I've decided to go with "casual woman of the world" attitude, and let the whole thing slide right off my back.

"Good for you, why settle down now?" Hillary jumps in. "You're about to be famous. Your range of prospects could get much swankier."

"I thought he sounded like a good guy, Hil." Naomi shakes her head. "A relationship might be a stabilizing influence as Lily begins this new adventure."

"Oh, *please*." Hillary smacks herself on the forehead. "Relationship nothing, she had a one-night stand. A fling. In our world, that is not automatically a prelude to a commitment ceremony. Please don't make me tell the U-Haul joke again, Mimi." Hillary is the only person Naomi lets call her Mimi. And the only straight person that Naomi will let tell lesbian stereotype jokes in her presence. I've always sort of thought that Naomi might have been in love with Hillary at one point or another, but maybe that's just my imagination.

"Hello? Ladies?" I interrupt before they really get going. "Can we please pay some attention to the topic of real importance? I'm going to be on television!"

"Good lord, you're a frigging diva already!" Hillary raises her glass to me. "May it be the next 'While You Were Out Trading Your Extreme Home Spaces with Queer Guys Who Know What Not To Wear'!"

"Much success, sweetie." Naomi smiles at me.

"Now that's more like it!" I grin at my friends.

Clink.

"Hey, Mom, it's me." I'd already left a message for my dad, who was probably on the golf course when I called, so it's time to check in with Mom.

"Hello, sweetheart, how are you?"

"I'm fine, how are you?"

"I'm doing fine, thanks for asking."

I love my mom. It is very important that I say that a lot, because as much as I love her, she drives me slightly batty. We just don't seem to see eye to eye on many things, and we're both too polite to actually bother to argue about stuff, so we've found that limiting our conversations to mostly mundane topics is the way to go. Most of the time we sound like we are making slightly awkward small talk at an office party. It's fine when she stays with me, we can talk about whatever she is in town to see, whether she should give up any of her subscriptions, and the latest adventures of my miniature cousins.

"I got the job."

"Really? Oh, honey, that's fantastic, I'm very proud of you. Wonderful news, and everyone will be so excited for you. Guess what Ethan said this morning?" Ethan being my cousin Ruth's oldest, a four-year-old hellion with a biting habit, and my mother's favorite.

"I dunno, Mom, what?" Her seeming lack of interest is not

really lack of interest, but a fear that if she asks me the wrong question it will come across as judgmental, and I will get defensive, and things will be uncomfortable. So she kvells for exactly four seconds and then changes the topic so that I will only offer what information is of interest to me. I'm so used to the way we communicate that I no longer take any sort of offense.

"He was looking through my wallet and saw the picture I have of you and he asked, 'Whose Mommy is that?' Isn't that funny?"

This would be a good time to point out that my mother loved Josh and had pretty much chalked up our marriage and eventual children as a done deal. When Josh broke up with me, she never explicitly stated that it was my fault, but she didn't NOT imply it either. And while my mother would never in a million years ask when she could expect grandchildren from me, she has no problem relating stories like this one. On the surface, very cute, the myopic vision of a four-year-old, in whose limited world every adult woman is somebody's Mommy. Underneath, a not so subtle, almost subconscious, substantiation that my suburban (read: married) cousins are sublime, and that my lifestyle is substandard.

"That's hilarious, Mom." Time for a return-to-subject segue. "So I have my first production meeting for the show in a couple of days."

"How wonderful, sweetie, I hope it is just a blast and that you'll have every success." And I know she means it, so this is the quote I will choose to remember from the conversation.

episode #1

Jake and Jill

Bravo *Wednesday June 7* 8PM–9PM

SWAP/MEET Pilot

The new American version of the popular BBC reality series by the same name takes two singles, their dreary apartments and lackluster selves, and makes them all appealing to the opposite sex. Their single friends get to weigh in on the transformations of home and hairdo, and see if they can score dates at the wrap party. Former Miss Louisiana Birdie Truesdell hosts the festivities.

"Hey there, dollface." One of the handsomest men I've ever seen is speaking. Presumably to someone else. I turn around and look behind me.

"I'm talking to you, darlin'. I'm Jake. Please tell me you're Ashleigh." He rises from the chair to a towering height, all shoulders and piercing blue eyes, and extends a hand. I shake it, feeling the rough calluses and strong grip. He smiles a twisted sort of smirk, and I can see that there is the smallest bit of crookedness to his front teeth, utterly charming. The kind of smile that makes me acutely aware of the current size of my ass, hovering these days somewhere between "Baby Got Back" and "Baby Got Backhoe."

I'm not usually too self-conscious about it. I'm built like a Russian peasant, and as long as I'm somewhere between a size 12 and 14, I come off as plump, curvy, and solid. But I'm wearing the size 14 black trousers today, a little tighter than usual, and suddenly wishing I hadn't eaten and drunk so much in the past week of celebrating the new job. I extend my hand to grip his.

"Lily. Allen. Lily Allen." I hope I'm not staring.

He runs a hand over the two-day scruff of beard on an impossibly square chin. "Pity. I was hoping you were my new mistress. Still, a pleasure to make your acquaintance, Lily Allen."

"Is that so?" Mistress? Is this guy for real?

"Yep. But I'll still let you order me around if you want. As long as you promise to spank me now and again to keep me in line. I can be something of a naughty boy." He winks conspiratorially, clearly unaware that the brief smoldering attraction that had been building in my gut and parts southerly had just been instantly and thoroughly doused.

From that simple exchange a couple of things became patently clear to me. One, he knows exactly how good-looking he is and uses it with ease. Two, he is accustomed to women fawning all over him. Three, the next girl to walk into the room would get the same treatment.

"Well, Jack, if I have any heavy lifting for you, I'll be sure to let you know."

The smile leaves his face. "Jake. It's Jake Kersten. I'm one of the carpenters."

Lily's Rule #45: Nothing deflates a narcissist's ego better than calling them by the wrong name or forgetting that you have met them.

I called him Jack on purpose, and his reaction tells me that it was a smart move.

"Sorry, *Jake*. Well, I'm going to get some tea, excuse me." I leave him and head for the table across the room, which is laden with the makings of a continental breakfast. Other people start coming in, and introductions are flying at a furious pace. I surreptitiously refer to the cheat sheet I cribbed out of the information packet I got on my new colleagues.

"Hi, I'm Bryan and this is my partner, Joe. We're the fashion czars." Two small, wiry, platinum blond boys in their mid-thirties, with leather cuff watches and tight low-rider jeans, Bryan LeClerc and Jou (pronounced *Joe*, apparently) DuFresne would be handling the personal makeover section of the show. They could be brothers, and I make a mental note of the small freckle above Bryan's right eye to help ensure I don't accidentally get them confused.

"You must be Lily." A well-manicured hand is extended in my direction. "Ashleigh Benning. I'm the other designer. What an interesting satchel." I know of Ms. Benning by reputation. The first of her wealthy husbands had bankrolled her in a posh interior design business; rumor has it to keep her busy so he could pursue a series of young blond personal assistants. While she has a certain artistic eye, it is untrained, and she's had to rely on the social pressure of her intimate circle of acquaintances to keep the business going through three marriages, the last of which ended just a few months ago. I've been asked by more than one of her former clients to come re-tweak a room once she's finished with it. Usually the major pieces and color stories are quite good, but she has problems with layout and accessories, and some of the oddest window treatments I've ever seen. She is tall, coiffed and chilly, with perfectly highlighted ash blond hair, and I'm pretty sure that her face has been lifted at least once. Her clear disdain of my battered leather backpack, which I bought in a flea market in Florence, hasn't exactly endeared her to me on first impression.

Paul comes over to kiss me, smelling like a distillery. "Darling, hello, hello, come meet Birdie. Birdie, love, this is Lily." Eight feet of legs lead to a pink froth of dress small enough to have been purchased at the American Girl doll boutique, barely containing a truly awe-inspiring rack.

"Hey there, Lily, it is so very nice to meet you." Birdie Truesdell, the "hostess" of the show, was Miss Louisiana last year, and second runner-up for Miss America. Her blue eyes sparkle, the caps on her teeth are blindingly white, the cascade of strawberry blond waves a perfect contrast to porcelain skin, and the accent is like cream over warm peach cobbler. Couldn't you just spit? It's official. I'm going on a diet. I'm a short little roly-poly girl with frizzy hair who has no business being on television.

The smile beams as she continues to gush. "So you're one of the decorators. I bet that is just the neatest job. You must have had the cutest dollhouses growing up, din't choo?" Bless her heart. She giggles and tosses the hair, while Paul looks up at her adoringly, just about eye level with her gravity-defying breasts. If he isn't careful she might take out his eye with a nipple.

Before I can answer her, Paul whisks her away to meet someone else, and I turn to find a seat at the huge conference table. There is a man at one corner whom I haven't met yet, sitting quietly and looking over plans that I recognize as my own handiwork. He must be my carpenter, Curt Hinman. I take my tea and poppy seed bagel over and sit next to him.

"Hey, you must be Curt. I'm Lily." I extend my hand. He doesn't even look up at me.

"Your plans are okay, but it would be helpful if next time you could do a supplies breakdown for me, since I have to put together a materials list for the PA."

I'm a little taken aback. "Sorry, I didn't know, I just figured you could do it from my measurements."

"I'm not your assistant, I just do the build out." He is older, probably early forties, slightly balding, with heavy features. Even sitting down I can sense the power in his arms and shoulders.

"Well, I can get you a list later today, if you like . . ." Perfect for me to get off on the wrong foot with my carpenter.

"Don't bother, I already did it, just do it next time, okay?" He finally looks up at me, without even a hint of a smile.

"Will do, sorry again, I just didn't know." I smile at him in hopes of mending fences.

"No problem. And you have poppy seeds in your teeth."

"Um, thanks." Great. Not only am I an idiot, now I'm an idiot with poppy seeds in her teeth. Everything today is conspiring to make me feel as unattractive as possible.

Paul calls the meeting to order, and there are introductions around the table, directors, film crews, extra hands who won't be seen on camera: the assistant carpenters, seamstresses, location coordinators, and production assistants, nearly thirty-five people in all. We get debriefed on the first two participants, a slightly nerdy banking guy named Ken and a fourth-grade teacher named Jill.

The photos of the apartments, which I've already seen, are pretty stereotypical for this kind of show. His is messy, full of electronics, hers is girly pink and flowery. We do the design presentations, going for geek chic on his end and a more sophisticated city girl for her. Paul's assistant Ginny hands out the filming schedule, and the group is dismissed until the following week.

I'm given a corporate credit card for my allotted budget. I get $4500 to re-do the apartment, plus $500 for Curt's building supplies. I try to catch Curt again before he leaves, but Jake grabs me before I can get to him.

"So, wanna grab a coffee or something?" The emphasis is on the "something."

I shake the remnants of my tea at him. "Don't drink coffee."

"Tea then?" He reaches a hand over and starts rubbing my shoulder. "We should get to know each other, now that we are working together."

I shrug off the hand. "Actually, you and I will probably see very little of each other, since I'm working with Curt. Maybe you and Ashleigh should get to know each other." I point across the room, where she's standing with Jou and Bryan, and when Jake looks in that direction, I slip out the door.

📺

The filming is a blur. I have never worked so hard or been so exhausted in my life. After avoiding the intense catered breakfast buffet (three kinds of eggs and a vat of bacon, biscuits, muffins, yogurts, and fruit), and getting a lay of the land, the insanity begins. Whoever thinks that television isn't backbreaking labor has never done a reality shoot.

I'm assigned to work with Ken on fixing up Jill's apartment.

We encounter several problems. Firstly, Ken, who may in fact be a banking whiz kid, cannot actually do anything handy. We get the two rooms we are tackling, bedroom and living room, loaded out, and then take a break while the production assistants prep the space. We start the painting in the living room, a rich camel color I have chosen as a backdrop for chocolate and cream furniture with occasional pops of a peachy pink in accessories and one accent wall behind the fireplace. But Ken can't paint to save his life, or mine. Splotchy, streaky, drips everywhere, divots on the ceiling. We have to have the PA's come in and totally redo it after we film our segments.

The one requisite "art segment," which I'd envisioned as a fun project to create our own chandelier for the bedroom, turns into "Let's spend forty-five minutes finding the crystals that Ken has accidentally thrown onto the lawn." In all fairness, he got too close to the boom mike and his personal microphone pack squealed so loudly with feedback that it scared the bejesus out of him. The fact that he screamed like a girl and threw the box of crystals ten feet in the air is, I suppose, not really his fault.

video diary confession:

"Okay, so it's the middle of the afternoon of Day One, and things have been going a little wonky so far. Ken is a very nice guy, but as you have seen, he is sort of a disaster when it comes to helping out. I'm starting to get a little bit nervous about getting everything done, I mean, after all, my goal here is to do the highest possible quality work. I have no idea if tomorrow will go any better, but I do know it couldn't be any worse. Oops. My mother would tell me I just jinxed myself. Oh well, can't be helped now. Anyway, I've got to go make sure Ken hasn't broken anything else, so I'm going to sign off for now. Bye!"

We finished the chandelier just in time for lunch, an equally expansive spread of equally not-so-healthy food. I'm really going to have to be careful about my eating on the set or I'll really be the size of a truck in no time.

After lunch, I thought I had the perfect thing for Ken's one-on-one segment with Birdie, the two of them were supposed to put together a small bookshelf unit I had purchased at IKEA. Simple. Two sides, a top, a bottom, a back, three shelves. Just follow the clear instructions. But the electric combination of Birdie's slightly below-par intelligence, Ken's general ineptness, and the fact that he is staring so intently at Birdie's chest that Bob the director has to stop filming twice to get him to look up, it's an unmitigated disaster. They put every piece on either upside down or backwards, have to totally disassemble it twice, and nearly two hours later, the whole piece is a wobbly mess because they have stripped half of the screw holes. I feel so badly that I sneak out to Schaumburg to the IKEA after we wrap for the day, buy another one, and put it together myself at home in about fifteen minutes. First thing in the morning I swap it out while everyone else is eating Krispy Kreme donuts.

Day Two is no better. The seamstress sews the curtains with the liner fabric on the outside and the expensive decorator fabric on the back, so we have to totally do them over. On Curt's recommendation we decide to skip having Ken help with any of the carpentry, since Ken and power tools appears to be a potentially deadly scenario. The large window seat I designed for Curt to build for the bay window in the bedroom is beautifully made, but turns out to also be too big to fit through the door, so we have to cut it in half and reassemble it inside the room. Curt shoots daggers at me as if I purposely forgot to take measurements of the doorway just to annoy him.

Ken breaks a vase, a picture frame, and a large decorative bowl. I can only hope Ashleigh is padding his apartment and giving him rubber mats for flooring. But finally, it's done. I don't even take a couple of minutes to bask in the glow after we wrap, I just thank everyone and head home to a big glass of pinot noir and a hot bath.

I'm totally conked out until nearly noon the next day, but I meet Hillary and Naomi for a late lunch to fill them in on the first shoot, and then spend the afternoon getting some work done on my other projects. Thursday afternoon I get dressed and head over to Jill's to film the reveal segment.

"I'm so nervous," Jill whispers to me from behind her blindfold, as we stand outside her door awaiting our cue to go inside.

"Don't be, it looks great, I just hope you like it." I, too, am nervous. After all, if she hates it, I have to be a witness to her misery. "Besides, you look fabulous." And she does. Bryan has coordinated a very stylish outfit, adorable new haircut; Jill has gone from the little schoolteacher next door to urbane sophisticate.

"All right, now, darlings!" Paul yells out at us from down the hall.

"We're speeding," Bob calls out. "And action."

"Go on in," says the assistant director behind us.

I open the door. I lead Jill inside. The living room looks amazing, candles have been lit everywhere, paint has clearly been touched up, fresh flowers in all the right hues, the team has perked up everything wonderfully.

"Okay, Jill, go ahead," I say on cue.

Jill removes her blindfold. She gasps in delight and begins to jump up and down.

"I love it! I just love it!"

Whew!

I give Jill some of the highlights, and then take her down the hall into her bedroom. I've replaced her eighty-five shades of pink and rose with pale gray and lavender, with hits of eggplant, soft celery green, and silver accents. The chandelier sparkles over the bed, the mountain of pillows on the window seat beckon.

"OH MY GOD!!!!" Jill shrieks in delight. She hugs me so tightly I can barely breathe.

I'm grinning like an idiot. It's official. I love this job.

Jill and I sit and chat while they are setting up for her girl-friends to come check out her new digs before we head to the party. She tells me that she has had a great time, and that the best part was shopping with Bryan.

"Well," she says, blushing a little bit. "Almost the best part."

"Sounds like there is dish there," I say, prodding for gossip. (For which, I have to admit, I am a total whore.)

"You can't tell though. I don't want to get anyone fired." Sounds juicy.

"Of course, what happened?" I encourage her.

"I slept with Jake!" I can tell she has been dying to share this information.

Lily's Rule #54: Part of sleeping with the really really *hot guy has nothing to do with the guy himself. Gorgeous men are notoriously lousy in bed. It has to do with being able to tell someone, ANYONE, that you bagged him. That of all the people anywhere, he went home with you. We are no different than men in that respect, and any girl who says different is lying through her pretty little teeth.*

"You did? When?" I prod her along, although clearly, she needs very little nudging.

"He let me help him on a carpentry project on the first day and totally flirted with me, but I thought it was all for the cameras. But after we finished the apartment he offered to drop me off at the hotel, and then asked if I wanted to have a drink in the bar, and we did and before I knew it, I was inviting him up!"

Not likely. More likely he was inviting himself up and making you feel like it was your idea. "Wow. I guess it must have been great." Poor kid.

"It was all right." Suddenly little Jill doesn't seem quite so innocent. "I mean, you know guys like that. Not the end all be all. But this show is going to be a hit, and with his looks, he is going to be a star, and my friends are going to be GREEN with envy!" The evil twinkle in her eye makes me really like this girl.

"Good for you," I say. We are still laughing as her friends start to arrive.

We spend just about forty-five minutes getting footage of everyone's reaction to the apartment, to Jill's new wardrobe and haircut and then we're all loaded onto a charter bus that takes us to the Hard Rock Hotel, which is hosting the meet-and-greet party. Jill and Ken meet for the first time and are filmed conversing about the experience while all their friends mingle with cast and crew. A few numbers are given out, a couple catty comments are made, but more importantly, by the end of the party, Jill and Ken are seen quietly smooching in the corner. What a little minx she is!

Bingo. Got 'em.

"Hey there dollface, brought you a cocktail." The whisper in my ear from Jake is maddening. I think he's disgusting, self-absorbed, and a total waste of time, but no one seems to have notified my body, which responds to the whisper by going all tingly on me. Down girls. We don't like him.

I turn around and show him my half-full wineglass. "Already have one, thanks."

"C'mon, how about a real drink?" He wiggles a neon green concoction in a martini glass at me.

"I can't imagine what that is, but I'm fine with my wine, thank you. If you'll excuse me." I beat a hasty retreat to the other side of the room. Curt has his back to me, talking with some of the crew. I head in his direction.

"I mean, who doesn't measure the fucking door?" He is saying harshly as I arrive. The crew guys give him a shut-up-she's-right-behind-you look. He turns.

"I just wanted to say thanks for helping me get through my first show." Then I turn and leave before he can say anything. On my way out, I run into Bryan and Jou, who decide I need to come with them for the rest of the evening. We end up at Sidetrack, for comedy Thursday, which is just what I need: three hundred gay men drinking slushy fruit drinks and watching comedy video clips.

We close the bar and end up having a 3:00 AM breakfast at Melrose. Bryan and Jou are really funny and sweet, with just enough bitchy for spice. They have all kinds of gossip about Ashleigh playing the diva, about how stupid Birdie is, about which of the crew guys are hot and who is gay, about Paul's liver probably falling out before we finish filming the next episode. I find out that they have been together for eleven years. They make me promise to come over and check out their Roscoe Village apartment to see if there's anything to be done with it, and I readily agree. I get home just after 5:00 AM, ignore the blinking light on the answering machine, and crawl into bed, where I dream about room after room, all blank walls and open floors, and endless potential.

We Three Queens of Disorient Are

Naomi and Hillary meet me in the small locker room at HiFi to get ready for our workout. It's a gym that's solely for the use of personal trainers and their clients. The three of us hired Giorgio to tackle our cellulite as a team, in part to cut down on the exorbitant cost of one-on-one training, and in part to guarantee that we see each other at least two hours a week. We're all supposed to do some sort of extra cardio three additional days a week, which Naomi does religiously, I do occasionally, and Hillary does not at all.

We hit the treadmills to warm up for five minutes before Giorgio begins to lead us through our usual grueling hour of stretch bands, free weights, plastic steps, and endless push-ups and crunches. Giorgio is flipping gorgeous. Tall, sculpted muscles, dark wavy hair, strong jaw, and piercing greenish hazel eyes. He has the kind of bottom lip you want to suck on for about an hour. We all love and hate him, as you do with any good trainer. Plus he has become sort of a therapist for us, since he gets to hear all about

29

our various trials and tribulations, and is able to give us a male perspective on things when we ask for one.

"There are my girls. Are we ready to punish ourselves today?" Giorgio stations himself between my treadmill and Naomi's and grins at us like a wolf looking at a small herd of sheep.

"Wipe the smug look off your face, George. You punish us too hard and none of us will have the strength left to write your check." Hillary always calls him George. He is third generation Italian-American, and she likes to goad him about the traditional name. She also slept with him for about three weeks two years ago, which is how we came to acquire his services at a pretty bargain-basement rate. I think it isn't unlikely that he has been waiting all this time for a second shot at her. Hillary has that effect on guys.

"We're ready, Giorgio. Let's do it!" Naomi would be such a suck-up if she didn't mean it.

"Okay then, that's the attitude, let's get down to work!"

The four of us head down the hall to a small room where Giorgio has set up three plastic steps, three sets of workout bands, and three sets of dumbbells—five pounds for me and Naomi, eight pounds for Hillary who is naturally strong as an ox. We start on the steps, up and down, following Giorgio's easy rhythm, catching up as we go.

"So," Hillary asks, "you're feeling good about the new gig?"

I think about it for two steps. "I am, so far. I feel like I learned a lot on the first shoot, and people seem to be relatively cool. Plus, if it's a bust, I still have my business. I mean, it isn't like I've been hankering for a television career. When it stops being fun, I'll stop doing it."

Naomi adds a little hop to the top of her step, since just going up and down isn't quite enough to get her heart rate up. "And how is the business going, still steady?" she asks, not even out of breath.

"Still steady. I sat down with my financial guy, and we figured out that with the income from *Swap/Meet*, I can reduce my private client list by forty percent and still post a nice profit for the year, so I'm going to be getting somewhat less aggressive in soliciting new business until I figure out exactly how much of my time the show is going to take."

"Are you also anticipating a forty percent decrease in your social life?" Hillary smirks at me.

"I certainly hope not," I quip back.

"Good. I was very proud of your little fling. It was time you got back in the saddle after Josh." Hillary doesn't believe in celibacy. She also doesn't really believe in relationships. She has had only one serious boyfriend, a much older lawyer named Kip, of all things, who was on the other side of her first big case. She was only second chair, but he complimented her on her work, even though she and the partner she was supporting lost the trial. They dated for nearly two years before she broke up with him, and to this day she has never said anything about the breakup other than it was her decision, and that they wanted different things. That was three years ago.

"All right ladies, good start, now let's work the upper body!" Giorgio picks up his set of weights and begins demonstrating a series of movements.

Naomi, on the other hand, believes strongly in relationships and has been very melancholy since she and Toby split. This makes her even pushier when it comes to my lack of a dating life. "I still think he could be more than a fling!" she says excitedly, doing bicep curls with the dumbbells while marching in place.

"How on earth did we get on the subject of my social life?" I ask, picking up my own set of dumbbells and trying to follow Giorgio's moves.

"All work and no sex isn't good for you," Hillary says.

"We just don't want you to be lonely," Naomi adds.

"I thought I was going to use the TV gig to land a better quality of guy?" I reply.

"See that you do," Hillary says. "Hey, George, slow that shit down or I'm going to whack you in the throat with this here dumbbell."

We laugh at Giorgio's obvious consternation. "Come on, girls, we have to keep up the pace! Otherwise we aren't getting the full benefit of our time together!" His eyes plead with Hillary to be nice. "I almost forgot," he continues. "Fabio cut his hair!"

Fabio is our name for one of the other trainers. He looks a lot like the cartoon prince in *Shrek 2*. Tall and beefy, but in a way that appears as if he might deflate if you stuck him with a pin. His mane of blond hair was the reason for the moniker, and the fact that he never seemed to have actual clients, just wandered around the gym, lifting heavy things periodically with a bored expression and checking himself out in the mirror a great deal.

"No way!" Hillary says. "Won't he lose all his powers now?"

We laugh. Giorgio loves to keep us distracted with tales from the gym. We always know which trainers are sleeping together, which clients don't bathe, who's using steroids, and whose checks are bouncing. Plus we always get the Marc update.

Marc is a very hot young trainer, African-American, only twenty-four or so, and an amateur boxer. Ripped. With a quick wit and a wicked smile. He's a huge flirt, and we all have tiny crushes on him, even Naomi. He is just the kind of guy that makes you smile, the one who always notices a new outfit, shares my personal addiction to Pumas, and always compliments us to his clients. Plus, he is a real ladykiller, and he and Giorgio frequently go out together, so we can always hear about his escapades. It makes the sessions go by pretty quickly.

"It's pretty short, too; you might not recognize him," Giorgio says.

"I think we'd recognize his ego anywhere!" Naomi pipes in.

Hillary gives her a high five and collapses on the mat. We all lie down to do some abdominal work.

"How do your folks like the new project?" Naomi asks between crunches.

"Dad is fine, you know him. He finally called me back from his cell phone from the bar at the club to congratulate me, offered his usual plane ticket for a visit, didn't ask about Mom, and then got off the phone as quickly as possible."

"It's really weird how he checked out," Hillary says. "He always seemed reasonably involved when we were growing up."

"I dunno," I say, thinking about it. "He was there, but when I think back, he wasn't really THERE, you know? He worked all the time. I was always hanging out with you guys. We vacationed with the Kellers until they moved away, and by then I was in college." I let my legs flop back on the mat.

"He never really seemed terribly comfortable talking to us when we were over at your house," Naomi says. "I mean, he was plenty nice and all, but not, you know, at ease."

"At this point, I'm happy for him. All those years in the lab made him kind of awkward with normal people. He has his golf, and the condo, and enough retired science geek friends to keep him busy. And I think he may be seeing someone, or at least my mom does, but I don't have confirmation yet."

Dad was a neurobiologist specializing in myelin research at U of C. I was neither surprised nor really upset when he and Mom divorced, since they had always behaved like colleagues and not like actual married people.

Not like Hillary's and Naomi's folks. Hillary's parents are the original hippie lawyers, doing so much pro bono work that sometimes their electricity got shut off. They still smoke pot, still march in protests, and according to Hillary, still "get it on" with sickening regularity. They are forever trying to get Hillary to quit the firm and join their crusade. Luckily for Hillary, her older brother is taking care of that, having stopped following the Grateful Dead long enough to get a law degree, marry a willowy textile artist, and squeeze out two blond daughters named River Rain and Summer Snow. Hillary says it doesn't matter what you name those kids, nothing really goes with Ganderberg anyway.

Naomi had such a Donna Reed upbringing we used to tease her that she should be in black and white. Dad was a VP of marketing for Kraft International, Mom was a homemaker who did tons of volunteer work for the JUF and Children's Memorial Hospital and was on the Board of Trustees for the Lyric Opera. Naomi and her two younger sisters always got along, and the family used to have things like weekly game nights and they'd feed the homeless together on the holidays. They laugh a lot, and seem to all really like each other, and once a year they all take a huge vacation for two weeks, which they love, even though it sounds like a form of torture to those of us with normally dysfunctional families.

"George, I'm going to puke if you don't let me stop these fucking crunches." Hillary moans.

"C'mon, you can do it, just five more!" He encourages us. "Marc was just telling me the other day how great you were all looking, you don't want to let him down, do you?"

Sigh. He always knows how to get us.

Naomi sits up and begins to stretch. "What'd Mom say?"

"She said she was proud and then told me an adorable story about Ethan." I try not to be bitter in relating this.

"Still with the fucking grandchild crusade?" Hillary gasps. "Renee needs to get a grip. She should be so stoked for you."

"It's fine. I'm used to her." Which I am.

Giorgio stretches Hillary while Naomi stretches me.

"Is everyone good for brunch this week?" Naomi asks. Her folks have invited us to family brunch on Sunday. Every week the sisters take turns inviting guests and on the fourth week they are just immediate family. I know, sick, right?

"Are you kidding?" Hillary smacks Giorgio away and stands up. "If Barbara is making that blintz soufflé, I'm coming."

Naomi helps me up. "I'm in, too. No one makes a Bloody Mary like Mike."

"Good work today, ladies, good work. Let's try and get some cardio in this weekend, what do you say?" Giorgio walks with us back down the hall toward the main gym.

"Thanks, George, see you next week." Hillary dismisses him as we head for the locker room.

"Bye, Giorgio, thanks for a great workout!" Naomi yells over her shoulder.

Fabio, indeed shorn of his flowing locks, is standing in front of the large mirror doing curls with the biggest dumbbells in the universe. The three of us make meaningful eye contact as we pass him.

"Ladies, ladies, ladies." Marc crosses the room to greet us each with a kiss on the cheek. "Looking good, babes, looking good."

We all grin like idiots and head into the locker room.

In the shower, with the muffled sounds of Hillary and Naomi talking, I wash my hair vigorously and try not to think about my parents and their lack of interest in my new job. After all, my friends are excited, and I'm excited, and in the long run, it just doesn't matter what Mom and Dad think. Right?

when Barry met sally

Bravo *Wednesday June 14* 8PM–9PM

SWAP/MEET Barry and Sally

A recently divorced gent and a newly svelte girl step up to the plate for a fresh start. Highlights include a new fireplace mantel for him and a sexy new look for her. Designers Ashleigh Benning and Lily Allen perform decorating divinity while stylists Jou DuFresne and Bryan LeClerc are in charge of makeover magic.

"Can I sit with you?" Bryan asks, sidling into the open chair on my left at the production meeting.

"Of course." I lean over to receive the requisite kiss on my cheek. Across the room I see Jou looking in our direction, as he takes a seat next to Ashleigh on the opposite end of the table. "Bry, what's up with Jou?"

"We're taking a break," Bryan says coldly.

"Well, I can see that it would be hard to work together and

live together, probably best not to be attached at the hip twenty-four hours a day." Because, of course, I'm a very, *very* stupid girl.

"No, honey, we're taking a break from our *relationship*." Bryan sighs dramatically.

"Oh, Bryan, I'm so sorry. But you guys seemed fine when I was over last week, what happened?" They had invited me for a small dinner party, which, while not exactly a place to meet potential dates, was nevertheless a lot of fun. And they'd seemed as happy as ever. In the last few weeks we'd been hanging out a little bit, and I'd come to really enjoy their bantering company, not to mention the kicky new haircut and wardrobe additions they had finagled for me.

"Let's just say that he needs to get some priorities in order, and until he does, I'm not going to put up with him." He looks down the table at Jou and Ashleigh, their heads close together, whispering. Then he half-yells, "And SOME of us don't need to bring our POISON into the WORKPLACE!"

I jump, and everyone else in the room stops dead and begins to look extremely uncomfortable.

"Well, you've done a FANTASTIC job of keeping things PROFESSIONAL," Jou fires back. "Now EVERYONE is feeling MORTIFIED!"

"At least they can feel SOMETHING, unlike SOME people I know!" Bryan stands up.

Jou stands as well. "At least what THEY feel is EMOTION, and not some sad little LANDSCAPER'S ASS!"

"I NEVER DID!" Bryan pounds his little fist on the table.

"I FUCKING SAW YOU!" Jou throws his hands in the air.

Paul walks over to Jou and takes his arm. "Jou, darling, let's take a walk, hmmm? Get some fresh air, all right, love?"

"FINE!"

"Really, with the yelling, really?" I can hear my director, Bob, whisper to his assistant.

They leave together, and Bryan slumps down in his chair. I put my arm around him. All around us a low buzzing begins, as our colleagues begin mumbling opinions on the outburst.

"I didn't fuck around with that landscaper, you've got to believe that, Lily." Bryan's eyes are full of tears.

"Of course you didn't. I'm sure this whole thing is just a big misunderstanding." Why I'm saying this, I have no idea. I really don't know them that well, what sort of judge am I?

"Thank you, sweetums, it means a lot to me to have you in my corner." Bryan excuses himself to fetch a napkin and some more coffee.

In his corner? There are corners now?

Paul returns, sans Jou, which everyone pretends to ignore, and we get down to the latest episode. Barry is a late-thirty-something divorced CPA getting back into the dating scene, and Sally is an early-thirty-something who has recently lost over seventy-five pounds and is still hiding in oversized clothes. His apartment is very spartan, since his ex-wife kept the house and the furniture, and Sally's is entirely furnished with hand-me-downs and things found curbside. Design presentations are pretty straightforward: I'll do classic and traditional basics for him, and Ashleigh will be going for French country for her. Jou reenters the room in the middle of Ashleigh's presentation. I squeeze Bryan's hand, and he whispers that he is a professional.

Then Bryan gets up to present his thoughts on Barry's new style, which he sees as conservative with a twist. He wants to replace the glasses with contacts, get him away from pleated front pants and navy blue blazers, make him look a little hipper, without being over the top. Jou describes his goals for Sally as "dump the frump," and wants her to embrace her new sexy body inside as well as out. Everyone seems to be holding their breath, but both men seem to have gotten the desire to snipe at each other out of their system for the moment.

"I have to get out of here quick, honey," Bryan whispers in my ear. "Call me later on my cell, okay?"

"Okay, Bry, I will, I promise." I give him a hug, and he makes a break for the door as soon as Paul dismisses us. Jou flies across the room to my side.

"Whatever he said about me isn't true, you have to know that." Jou seems nearly frantic.

"All he said was that you were taking a break, honest. I'm really sorry about the whole thing." Why these guys are remotely interested in my loyalty, I have no idea.

"Not nearly as sorry as I am, wasting eleven years on that lying little bitch." There is real venom in Jou's tone. "I mean, I saw him chatting up his little bit of stuff in front of my own eyes, and then HE tried to make it all about me being closed off emotionally! Classic transference, but he never did believe in therapy."

"Jou, I adore you both, and I hope this is just a rough patch. I promise I'm not taking sides here." Which seems like a clear-headed thing to say.

Lily's Rule #17: Never take sides in a fight between two friends; they'll always end up uniting against you later.

"Well honey, you'll find out soon enough which side you are going to want to be on, and trust me, it isn't Bryan's!" He stomps off.

"I guess that is why they call them Drama Queens, huh? How about that show!" Why Jake is forever sneaking up behind me is beyond my comprehension at the moment.

"Jake, if you don't mind, I have to get going." I turn to leave and he grabs my elbow.

"C'mon dollface, I didn't mean to offend you, it was just a joke. How about you let me make it up to you? Dinner? Back rub?" He winks at me lasciviously. I shrug off his hand.

"Jake, really, I don't think so. Gotta run."

I twist away from him quickly and head to the door where I smack right into Curt, whose coffee spills all over him.

"Jesus Christ! Look where you're going, would you?"

"Curt, I'm so sorry, I was just trying to get away from Jake, and I . . ."

Curt snorts derisively. "Yeah, right, get away from Jake. Couple pieces of advice: one, don't shit where you eat, and two, don't shit where I eat." He stalks off before I can reply.

"Heck of a day, huh?" Hillary asks around a mouthful of veal at Buona Terra.

"You poor thing. Trapped, that's what you were. Trapped . . . like a baby calf," Naomi says pointedly in Hillary's direction.

Hillary won't take the bait, but instead licks her lips with relish and continues, "Sounds like you have a bunch of crazies over there."

"You have no idea," I mumble, enjoying a huge bite of the house specialty pasta. "And what is worse, I really don't want to take sides with Bryan and Jou, and I really do want Jake to leave me alone, and I really, *really* want Curt to at least respect me. But

I think the boys aren't going to rest until I tell one of them I think he's in the right, Jake is going to plague me, and Curt thinks I am a featherbrained nincompoop, and always will."

"Could you tell them both secretly that you think they are in the right, but that you feel you have to be nice to the other one for the sake of the show?" Hillary asks.

"That isn't very honest, Hil." Naomi does her little head tilt "I am encouraging you to make the right decision on your own" thing.

"Actually, honest or not, it might be a good idea. That way they both think I am 'in their corner,' but I can keep them both as friends. It's certainly worth a shot."

"Good plan." Hillary is patting herself on the back already. "Now, about this Jake thing, are you sure you are not protesting too much on that front? I mean, if he's as hot as all that, don't you just maybe like him sniffing around?"

"Of course she doesn't!" Naomi snaps. "He sounds obnoxious. Some people aren't flustered by good looks, they need someone principled, too."

"Of course I don't." I jump in before Naomi really gets going. "He's totally full of himself, it's gross. Don't forget, he slept with the first episode girl and has probably had half the women on the crew by now! I really do wish he would just sniff elsewhere. And before you ask, no I'm not worried about Curt because I find him attractive, I am worried about Curt because we are working together and he is smart and good at his job and I want him to appreciate me as a professional."

Naomi and Hillary exchange glances. Hillary pounces first. "He's attractive?"

Oy. "You know what I meant, you guys make everything about

everything that it isn't!" It's criminal the craft with which my cronies can give credence to any crumb of a possible crush, credible or no.

"I don't think she answered the question, counselor." Naomi sparkles a little.

"No, Mimi, I don't think she did." Hillary grins at me.

"I do not, for the record, find Curt Hinman attractive. He is a brusque, grumpy, tedious, patronizing man, and I just want him to respect my work. End of topic."

"Fine, new topic. Why haven't you returned Ron's calls? Dave was up my ass all week at the office," Hillary chides me.

"He called? When did he call?" Naomi perks up. "Why didn't you tell me he called? That is so great!"

There have been three messages so far, all of which I'd managed to conveniently ignore. "Look, Ms. Butt-in-ski. First off, since you're so curious, he didn't call me for SIX DAYS after I slept with him. Almost a week. That is just bad form. But ultimately better for me, because it gave me time to really think about whether I wanted to see him again, and I realized that I genuinely don't have time to begin a relationship with anyone, even if I were so inclined. If you want I'll call him back and tell him I can't deal right now, okay? Will that get Dave out of your delicate ass?"

I still haven't told them about Ron's little comments, the fact that not only didn't he see me home but he didn't even come down to be sure I was okay, and that his apartment could get shut down by the health department at any minute. I could have probably gotten past all of that, but to not call for six days after sleeping with me, that was the straw of humiliation that broke this camel's back.

"Fine. Whatever you want." Hillary smirks. Naomi pouts.

"What I want is tiramisu." Which is true.

Hillary waves the waiter over to order dessert. "Let's be sure the lady gets at least one thing she wants today!"

Which I will not be arguing with.

📺

"Lily, darling, delicate question for you." Paul has steered me into a corner of Barry's apartment, which is rapidly becoming a much more attractive place, if I do say so myself. Paul is weaving slightly as he walks, and carries his usual Eau de Single Malt aroma.

"Sure, Paul, what's up?"

"Could you be a love and do the art project segment with Sally and Birdie? I know they're supposed to work alone, but the poor girl is out of her element already, and you know what happened last time. We really can't afford two hours of filming just to get a little splash of color over the fireplace." Paul smiles up at me expectantly. It's unclear which girl he is referring to being out of her element: Sally, who has tried as much as possible to hide from the cameras, or Birdie, who seems to be setting a world's record for takes. Fourteen alone for the intro. She kept saying that Barry was a GPA instead of CPA. My guess is that her own GPA was somewhere in the negative digits.

"Sure, Paul, no problem." I was counting on that time to work on the slipcover for Barry's couch with May, the off-camera soft-goods specialist, but I'll have to find another time.

"You're an angel! I'll get the shot set up, and we'll see if we can hammer it out quickly, shall we?" Paul teeters off to talk to the director about the segment, and I head to the bathroom to check my makeup. I open the door to find the room occupied. The occupant bellows much like an old bear.

"JESUS, DON'T YOU FRIGGING KNOCK WHEN YOU SEE A CLOSED DOOR?" Curt yells.

"Oops, sorry, thought it was empty." Why Curt? Why did I have to walk in on CURT of all people? Especially at such an *indelicate* sort of time. Then again, why hadn't he locked the door? I start to leave, to alleviate some of my embarrassment, when the door flies open. I brace myself for a tongue-lashing.

"Hey, um, sorry I yelled, I guess I forgot to lock the door." He sounds almost genuinely contrite. "You just, um, surprised me is all."

"No, Curt, you were right, I totally should have knocked." I can't believe he is being nice to me.

"Yeah, well, I suppose if we're working together like this, these things are bound to happen." It is like invasion of the carpenter snatchers.

"Let's just pretend it didn't happen." I'm so relieved.

"Yeah, and, um, your fireplace surround, it's done, so I'll send the boys in with it." I had ripped out Barry's developer-standard white marble tile, and had Curt do a traditional wood surround with half-columns and an elegant mantelpiece.

"Great, I need to get it stained and sealed before you install it."

"I did it already."

"Really? I thought staining and stuff was my responsibility." Actually what Curt had said on the last shoot when I asked him to stain a floating wall shelf was "I build it, you gild it." Sort of a poet, really.

"Well, you didn't ask for too much, I had the time, figured I'd help out. Anyway, I'll send it in and come by to install when you're done with the paint touch-ups."

"Thanks, Curt, I really appreciate it. And sorry again about walking in on you." Maybe we have turned a corner here.

"Yeah, forget it. See you later."

He heads out and I zip into the bathroom, carefully locking it behind me.

"Birdie, sweetness, let's try it one more time, okay love?" Paul massages Birdie's shoulder as she sighs deeply.

"Paul, sugar, I just don't know what I'm doing wrong."

There is serious concern in her voice. As well there should be. We have been trying to do a small art project for almost forty-five minutes. Not a difficult art project. Taking one of the small elements from the throw pillow fabric and enlarging the image on canvas in acrylic paint. I could have done six of them by now. Except I'm not supposed to do the project, I'm supposed to explain it to Sally and Birdie who are supposed to execute it without me.

First, Birdie thought that she was supposed to paint WITH the pillow, instead of using it for visual inspiration, and only quick thinking on my part snatched it out of her hands before she dunked it in the paint. Take Two: Birdie and Sally are using brushes to lightly sketch out the design, and Birdie leans over accidentally dunking her breasts into the paint palette, requiring a quick wardrobe change, and a reshoot of my explanation of the project, since now Birdie is in a new shirt. Take Three: Birdie and Sally manage to get the pattern onto the canvas and begin painting. Sally says she likes the way the colors are so organic. Birdie agrees that orgasmic colors are her favorites, too. I thought Bob the director was going to either smash his little portable video monitor over her head, or break down and cry.

"Really, with the eighteen takes, really?" he says, in his monotone voice.

"Just relax, darling, you are doing great. Just great!"

Sally rolls her eyes at me. Behind me I hear Bob whisper that we probably won't be able to use the segment at all. At this point all I really care about is that we get the stupid canvas done so that there is something to hang over the new fireplace mantel.

During the last take Birdie tells Sally how impressive it is that she has lost so much weight, and that she must be enjoying the improvement in her dating life. Sally snaps back that actually her dating seemed easier when she was heavy, and that was part of the reason she applied for the show to begin with, that she doesn't seem to know who she is anymore, so meeting men has become uncomfortable. "Plus, I bet none of the guys who ask me out now would have asked me out when I was fat, so then I have to wonder if it is me they really like, and what they would do if I gained the weight back!" Then she bursts into tears and runs off camera.

"That's a wrap on this segment, kids; let's take fifteen and then set up for load in," Bob yells, then calls Raoul the lighting guy over to discuss some ideas for the reveal segment. Birdie looks confused, while Paul hustles her off to shuttle her to the other apartment. I head inside to find poor Sally.

"She's in the john, you know where that is," Curt says as I come down the hall. "And your fireplace is done."

I forget that I should be comforting Sally and instead head into the living room where the fireplace mantle gleams a deep walnut.

"Curt, it's beautiful, thank you so much." He really is a very talented man.

"No big deal. You'd better go find Miss Sniffles, we need to load in, and they are going to want her in the footage."

"Right." But before I can get out of the living room, Bob motions for me to go over to the kitchen to film my video diary.

video diary confession:

"Okay, so I have to just put this out in the universe. Curt is amazing. Have you seen that fireplace mantel? It's a miracle of deliciousness. I can't believe how beautiful it is. Now I know that it seems a little over the top to gush about such a thing, but here's the deal: it's no small thing to find a true craftsman these days, and when a designer puts something on paper that another person can turn into a real lasting piece of art, that is just so very gratifying. Just don't tell Curt I said so, it'll give him a big swollen head!"

Just as I finish, Sally enters. She looks fine, a little embarrassed, but not too puffy-eyed.

"They aren't going to show that, are they? I'd be mortified," she asks me.

"I think Birdie screwed up too many times to salvage it, so you should be safe. Feeling better?"

"Yep. I guess I didn't realize how emotionally draining this is. And there are still two more days!" She shakes her head.

"Don't you worry, tomorrow you get to be a princess with Bryan, and he's so much fun, and he'll be sure you're pampered within an inch of your life and that you look fabulous. And then Thursday you get to see your new place and have a big party."

"Thanks, Lily, it has been fun working with you, and I just hope my place looks as good as this place. Barry is a lucky guy."

I give her a hug, Bob yells that we should do the bedroom footage first, so Sally and I start the two hours of schlepping that will be sped up and edited to look like the room came together in about ten minutes.

The magic of television.

Bryan and I are on my couch splitting a bottle of Chilean red, and I'm listening to eleven years' worth of pent-up Jou hostility. He invited himself over after the party, where both Barry and Sally were looking great and introducing their respective friends.

"I mean, who does she think she is kidding, Ms. Jou DuFresne. You know her real name is Jonathan Friedman!" Bryan cackles.

I don't know that I will ever get used to this alternative pronoun stuff. "Funny, he doesn't look Jewish." It's all I can think to say.

"NOSE JOB!" Bryan snaps his fingers in the air. We laugh. My phone rings.

I motion to Bryan to top off his glass.

"Hello, this is Lily."

"Lily, Jou. You left the party so fast, I never got a chance to talk to you! Great job with the apartment by the way, I saw the after shots." Uh oh.

"Thanks, and you did a great job, too." I'm trying to be vague, since Bryan is watching me carefully.

"Thanks! I was thinking of heading out for a nightcap, want to come meet me?" Crap.

"Um, I can't tonight, I, um, have a friend over. Maybe this week sometime?"

"Mmmmm, friend friend, or is there potential there?" he asks.

"Friend friend." Which is the wrong thing to say because a slightly tipsy Bryan decides to jump in.

"No nookie from me!" he shouts out. "I'm not that desperate yet!"

There is a venomous pause on my phone. "Is that Bryan? Do you have Bryan over there?"

"Um, yeah, I do." I figure I'd better go with honesty.

"Well, I guess now I know which side your bread is buttered on."

"It just sort of happened . . ." I start, but Jou cuts me off.

"No problem. No problem at all. Just remember, there are two sides to this story, and he is the one with the monogamy problem."

"I know that everyone has their own perspective. Can't we talk about it later this week? I really want to." I don't really, but I also don't want him angry with me.

"Maybe. I'll see. I have to go. And you shouldn't neglect your guest."

He hangs up. I'll have to call him tomorrow and put plan "I'm on everyone's side" into effect as soon as possible.

Luckily, Bryan doesn't ask whom I was talking to. We finish the wine, and another round of Jou-bashing, and just after eleven I put him in a cab. When I get back upstairs, my phone is ringing again.

"Hello?" Who the heck is calling me at this hour?

"Lily, you're alive." I don't recognize the voice.

"So I am. Who is this?"

"Ron." Ohmygod. Package Boy.

"Ron, hi. How are you?" Crap.

"I'm good. How about you? Not in a coma?" All right, I deserve that, he has called and I've been rude. Clearly not unforgivably so, since he is trying again. Then again, since I'm obviously a "sure thing" it isn't that surprising.

"I'm sorry Ron, it is just a very weird and busy time for me. Thanks for your messages though."

"Well, I'll let you make it up to me." Which sounds a lot too cocky if you ask me. "Dinner?" Oh.

"I'm supposed to buy you dinner for not returning your calls?" Cheeky.

"You're supposed to let *me* buy you dinner for not returning my calls." Oops.

He was nice, before the comment. But I know guys, he just doesn't want to work too hard to get laid. "Ron, that is so sweet, but I'm sort of working two full-time jobs right now, and I'm afraid I wouldn't be good company. Thank you though. Why don't I call you when things settle down a little for me." Like I'm gonna do that!

"I see. Well, okay, I'll hope that you do that then." He sounds sort of miffed. Which I probably would be if I was in his shoes; all work and no nookie makes Ron a sad boy.

"I will, I definitely will, it may just be a few weeks until I get my head above water." By which point you will have forgotten all about me.

"Okay, Lily, I'll talk to you in a few weeks then. I hope all your stuff gets straightened out."

"Bye Ron, thanks for calling."

I'm going to kill Hillary for giving Dave my number. This is an aggravation I do not need right now.

Fun With Rick and Jane

Bravo *Wednesday June 21* 8PM–9PM

SWAP/MEET Rick and Jane

Swap/Meet takes over for a good ol' Southern boy and a quiet office manager. Watch the sparks fly on this episode, when taxidermy becomes a four-letter word, and a cat named Lucy shakes things up. Studly carpenters Jake Kersten and Curt Hinman sound off on the relative benefits of MDF over wood, and designers Lily Allen and Ashleigh Benning take their licks. Highlights include the honest appraisals of participants and their friends.

Tomorrow we start taping the third episode of *Swap/Meet*, and I feel like I've begun to find a method to the madness that is television. This time I'll be working with a guy named Rick, a Tennessee transplant who works in the steel business, and Ashleigh will be working with Jane, an office manager for a local printing company. Ashleigh has some insane plan about bringing Rick's

Tennessee heritage home, and let's just say the word taxidermy
was bandied about in a very casual way at the production meeting.
Jane's place is deadly dull, beyond stark into austere, so I figure
she could use someone helping her do minimalism the right way.
I'm very excited about the plans, which include a Zen rock garden
in her bay window alcove, and some wonderful subtle art projects
for both the living room and Jane's bedroom. I just hope Rick isn't
all thumbs like his predecessors.

I've officially established a lovely little ritual for the night before filming, just to be sure I'm at my best for the cameras. I eat a
light dinner around 6:30, something with protein and some carbs,
since I'll need good energy tomorrow (tonight's entrée included a
halibut fillet and wild rice pilaf) and I limit myself to one glass of
wine.

I go over my notes and double-check my Time and Action
plan. With only two days to completely redo two rooms, and with
the different "required" segments, I've got to be very detailed in
how I budget out the filming hours. Both days are laid out in ten-
minute segments, with a breakdown of who needs to be working
on what. For someone who isn't terribly organized naturally, it's a
great exercise for me.

When I'm sure that I have my bases covered, I take a long
soak in the bath, rub some Badger Sleep Balm on my temples, and
climb into bed, warm, pink, and smelling of lavender and other
soothing essential oils.

The phone wakes me just after 2:00 AM.

"Lily? It's Hillary." Boy, does she sound drunk.

"Hil? What's up, are you okay?" Because if you aren't in some
sort of trouble, I may have to kill you. "Why are you whispering?"

"I'm at Chandler's. I'm in his bathroom. I have a COS situation with a twist."

Oh Lord.

In college Hillary and I came up with a set of secret codes, which allowed us to speak freely about sex even if other people were in the room. COS. Cock of Significance. Not the "Oh my, how pleasantly surprised I am to find that you are amply endowed in the genital arena, and won't this be fun" sort of thing. The "holy crap what the hell am I supposed to do with that monster" sort of thing. The twist reference means that there must be something additionally disturbing, a severe curve to the left or a downward hook or perhaps a piercing of some kind.

"Hil, what are you doing at Chandler's? You hate Chandler." I'm hoping in her stupor she will forget about her cock situation, since Chandler works out at HiFi at the same time as we do occasionally, and I really don't relish knowing more about his penis than I've already managed to ascertain from the way his track pants fit him.

Chandler is not Jewish. Enough said.

Hillary snorts. "I know I hate Chandler. Geez, Lily, he is a major schmuck. I totally should have gotten second chair on that Moretti case." Chandler and Hillary seem to always be in competition at the firm, and their rivalry never seemed in the least fueled by desire. "But we were working late, and then a bunch of us went out for drinks and then he offered to take me home, but we came here instead."

"Hillary Anne Ganderburg, that's the biggest bunch of crap I ever heard. Why. Are. You. At. Chandler's?" Hillary doesn't make spontaneous decisions about sex. Ever. Her sex life is always thoughtfully calculated, always designed to provide maximum physical pleasure for minimum emotional involvement, and she NEVER fools around with anyone she works with.

Hillary sighs. "I lost a bet."

"A bet?" This is getting worse by the minute.

"Chandler bet that this stupid decision would be upheld in the appellate, and I bet it would be overturned. If I won, he was going to have to take any pro bono case I asked him to, and if he won, I was going to have to go on a date with him. I lost. Tonight was the date. Is the date. It got a little out of hand."

"Hillary, you didn't say you would sleep with him if you lost, did you?" In which case I will have to protest, and proclaim that she has profaned eighty years of progress in the women's movement with such a promise of promiscuity.

"Don't be ridiculous, Lily, I just said I would go on a date. Which I did."

Whew.

"The fact that he turned out to be charming and sort of sexy and a really good kisser was totally unanticipated and accidental," she continues. "But what can one do? You go with the flow. And now I'm naked in his bathroom, and having a major issue, and I don't know what to do, so can we please address the cock at hand and deal with the other bullshit tomorrow?" Her whispering is ferocious, and still slightly slurry, and I'm tired as hell, so I've got to give in.

Lily's Rule #65: In any sex-related emergency, being a good friend takes precedence over being rational.

"Okay," I tell her. "Give me the particulars."

I can hear her exhale dramatically. "Thank you. Okay, here goes, first off, he is huge. Enormously huge. Possibly the biggest one I have ever seen." She sounds genuinely frightened.

"Bigger than Moose?" A football player she had a fling with, and heretofore the record for size.

"Makes Moose look like a mouse."

Yikes!

"And the twist?" I guess I should get all the info on the table.

"There's two things that are freaking me out. I mean the size is one thing, but I think the cap is on backwards." This woman is making no sense at ALL.

"The cap is on backwards?" I'm at a loss.

"Yes. You know, the helmet thing, it's facing the wrong way, like it got turned 180 degrees." I'm trying to picture this, unsuccessfully.

"Let me see if I understand you." I say. "If you are between his legs facing the beast . . ."

"Yeah."

"Then you should be looking at the upside-down V part of the helmet." I cannot BELIEVE I'm having this conversation.

"Right, like the little face part, but it isn't there, it is on the top by his belly, and then there is this hard bony thing under his balls on the sides. Like Jay Leno's chin." She sounds very serious, and I'm about to lose it entirely.

"Hillary, do you hear yourself? Are you actually calling me at two o'clock in the fucking morning to tell me that you are about to sleep with Chandler, but you are worried because he is hung from here to Friday, the head of his penis is on backwards, and he has Jay Leno's chin under his balls? Really?" I start to laugh.

Hillary giggles quietly into the phone. Then I hear some mumbling, and a flush, and Hillary whispers, "I have to go, I'll call you tomorrow. Wish me luck . . ."

"Good luck."

The last thing I remember thinking before I fell asleep was that at least Naomi never calls me with cock problems.

When the alarm goes off at seven, it feels like I've only been asleep for ten minutes. Goddamn Hillary and her lousy timing. I have to be at the apartment for Episode #3 by eight, and I know that I'm going to look like death-warmed-over on-screen. No amount of cover-up is going to minimize these bags. I get to Jane's apartment in Ukrainian Village and meet with Paul and the crew to go over the goals for the day. Curt and I have already met about my plans for him, building out the base for the rock garden, a couple of end tables, and a platform bed with built-in nightstands. But yesterday I decided I wanted to add a small bookshelf project, so I track him down.

"Curt, hey." I tap him lightly on the shoulder.

"Hey, Lily, all set for today?" He seems to be in an okay mood, for Curt that is.

"Getting there. I was actually wondering, any chance I could add a small item to your list?" I smile at him in what I hope is a very winning way.

"Lily, I told you yesterday, you can do what you want, but this is a lot of carpentry, and it will be tight to get it finished in time." He sounds even less sure of things than he did at the production meeting.

"But still doable. With your magic." God, I sound insipid.

"I think so, but no promises. You gave me the priority list, I'll tackle stuff in order. You'll definitely have the bed and the rock garden base. Anything else will be up for grabs." Not exactly a reassuring thought.

"It'll be great. Here is the plan for the shelf. If you have time to get to it, great, if not, I can lose it, no big deal." Maybe I'll get lucky.

"And you know I'm using MDF on all this stuff; cabinet ply was too expensive for the budget."

Medium-density fiberboard, the necessary evil of television home improvement. Easy to work with, cheap, easy to paint, totally not attractive on its own. Cabinet-grade plywood, which has a really nice stainable veneer on one side, is as much as $45 per sheet, and I need so much wood for this shoot that it just wasn't cost effective.

"I know, Curt, and I promise, next time, smaller projects so you can work with real wood!"

"I'm just the carpenter." Curt shakes his head at me and goes off in the direction of the carpentry tent, hopefully to start building my bed.

The morning runs relatively smoothly, all things considered. Rick is a really great guy, and very easy to work with, not to mention actually competent. We got the walls painted in both rooms, a soft sage green in the bedroom and a buttery cream in the living room. And the art project for the bedroom, a large simple watercolor suggesting grass and sky, turned out really cool. Jenna, the soft-goods assistant, has managed to get one of the window treatments for the bedroom sewn, and assures me that once she is done with the second, she and May will get on the duvet cover. We're breaking for lunch while the production assistants set up for the afternoon segments, the Birdie piece, and the "Rick visits the land of carpentry to help Curt use power tools" piece. I'm tentatively optimistic, and decide to check in on Hillary while eating my ubiquitous turkey sandwich.

"Zapp, Standish, and Stein." The ever-efficient monotone receptionist at Hillary's office. Dulcet, not so much.

"Hillary Ganderburg, please."

"Who may I say is calling?"

"Lily Allen."

"Will she know what this is regarding?" I'm tempted to say it is regarding the enormous penis possessed by one of her colleagues, but I resist.

"Yes, she will."

"Please hold one moment while I put you through." The muzak version of Cyndi Lauper's "Time After Time" may actually be murdering brain cells.

"Lily, I'm so sorry for waking you up, and there is already a huge floral monstrosity awaiting you at home." Hillary keeps Robert Daniels Florist in business, she is very big on sending flowers. And cookies. The fact that Cookies By Design will actually make a floral bouquet out of cookies was like peanut butter meeting jelly for Hillary.

"No need for the greenery, but I'm sure it will be a lovely thing to come home to. How are you doing today?" I can hear her walking around her desk to close the door of her office.

"I am hung. A two-McMuffin day." Ouch. That means one Egg McMuffin on the way back from Chandler's, promptly thrown up upon reaching home, and a second on the way to work. A two-McMuffin hangover is the worst.

"Poor thing. How'd the rest of the night go?"

Hillary sighs. "Interesting."

"Please elaborate." Interesting is never a good description of anything.

"Well, when our call was interrupted, it was Chandler coming to see if I had passed out in his bathroom. We returned to the bedroom and resumed our activities. He was very attentive, about a seven on the oral-sex scale, which is pretty good for a first time, so I was inclined to return the favor."

"Well, that is a good sign, but weren't you worried about the gag reflex issue?" When Hillary was with Moose, oral sex became a problem. Giving, not receiving. His size made for some tricky situations, and Hillary eventually stopped giving him head altogether.

"I was concerned, yes, but it was a moot point."

"Why?"

"No erection."

"I thought you guys were all hot and bothered?" No erection is very weird.

"I thought so, too. He certainly didn't have a problem when we were fooling around before I called you, and even after, I could definitely feel that he was excited, but then nothing. Do you think I give such a bad blow job that he got turned off?" This may be the first time in our lives that Hillary has questioned her own prowess in bed.

"Hillary, he's a GUY. The only BAD blow job is NO blow job." Which she knows as well as the rest of us.

"I know, I know. I just don't get it. I eventually gave up, we fell asleep, and I left at around five-thirty. Thank God he is in depositions all day. I can't bear to face him. It was a huge mistake, wasn't it?"

"I dunno, Hil, was it weird this morning when you left?" Intramural sports can be fun, but they do require a great deal of caution.

"No, actually it was sort of nice. I slept okay, he was very cuddly and affectionate, brought me coffee in bed and offered to make breakfast, which I declined. We kibitzed about being hungover, he asked if we could have dinner later this week, kissed me good-bye, and left me a message before I got to work."

"Don't overthink it. You were both drinking; maybe it affected his performance. Do you want to go out with him again?" I'm hard-pressed to imagine Hillary actually getting involved with him in any serious way.

"Well, he could make for a good Shabbas Goy. . . ."

The Shabbas Goy. Code for fuck buddy. When I was in design school I got connected to a sort of boring Wasp-y guy named Brandon with whom I had nothing in common, and yet shockingly, a fierce sexual compatibility. I would go to his apartment on Friday nights after classes, we'd have a drink, order takeout, spend two to three hours in bed, and then I would go home. We never dated, weren't even really friends, and whenever either one of us was seeing someone else, we would take a sabbatical. He met a lovely gal named Holly or Molly or Golly or some such thing and I believe they are happily wed.

Naomi is actually the one who named him the Shabbas Goy. Orthodox Jews used to have gentile boys board in their houses in exchange for doing all the things on the Sabbath that they themselves were forbidden to do . . . like turning on the lights or the heat, a goy to take care of things for Shabbat, hence the name. Since our dates were always on Friday evenings, and since he was taking care of some things for me that I couldn't take care of myself, it seemed fitting. And he was probably the best sex I ever had. Hillary's last Shabbas Goy, actually a nice Jewish doctor, but we didn't feel like changing the moniker, started seeing someone seriously about the same time Josh and I broke up, and she hasn't found a new one yet.

"Do you think that would be a good idea, since you guys work together?" Just want to be sure she is thinking of all of the potential problems.

"I think it is something we could explore. Provided the erectile dysfunction was alcohol-related and not an ongoing problem. And provided he knows what's what. I figure I'll accept his offer for dinner and see what happens." Hillary always bounces back quickly.

"Sounds like a plan. Did you tell Naomi?" Naomi, bless her heart, has always seemed just as interested in our guy foibles as she did when she was straight. Or when she thought she was straight. Or pretending to be straight. Or however that works.

"I called her before I called you, but she wasn't home . . ." Hillary trails off in a sort of seductive manner.

"Do you think there is a new woman in her life?" I'm surprised; if Naomi is dating someone, usually she would want us to know.

"I think Ms. Miller may have a Shabbas Shiksa!" The delight in Hillary's voice at the prospect is palpable.

"Really? We'll have to grill her Wednesday night." The three of us are meeting up at my place for dinner and to watch the first ever airing of the pilot episode of *Swap/Meet*.

"We will indeed. I believe there is dish there. We'll get it out of her." Hillary giggles in anticipation.

"Okay, well, I'll talk to you later, I have to go set up a rock garden."

Bob walks by. "Really, with the talking on the phone, really?" he says, meaning that I'd better get ready for the next shot.

"Okay, I'll talk to you later."

So much intrigue, so little time. Now where did the PA's put my sand?

Trouble. We've got trouble. With a Capital *T*, that rhymes with *P* that stands for predicament, which means FUCKED.

It is lunchtime on Day Two of filming, but I'm not eating, because this whole project has fallen into the crapper. Yesterday went pretty smoothly, all things considered, until about midafternoon. I'd just finished laying out the Zen garden, perfect white sand, punctuated with a few large-ish chunks of black volcanic rock, with calming swirly patterns all around, thanks to the Japanese rake, now perched decoratively in the corner of the window. Birdie and Rick managed to do the lamp project I had for them in only four takes, which is a new record for Birdie, and to Rick's credit, he seemed totally impervious to Birdie's assets. Then Rick returned from working with Curt to inform me that he had a great time doing the carpentry and hoped he'd be able to do it again today to finish up the bed.

The bed, with its built-in nightstands, is essentially the only piece of furniture in the bedroom. It is in need of a four-coat paint technique in order to disguise the dreaded MDF and make it beautiful. It was supposed to be finished last night so that the primer and first coat of paint could be dry for today.

"Rick," I said, using my very calm voice, sure that he misunderstood, and not wanting to jump to conclusions in front of the cameras, "isn't the bed going to be done tonight?"

Rick smiled at me. "Nah. Curt and I got the platform framed out, but those nightstand things won't be on there until tomorrow."

"What about the end tables for the living room?" My stomach was turning over.

"All we worked on was the bed. I don't know about any other stuff." Rick walked over to the window to look at my handiwork. "This rock garden thing is pretty cool, Lily. What a great idea."

"Thanks Rick. If you'll excuse me just one minute, I have to check in with Curt." I exited in what I hoped appeared to be a calm, businesslike manner, then ran down the stairs, out into the parking lot behind the building where the carpentry tent is set up.

"Curt, how's everything going?" I could see the platform for the bed, without a base on it, and nothing that looked like end tables or nightstands or a shelf for that matter.

"Hey, Lily, Rick was actually a help, such a nice change to have a contributor who actually can handle himself . . . I don't have to undo any of his work. You'll definitely have the bed by lunch tomorrow, and the end tables I can knock out in about an hour and a half, but I think the bookshelf may be a nonstarter." Curt seemed calm as he informed me of this.

"I thought I was getting the bed tonight. It needs priming and painting and more painting tomorrow . . ."

Curt heaves a sigh and shakes his head at me, and I can feel our little camaraderie evaporate. "I told you it was a tight schedule. Your little rock garden in the living room required that I reframe the floor joists because of the weight of the sand and stuff, and I had to put in a liner so that the fine sand you bought didn't seep through the flooring. This bed requires some serious finessing, especially with the nightstands built in. Without a headboard, we can't cleat it to the wall for extra stability, so I need to build it as a freestanding piece, which is always harder. I should be able to get the base on tonight, but no nightstands until tomorrow morning."

I didn't know what to say. He did tell me things were tight, and he did tell me that he was using MDF. I am totally SCREWED.

I thought fast. "Okay, Curt. What if we lost the nightstands?" Better something than nothing . . .

"Considering that the base was designed for them, it is going to look pretty weird if we don't do them." Curt walked me around the platform where I could see the notches where the nightstands would eventually go. It would look even more awful if we left it as is.

"Okay. I'll revisit my painting idea, but tomorrow the sooner I can get this the better." Trouble. With a capital *T,* that rhymes with *C,* which stands for CRAP!

"I'll try to crank it out tomorrow, but definitely not before eleven."

Sigh. "Thanks Curt. It really looks great, and the rock garden is terrific, I'm sorry I didn't think about the structural work."

"It's okay. I'd better get on it if I'm going to finish this base for you though . . ."

I walked back upstairs, headed into Jane's pretty little powder room, turned on the water, and had a quiet little cry.

video diary confession:

"Okay, so I have just finished having a nice little breakdown in the other room, as you can probably see from my red eyes. See, here's the thing. This show, well, it's about trying to make people happy. You know? The whole reason I got into designing as a career is because I think that life should be beautiful. Your home should be a haven, a sanctuary. Whatever bad things happen to you outside, however ugly life gets, when you walk in your front door, you should be safe and happy, and everything around you should be as beautiful to you as you can make it.

And I think my job is to help people create that beauty around them. To take their ideas and feelings and translate that into spaces that make them feel wonderful. And the point of Swap/Meet *is to do that for people, which is why I wanted to work on this show. Because we aren't about being shocking or provocative. We aren't about trying to find some awful thing to glue to your walls just to get a big reaction. We aren't interested in sloppy or shoddy work. And on this show, I'm doing sloppy and shoddy work. And that makes me embarrassed for myself, and very sad for Jane. So, for all you viewers out there, this wasn't a fix or anything, I really just*

miscalculated the use of time and resources. And Jane, if you are watch-
ing, I'm going to do my very best for you, but if it isn't totally successful,
know that I really did try, and I really did want to make you happy, and
I'm very, very sorry. Okay, that's it. Bye for now."

"Ducky, it's brilliant television!" Paul is petting me in the corner, prepping me to take Jane into her not-so-lovely, totally unfinished apartment. I'm mortified. Everything that could go wrong
on this shoot has. The paint we used this morning on all the wood
trim in both the living room and bedroom was apparently allergic
to the original paint, and over the course of the day has bubbled
and cracked and looks like some sort of mange. Curt did indeed
get the bed finished before noon, and we got it primed with the
tinted primer, a lovely shade of Pepto-Bismol pink, which would
have made the deep cranberry red (which was supposed to be the
base color for my paint technique) cover in one coat. Except the
MDF soaked it up like a sponge, and is just barely dry as it is, so no
paint went on at all. I'm leaving this poor girl with a hideous pink
platform bed, three quarts of paint, a quart of sealer, and my
solemn promise to return and fix it.

Curt did finish both of the end tables and the bookshelf, each
of which got a coat of white primer, and again, no time for a paint
coat. So the living room is equally unfinished. And about twenty
minutes ago, Jane's aunt dropped off Lucy, Jane's cat, who got out
of the carrier, walked delicately over to the Zen garden, hopped
in, and took an enormous dump. We finally got her back in the
carrier and locked her in the bathroom. I didn't know that Jane
even had a cat, and now I have presented her with the world's
largest litter box in the middle of her living room.

She is going to hate it. She is going to hate me. I am SO fired.

Paul rubs my shoulder and breathes words of whiskey-laden

comfort. "Love, it will be great. No one remembers the episodes with the perfect results. But everyone remembers that woman sobbing off-camera at her hideous brown room with the covered up fireplace, or the cherished wedding candlesticks painted speckled aquamarine. It will be the episode that makes everyone say, 'Did you see *Swap/Meet* last Wednesday? They totally ruined this woman's apartment!'" Why anyone—even a drunk man—would think I would find this soothing is totally beyond me. "Now, go get your girl, and let's do the reveal!" Evil little monkey dwarf.

I walk the blindfolded Jane into her apartment. I whisper in her ear that things did not go as well as planned, some projects are unfinished due to time constraints, but that I promise to return on my own time to help her finish things up. She whispers back that she is sure it will be great. Bob yells, "Speeding!" meaning the cameras have started to record, and then, "Action!" and I take off Jane's blindfold.

"What the FUCK?" is her first response. And I can't blame her. I try to be positive and upbeat, try to take her through the different elements of my design, and I can see her trying not to cry and to understand what it was meant to look like. But then she turns to me, and big as life says, "Is that SHIT in that sandbox thing?"

Yep. In the rush to finish things up, guess who forgot to remove Lucy's little contribution?

The bedroom was the final straw, Jane breaks down when she sees the awful pink bed, and we finally stop taping to set up for her friends to arrive.

"Really, with the crying, really?" Bob whispers to me as he walks past.

Then I get to sit on the sidelines while a group of women loudly slam everything I have done, and essentially call me a hack, which I certainly have to agree with at the moment. We finally get to leave to head over to The Grand Central for the party, and thankfully Bryan has saved me a seat at a table in the corner.

"Rough one, huh?" he asks when I sit down.

"The worst," I say. "I feel so awful, I'm not used to all of these restrictions and time pressures, and I totally messed everything up. And it was my own damn fault."

"These things happen, and it will probably end up being a really fun episode, especially with both rooms being fucked up," he says with a gleam in his eye.

"Both rooms?" I have been so focused on my own disaster that I hadn't bothered to even inquire about Rick's apartment.

"Ms. Thang may have gotten finished in time, but hers is worse than yours!" Bryan chuckles. "Apparently, there was some weird theme restaurant going out of business that had all these stuffed creatures all over, and Ashleigh bought the lot. That boy's living room looks like the zoo of the living dead. Plus, she bought about twenty leather trench coats at a local thrift store, cut them up, and upholstered his headboard and a wall in his bedroom with them. He walked in, took one look, asked her what the hell she was thinking, and promptly informed her that he is a vegan and animal rights activist. He didn't even want to come here, but Paul talked him into it . . ."

I start to laugh, which feels really good. "Oh my God, at least mine wasn't that bad! Poor Rick!"

"Well, they do get their moment in court . . ." Bryan points at the section of the room where Jane and Rick are filming the "participants meet for the first time" segment, and even from here I can tell that they are letting me and Ashleigh have it.

Curt approaches the table carrying a wrapped box, which he hands to me ceremoniously. "For you," he says, winking.

"Curt, I don't know what to say . . ." I begin to unwrap the rectangular package. It is a shoe box, and I remove the lid to reveal a plank of MDF, painted with pink primer, with a cat litter scoop screwed to it like a plaque. He grins at me expectantly. I start to laugh. Bryan leans over and sees what is in the box, and he starts laughing, too, and pretty soon the three of us are really cracking up.

"Thanks, Curt, I know just where I can put it," I say through my giggles.

"We'll get 'em next time." He heads back to the table where the PA's are. Just when you think you know someone, they do something totally out of character. Who'd have thunk it? I tell Bryan I'm going to see if I can leave. He promises to call me and makes me swear I won't put my head in the oven. I assure him that my oven is electric, and go to find Paul, who says I don't have to stick around. I sneak out without bumping into Jane and head home to a bottle of pinot gris, a hot bath, and a long dreamless sleep.

Let's Get Cynical

"And where is Hillary today?" Giorgio asks Naomi as we warm up on the treadmills.

"Big case, she couldn't make it," Naomi says, apologetically. Actually, Chandler and Hillary are celebrating a big win for him in a suite at the Four Seasons. For a Shabbas Goy, Chandler seems to be taking up some serious time. Naomi and I have vowed not to needle her about it, since we're both sort of hoping it might become an actual relationship. Not that either of us have any great love of Chandler. We just intuit that she shouldn't think herself invulnerable to relationships, and that she should be inclined to some sort of basic human instinct to find it an inoffensive idea to link herself to another person. At least until someone better comes around.

Giorgio looks sad that she isn't here, but resigned. "All right, then ladies, what do you say we really hit it hard today, show Miss Hillary what we can do without her complaining!"

"You got it!" Naomi enthuses.

We fill our water bottles, grab a couple of towels, and head down the long hallway toward our little private room.

"So, since the face of doom isn't here today . . ." Naomi begins.

"Yes?" Uh oh. I feel a lecture coming on. Hillary always nips these in the bud, so Naomi has to wait to get me one-on-one to play analyst. Which, to her credit, is usually beneficial to me in the long run.

"I want to talk about Josh."

"Why on earth would you want to talk about Josh? Josh is ancient history. Josh and I broke up three whole seasons ago. Single is the new black. I'm so over it."

"I want to talk about Josh, and why you guys broke up, and why you aren't taking dating seriously."

"Okay girls, let's start with step-ups!" Giorgio starts to lead us through the routine. I stay silent. "Okay, what's the topic for today?" he asks.

"Josh," Naomi says.

"Ahhh, the infamous ex. Much beloved by Mother Renee, much maligned by Hillary, and of seeming little consequence to Miss Lily. I have always believed there was more to that story," Giorgio pipes in, clearly eager for just the kind of conversation that always makes us forget how hard he is pushing us until we are crippled by soreness the next day.

"I don't know why you are even worried about him, really, that breakup was like a little blip on my radar."

"Lily. I love you very much. And I know that Josh wasn't the one for you. I just want to know if you know WHY he wasn't the one for you." Goodness, aren't we all mystical today?

"Look, Josh was fine, benign, good company, reasonably good in bed, and very tolerant of my little quirks. Yes, when he set that particular date to cook for me at his place, I did suspect he was going to suggest we move in together. I did not suspect he was going to suggest we move ON separately." I'm really stepping fast and hard now, as I get a little bit agitated. "But, as you may recall, I wasn't really sure that we ultimately wanted the same things, and I wasn't prepared to take that step. So, I was a little taken aback at the breakup, but not terribly devastated, and I have been POSITIVE ever since that it was the right thing to do." My vehemence in this matter is sort of surprising, even to me.

"Lily. I'm trying to really have a conversation about this, even though Hillary doesn't think it's a good idea."

Giorgio hands us each a stretchy band and we begin to do some upper-body work.

"You've been talking about this with Hillary as well?" The only problem with being a triumvirate is that inevitably two of us are discussing the third behind her back, and the assumption that it is critical is not irrational.

"Hillary and I agree that the Josh thing was a problem from the get-go, and we are both less concerned about the breakup, and more concerned that you spent so long with him to begin with, and then seemed shocked at the end, if not terribly disappointed. We worry for you. We want you to be happy. That's all."

"Okay, first off, Hillary should not be pointing fingers. And I thought you liked Josh?" But deep down, I know that Naomi was just being supportive of me, not necessarily of Josh specifically.

"You and Hillary are different. She doesn't want kids; you do, or at least you might. She doesn't necessarily want to get married. You do. Or at least, you either think you do or you think you should, but you keep dating these inconsequential guys for a few months at a time, just enough to keep your mother generally off your back about 'being out there,' and the one guy you got really

serious about was totally wrong for you, and even HE knew it!"
Naomi lets her band snap to the floor.

We go back to the steps for another set.

"May I say something?" Giorgio offers tentatively.

"Of course," I say.

"I think there are two men from your past that you need to be
worried about. Your father and Chuck. Both disappointed you,
both let you down, and if you are afraid to let yourself seek a permanent relationship, it is because you fear those results."

I fucking hate Giorgio.

Naomi claps her hands in delight. "EXACTAMUNDO!
Giorgio, you have hit it right on the NOSE. Your dad asked for a
divorce after nearly thirty-five years of marriage. Granted, a sort
of weird business-y marriage, but still, not horrible. What sort of
example does that set for you, when a pretty mild-mannered guy
can bail on his wife and kid after a whole lifetime? And Chuck not
only let you down, he did it in the most humiliating way possible."

Chuck.

Good old Chuck.

Chuck the Fuck.

Chuck seduced me during freshman year at Brandeis. He was
a big, bad sophomore, a know-it-all, a pain in the ass, and totally
my type. Genuinely tall, over six feet (as opposed to the usual
Brandeis-Jewish-tall of five-feet-nine-inches). Broad shoulders,
great legs, he was a power forward for the soccer team, and he
was the first guy I ever dated who had that nice a body on him.
Dark hair, already thinning at the temples, so he kept it cropped
close to his head. Brooding brown eyes, perfect teeth. Not gorgeous, but winningly attractive. We got fixed up at the annual
Screw-Your-Roommate Dance (a campus-wide blind date), and

after a fairly enjoyable evening, ended up talking all night in his room. When he walked me back to my dorm at sunrise, we stopped under the statue of Justice Louis Brandeis and he kissed me. Fireworks city.

Then we did what most couples in college do, we had a lot of sex, ate a lot of cheap food, fought, drank a lot of cheap wine, broke up, got back together, broke up again, slept with other people, got back together, and celebrated the weirdest anniversaries with pomp and circumstance. Four and a half months with no fight anniversary, two weeks of having sex every day anniversary, seventeen days in a row of spending the night together anniversary. Ah, to be young and dumb and in love for the first time again.

Brandeis is a strangely marital campus. Not that girls go there to get the old M.R.S. degree, it's too academically rigorous for that, but a lot of students start getting engaged to one another around junior year, and the monthly magazine is chock full of weddings and birth announcements from So-and-So Cohen '93 and What's-His-Name Goldstein '92.

Chuck and I were well on our way in that direction. We lasted almost four years. I thought we had a good plan. He applied to law school in Chicago. That would give us only one year of long-distance stuff, with him getting settled in my home city. Then I'd graduate and come home and go to design school, and we'd get a place together. Once we were both done with grad school, we'd get engaged.

We spent the summer after his graduation driving cross-country in his beat-up Saab, camping and having adventures. He registered at Kent for law school, found a seedy apartment in Uptown, and I went back to school.

He broke up with me over Passover break. He'd been seeing

someone else, a classmate. Also a Brandeis alum. Who just happened to be the ONE girl that I just couldn't fucking stand the sight of.

Heather Weierschmidt was my RA sophomore year in Shapiro dorm. We called her Hollywood behind her back. Or Fancy Pants. She was one of those nitwit girls who pretend to be much dumber than they actually are whenever a guy is around. She was a stuck-up social misfit from Beverly Hills who had never seen a person of color who wasn't a maid or a gardener. She drove a white BMW convertible with vanity plates that said "Prncz 1," and wore fucking Chanel pajamas and perfect outfits every day. Her dad was some minor player in the "industry," so she majored in name-dropping and sociology. She joined The Waltham Group, a campus organization devoted to community service, and then publicly made fun of the developmentally challenged people she was assigned to visit. She was a fuckwit cunt. Anyone, he could have dumped me for anyone, ANOTHER GUY even, but not Heather.

Apparently they were both particularly susceptible to the Chicago winter blues. They had both applied and been accepted for transfer to UCLA. He felt badly. I felt like hell. It is to this day a miracle that I managed to get through my finals and graduate. And since Hillary and Naomi had already planned on living together, but not yet found a place, we started looking for one big enough to accommodate all of us.

But Chuck was ancient history, my first real broken heart, to be sure. But even then I knew how young I was, and how slim our chances for real long-term success were. I'm sure I'm not harboring any residual fallout from that, and my dad left when I was thirty, not exactly making me a broken-home kid, which I clearly need to explain to my friends.

"Look, I know I'm in a dating slump, but I promise, Chuck isn't holding me back. My dad isn't holding me back. I just haven't found the right guy, and I'm too old to settle. When he comes, he comes. In the meantime, I have work to do, and a full life, even without dating."

Naomi and Giorgio exchange a glance full of not-so-hidden meaning.

"Oh, you guys!" They kill me. "I'm fine, really. And if family really becomes that important to me and I start to fear for my eggs, well, Giorgio can just beat off in a cup and Naomi and I can both go the turkey baster route and raise our kids together!" This finally makes them both laugh. "Now, can we get back to the workout, please?"

"You know, I know this great therapist who specializes in relationship stuff. Maybe just a couple of sessions, just to see if you have some deep-rooted stuff you aren't aware of?" Naomi gives it one last try.

"Might be good to talk to someone, just to see if it helps," says Giorgio.

"Look, I'll think about it, okay? I'll let you know."

"Fair enough." Naomi looks disappointed, and I wonder if she will be talking to Hillary about it later and if so, what she will say.

"Okay, my little chickadees, one last big push for Papa Giorgio!" He hands us each a set of dumbbells and begins the last cardio routine.

"Go easy, George! I'm dying here," Naomi says, in a perfect imitation of Hillary.

We laugh, finish the workout, stretch, shower, change, and head to the parking lot together.

"I just worry about you, you know that, right?" Naomi says as I'm putting my gear in the trunk of my car.

"I know. And I love you for it." Which I totally do. I give her a hug, and she heads to her car, which she purposely parks as far as possible from the door, just to get an extra bit of walking in. How sick is THAT?

I get in, tune the XM radio to the comedy station, and head home to finalize the design for the next episode. I'm feeling like I've got my sea legs, so to speak, television-wise, and I have some great and ambitious plans for the new show. The fact that this will allow me to not think about the men in my past or the lack of men in my present or even the dream of men for my future is something for Naomi to worry about. I just can't go there myself. At least not today.

episode #4

A Little Ditty 'Bout Zack and Diane

Bravo *Wednesday June 28* 8PM–9PM

SWAP/MEET **Diane and Zack**

An emotional *Swap/Meet* pays tribute to our fighting men and women in uniform. Two reservists, recently returned from tours in Afghanistan and Iraq, get new apartments and civilian makeovers to welcome them home. Sponsors Ethan Allen, Pottery Barn, and Bed Bath & Beyond provide everything from the floor to the rafters. Highlights include inspections from commanding officers, and a very special message from the commander in chief.

Okay, it's official. I hate sponsors. I mean, not really, you know, God bless them, and especially today when they are donating all of this stuff, but working through someone else's agenda is beginning to piss me off.

My design for Zack, who is twenty-six and works as an account rep for SBC when he isn't serving his country, was supposed to be very city slick and modern. Lots of leather, glass; I even have plans to make end tables out of concrete. The Ethan Allen people balked a bit, since they are currently highlighting their "Colonial West Indies" sort of look and so they wanted me to use that collection in the apartment instead. To say I pitched a fit is mild. Paul, to his credit, really gave them what for about the purpose of the show, and that sponsorship doesn't mean an hour-long infomercial, and that it was stifling enough on the creative energies of his designers to have to shop entirely out of their store to begin with. Then he got the executive producer on the phone to ensure that they would be cooperative. I didn't think the little tipsy fellow had it in him. The poor Ethan Allen rep looked like he was going to cry.

Then the truck arrived from Bed Bath & Beyond with all of the orders for both places jumbled up together. Every whisk, dishrag, bath mat, fork, and glass, in no particular order. And since Ashleigh and I were the only ones who knew what we'd bought, we had to go through everything piece by piece, together. This meant I had to endure a snarky play-by-play about all of my choices.

"What an interesting lamp, Lily. Are you planning on painting it to make the color less glaring?" "A brave choice on the chocolate brown towels, the dark colors are so notorious for lint problems. How many washings do you think they will need before Zack stops looking like a hairball after every bath?" "Oh look, they must have sent this rug by mistake. No? You picked this one out? Hmmm."

Lucky for me they weren't filming, since they felt it wouldn't be the most flattering product placement. It took all of my strength not to smack her. Finally, after sorting through everything, and gamely ignoring Ashleigh, determined not to stoop to her level, we are able to get started.

Bridget, the location coordinator, has Curt remove the address number from the front door so that we can film the entrance segment without splashing Zack's actual address all over TV. And even though we've been hanging out in the apartment for a couple of hours, Birdie and I are hustled outside to ring the doorbell. Diane is instructed to answer the door, and to greet us as if we haven't met. Of course, we'd all hit the breakfast buffet together, and have been prepping for the day, but it looks better when they cut the show together to have the meet-and-greet moment at the front door.

Bob heads over to stand behind the camera guy, tripping over a cable on his way.

"Really, with the not taping shit down, really?" he shouts at the nearest PA, who runs to get some gaff tape to control the cables.

"You excited about next week?" Birdie asks me, fluffing her hair and waiting for the director's cue to ring the doorbell.

"I guess." We are planning on doing a "local celeb" episode with a new White Sox rookie and a reporter from WGN news.

"That Samuel Diaz-Perez is so adorable, don't you think?" she gushes at me.

"I'm not really a baseball fan." I can smell the danger brewing. It's hard enough to get through a day of shooting with Birdie without her having a crush. Figures I would be the one assigned to him. She'll be underfoot for the whole shoot, I just know it.

"Okay, Birdie, knock away," Bob calls out.

Birdie knocks on the door, and we're off and rolling.

Midafternoon and I'm headed out to the land of carpentry to check in with Curt. Lucky for us both, they are trying to get the end of Day One wrap-up out of Birdie, so there is no crew hovering about.

Things are surprisingly peaceful out in the parking lot of Zack's condo where the tents are set up. I know that on TV we always look as if we must be hustling about like chickens all day, but there are moments of calm that are always lovely and unexpected. As I get to the bottom of the stairs, I can't help but be mesmerized by Curt, who is building an entertainment center for the living room. Watching him work is very much like watching someone do tai chi. Simple, spare movements, running the wood through the table saw, sanding the edge, sliding it into the groove in the other piece of wood like butter.

I hadn't ever noticed how strong Curt is, but the muscles in his arms are sort of spectacular. Not in that "I spend a lot of time in the gym lifting barbells" sort of way. In that "I'm a man who works with his hands and is strong because of my generally active lifestyle" sort of way. And while I hate to burst the bubble of all the gym rats out there, women in general prefer the latter in terms of body type. It's more naturally appealing. More solid. I seem to find that the guys who pump up at the gym always look as if they are made of foam. Whereas guys with physiques like Curt's, they look like they will hold up to a lifetime of use. Finally he looks up at me.

"How long have you been there?" he asks, removing his safety goggles and wiping the sweat off his brow with the back of his hand.

"Just a few seconds," I reply, suddenly self-conscious that I was admiring his muscles. "How's the entertainment center going?"

"So far so good." He swigs from a handy water bottle. "Should be done in about an hour for stain."

"One thing about all that donated furniture, we get to spend the budget on nice wood!" The cabinet is beautiful walnut veneer ply, which we are staining a deep sheer eggplant purple.

"Lucky for you, no primer!" Curt grins at me, and we both laugh.

"My first disaster," I say. "And probably not my last."

"For sure not your last. Nor your worst, if I know how the universe works." Curt winks. I wonder why I never noticed his eyes before? Sort of a sparkly greenish hazel. Lovely, really.

"How's everything inside?" he asks, breaking me from my pondering about his eyes and returning me to the task at hand.

"So far so good. Birdie is doing the Day One wrap-up, so we have at least an hour to chill."

"Poor kid." Curt's brow furrows. "She is so out of her element here, and Paul is too smitten with her to see that it's bringing the show down a notch. He should have gotten one of those 'guy-next-door' types to host. The ones that're smart and skilled enough with a drill to hang with the guys, and handsome-charming-little-brother enough to hang with the girls but not make them incoherent with lust. Birdie is too dumb to be anything but a nightmare on site, too gorgeous to be anything but a distraction to the guys and a source of withering jealousy from the girls."

"Wow, I never thought of it like that," I reply. "I have just been too busy praying she doesn't screw something up that I can't fix later."

"You're getting through it pretty well so far." He pauses. "For a rookie."

"Oh yeah?" I quip back at him. "I don't recall seeing your laundry list of television credits. Seems to me you have a small cabinet-making and custom furniture business somewhere in the sticks, and the occasional rehab property."

"Piece of advice, in this business, don't list anything on your resume that wasn't ultimately at least a little successful or well-respected. If you've done a bunch of stuff and none of it went anywhere, and they haven't ever heard of you, makes 'em wonder if you are some kind of jinx." He slides the safety goggles back on and gives me a two-finger salute. "And now, my little taskmaster, I had better get this knocked out so you have plenty of time to stain it that awful purple."

"It's aubergine, and it will be gorgeous," I yell over the noisy sander.

"Aubergine my ass, it is purple, and you're ruining this wood with it!" He is using his irritated voice, but I can see the mischief in his eyes.

"Well, when you acquire enough taste to be a designer, you let me know and I'll come out here and play with power tools, and you can be the one with your butt on the line for the reveal!" Curt holds his dusty hand out to me. I take it, feeling the calluses under the gritty sawdust.

"That's a deal, peanut."

I head back across the parking lot to Zack's apartment wondering if Curt and I were actually getting to be friends, and why the hell he had called me "peanut."

video diary confession:

"Okay, so I just have to say that this shoot has been a real eye-opener. Frankly, I've never really known anyone personally who was in the military, and the willingness to put oneself in harm's way out of patriotism is an impulse I appreciate in others, but cannot really comprehend myself.

*And especially as a woman, I just could never imagine going through
everything that a regular soldier has to go through, plus all of the extra
difficulties inherent in fitting in as a female. But listening to Diane's story
these past couple of days has made me understand things a little bit better,
and I'm more grateful than ever that we have such brave and heroic people in this country who put their lives on the line every day to make me
safe. I thank you all. From the bottom of my heart, and with all humility,
I thank you."*

At the wrap party, I find a quiet corner table away from the
bedlam in the middle of the room. Jou has come to join me, I suspect because Ashleigh is flirting like mad with Zack's commanding officer, who came for the reveal to surprise Zack, who hadn't
seen him since Afghanistan. We get to watch the taped message
from President Bush welcoming Zack and Diane home and
thanking them for their service, sort of moving in a "support the
troops" non-partisan sort of way. Poor Bryan, who has become
very accustomed to being my date at these shindigs, is standing
with Birdie, and looking forlorn. I wink at him when Jou isn't
looking just to let him know I'm still not taking sides.

Not that Jou sees the seating arrangement that way.

"Do you believe that little bitch STILL hasn't gotten all of
her stuff out of the apartment?" Jou snarls. "I'm tripping over her
god-awful collections EVERYWHERE. If it isn't a *Wizard of Oz*
figurine, it is a 1950's lady's head vase. You would think she would
want to move on with her life already."

"Jou, it's only been a few weeks, and I assume deep down
Bryan probably believes you will work things out. Leaving some
of his most precious items behind is a way of saying he still trusts
you and wants to return." I'm such a capable therapist. For a designer. "Besides, you can complain all you want, but the first time

you guys had me over for dinner, you glowed with pride at those collections."

"Maybe. But still. If she wants to come back, there is a lot of work to be done. Can't just pretend it's all water under the bridge, you know. Things have been DONE. Things have been SAID."

"I'm going to give this one more shot, because I care about you both. My friend Naomi works with a really great doctor who specializes in couples therapy for same-sex partnerships. He's gay himself, and Naomi says he's saved some really broken relationships. Will you at least call him and see if you could meet with him for an introductory session?"

"Will she do it?" Jou says, gesturing with his Manhattan at Bryan.

"Of course he will, he misses you." I'm assuming.

"All right. If Miss Thang agrees, I'll go to one appointment. Just to see. No promises."

"I'll talk to Naomi and Bryan and we'll get it set up. You'll see, it will be a very good thing." I'm deeply and importantly proud of myself. Love getting everything fixed for people.

"Okay. Just let me know. I've got to get out of here, all the uniforms are making me crazy. I don't suppose you want to head up to the Eagle?" Jou teases me, since the leather bar is not exactly an appropriate place for me.

"I think I'll pass this time, I have a friend meeting me in the back room of the Cellblock!" Another place I have only heard about and will never see in person.

"Have fun then, sweetie. And remember, you have to play to win!" Jou drains the last of his drink and smiles at me with the cherry between his front teeth.

I look down at my nearly empty wineglass and debate whether

I should have another or just head home. My cell phone vibrates on my hip.

"Hello?"

"Hey, it's Hillary." Who is obviously someplace loud.

"Where are you?"

"Thirsty's. Naomi and Alice are here, so are Chandler and Dave. Come meet us."

"Perfect. I'll be there in twenty."

"Bring smokes, we're nearly out."

"Got it."

I make my rounds fairly rapidly, and head out, stopping by White Hen for a couple of packs of Parliament Ultra Lights. None of us smokes unless we are drinking, and these days, fewer and fewer bars have cigarette machines. Usually one of us picks up a pack on the way to the bar and we share. Must have been a long evening already, if they are out. When I get there, I find the group sitting at a big table near the front window. Hillary hugs me tightly, hands me a lemondrop shot, and tells me I need to catch up. I throw back the sweet-tart drink, feeling the tingle all the way down, and Chandler returns from the bar where he has gotten me a cocktail.

"SKYY Citrus and soda, Hillary said that was your poison." He hands me the drink.

"It is tonight." I'm glad to be here with my friends; it's comfortable and anonymous and I have a really nice buzz going.

"Hey!" Dave shouts, waving his arms over his head. "Over here!"

Everyone turns to see who he is yelling at. Everyone but me. Because there is only one person that he could be yelling at.

"Hey everyone, what's going on?"

Package Boy.

Ron makes his way around the table saying hello and finally gets to me. He leans over and whispers in my ear.

"I promise I'm not stalking you. But I'm not giving up on you yet, either." Then he kisses my cheek lightly, right near my ear.

Even if I've been avoiding him, that makes me very sparkly in all my girl parts. After about an hour, Naomi and Alice have left, with the number for the therapist safely entered into my Palm for Jou and Bryan. Hillary and Chandler are clearly getting ready to leave to "light the Shabbat candles," and Dave is hitting on one of the waitresses, leaving me and Ron to our own devices.

At the moment, those devices appear to be his hands, which are clever for sliding up and down my spine, and my hands, which seem of their own accord to be kneading the very strong muscles of his thigh, firm under worn jeans. I realize I never asked him what he did at the packaging company, and wonder if he works in the warehouse, lifting and carrying, and building these lovely thighs. He leans close to me and whispers in my ear.

"I think we are making a spectacle of ourselves."

I laugh. "Probably so. Perhaps we should behave more demurely." He leans back, and I unhand his leg.

"So how is the show coming along? Are you enjoying it?" he asks, fiddling with the paper coaster.

"It's great, so far. I mean, it's a lot of work. I still don't have my head completely around it, but it's fun, too. And the people are great. And I get to be constantly designing something new and fresh, which is my favorite part." I finish the dregs of my drink.

"I have this friend who is a hairdresser. She said that whenever she sees anyone, her friends or strangers on the street, she's always picturing them with the hair she thinks they should have. Do you do that in rooms? Like, do you come in here and imagine how you would rearrange the furniture or change the paint color?"

"Well, it depends how you mean. If you mean do I obsess about design to the exclusion of all else, having weird visions all over the place, the answer is no. If you mean do I frequently see a better version of a space float magically before my eyes for a second or two, the answer is yes."

"Oh, man!" he exclaims.

"What?"

"I can't imagine what must have floated magically before your eyes in my place! It's embarrassing enough with normal people!" He laughs at himself, which is sort of endearing. And good that he knows he's living like a total pig.

"Well, you certainly could use some organization and cleaning. I couldn't even have a design come to mind, it was so crazy!" Might as well call him on his shit.

"Maybe I just need the right influence and a designer with vision." He leans over and kisses me, which is really yummy.

"You need a designer with a can of kerosene and a blowtorch." I kiss him back.

"I think I should take you home."

"I agree." Déjà vu all over again. And I try not to think about anything except how good it feels to have someone interesting interested in me.

I call Hillary, not knowing if I should be furious or dejected or relieved. I do not pay attention to the time. She points this out to me immediately.

"It's three o'clock in the fucking morning, Lily." Oops.

"Sorry, Hil."

"Whassup?" I can hear her moving around, and assume that she is slowly getting out of bed and trying not to wake Chandler.

"He left."

"Who left?" I hear fabric rustling and can picture the robe sliding on.

"Package Boy. Got me all hot and bothered, came home with me, came upstairs, made out with me on the couch for almost an hour, and then when I stood up to take him to bed, he said he should go, and left!" I was still in shock.

"That's weird," Hillary says. "Maybe it's payback for you blowing him off?"

"That's what I thought, but what guy thinks of that when he is half drunk with a hard-on and a girl trying to get him in the sack?" I mean, honestly!

"None that I can think of," Hillary says. "Did he say he would call you?"

"Yes."

"Do you want him to call you?"

"I dunno. I mean, the first date was mostly fun, tonight was fun, sex would have been fun, but you know I'm not thinking about dating these days." Plus I can't forget how that first date ended, and how it made me feel. And how long it took him to call. And that he knows I'm a slut.

"Well, maybe he is. I mean, he has tried a couple of times to take you out properly." Hillary pauses. "Maybe he felt sort of used."

"In other words, you think I was using him!" Bitch.

"Look, you know I'm a big fan of keeping sex and relationships in their proper perspective. However, if you look at the facts, you got drunk on your first date and went home with him. But you bolted in the middle of the night, and no matter how many times you tell me that it was because of your morning meeting, I still think something is fishy there. Especially since you proceeded to blow off all of his attempts to take you out again. Then tonight, he shows up unexpectedly, and you start drinking and try to sleep with him again. Noticing a pattern that might be confusing to him?"

"I hate when you are logical in the middle of the night, counselor." Of course, Hillary is right at all hours of the day.

"I know, sweetheart. Look, get a good night's sleep and we'll continue tomorrow. And my recommendation is that, this time, if he calls, just fucking have dinner with him."

"Maybe." I yawn. "Thanks, Hil, sorry for waking you."

"Quid pro quo, kiddo. Not like I haven't done it to you a billion times. I'll talk to you later."

" 'Kay. And Hil?"

"Yeah?"

"How was your night?"

"Full of mitzvahs." She giggles.

"How many mitzvahs exactly?"

"Four."

"Slut."

"G'nite."

"Bye."

I climb into my bed, still vaguely irritated to be alone, still half-drunk, reach for the new toy I bought at G-Boutique, have a quick mitzvah of my own, and fall asleep immediately.

♥ My Big Fat Geek Wedding

"Naomi, hurry the hell up, would you?" Hillary is honking the horn of her sassy new Audi and screaming at the outside of Naomi's condo.

"Relax, we're eons early as it is." I try to calm her down. The three of us are heading to the wedding of the year. Not in terms of social importance or glitz or glamour. In terms of living proof that there is indeed someone for everyone. Every year or so, a couple gets hitched that gives the rest of us reason to believe that we are not going to spend our lives alone. And Clifford Daniel and Lang Shelby are that couple. Cliff is about five-feet-four-inches, balding, round as a beach ball, and no matter what he is wearing, it is rumpled, half untucked, and frequently smells sort of musty, like old books. Lang is five-feet-eleven-inches in her stocking feet, thin as a rail, with frizzy mousy-brown hair, terrible skin, and bug eyes sort of like Marty Feldman. Cliff has a tendency to wax poetic about the intricacies of tax law, and Lang likes to get out the slide projector when company comes over to give lectures on her travels in South America. Cliff is thirty-three. Lang is forty-six.

Hillary met Cliff in law school when they were assigned to a Torts study group together. In spite of his shabby appearance, Cliff is smart as a whip, and it became clear that working with him would do Hillary a world of good academically. In return, she started including him in some of our outings, gradually giving him access to an actual life outside of school, which did him a world of good socially. Especially last year, when Naomi brought Lang, a fellow therapist she met at Hazelden, to Cliff's Fourth of July party. Love at first sight. When they announced their engagement six months later, we were not surprised. And instead of being depressing, the way weddings can sometimes be, that whole "why them and not me?" syndrome, this one is just joyous. Because if these two can find true love, then there really is a lot of hope in the world for the rest of us.

Hillary honks at Naomi's building again, just as the door opens and she flies out carrying the enormous box that holds our joint gift, a KitchenAid stand mixer. We always buy people the KitchenAid stand mixer. Always the five-quart, even if they registered for the four-and-a-half-quart. Always in either deep cobalt blue or bright red, even if we are tempted by the new color choices of the season. (The lavender and spring green this year were particularly difficult to resist.) I think that deep down, all three of us secretly want nothing more than to own a five-quart KitchenAid stand mixer.

Lily's Rule #23: Buying a KitchenAid mixer for yourself as a single woman in her thirties is tantamount to potential marriage

*suicide. It is throwing in the karmic towel. The KitchenAid mixer
is a wedding gift, period. You buy one for yourself, you tempt the
gods.*

Naomi gets in the backseat, apologizing for not being downstairs.

"I'm sorry guys, I was on the phone and lost track of time,"
she says, breathlessly.

Hillary snorts. "Talking to the new babe?"

Naomi blushes, and says, "Yes, in fact, it was Alice, and she
says hello to the both of you."

Hillary's instinct about where Naomi was the night of the
Chandler debacle was dead on, and after she brought Alice to
Thirsty's we were pretty sure we knew what was up.

So last Wednesday, after watching my television debut and
drinking gallons of champagne, we got her to confess. Turns out
Alice, who is studying to be an art therapist as well, had been assigned to Naomi as part of an observation requirement for
school. Naomi was pleasantly surprised to discover that Alice was
not only attractive, smart, and Sapphically inclined, but also single and immediately drawn to Naomi. They kept their mutual attraction under control just long enough for Alice to finish her
observation requirement, and for Naomi to file a glowing recommendation with the school. Apparently, they have been in bed
ever since.

We all met up for dinner at MK last night, and both Hillary
and I agree that she is a lovely woman, and she has our total support. Toby was sort of a pill, and Hillary and I were enormously
relieved that this time around Naomi seems to have paired herself with someone we can actually have a conversation with.

Naomi winks at me. "And speaking of new romances, how is Chandler these days?"

Hillary turns the car back on. "He is fine, thank you for asking. However he is not a romance, he is sex. Like a decent vibrator, but with kissing. Don't start planning MY nuptials, just because we are off to see Cliff and Lang walk the plank. Got it?"

"Got it," Naomi says.

"All right girls, off we go," Hillary announces, pulling into traffic and heading for The Fairmont.

The wedding ceremony is simple and sweet, even if the bridal party does look a bit like an Addams Family reunion. Cliff's best man, some guy he went to camp with, actually looks a lot like a male version of Lang, which we all choose not to comment upon, especially since Lang's sister, Elodie, serving as the maid of honor, bears a striking resemblance to Cliff, thinning hair included, poor thing. There are three other groomsmen. Cliff's first cousin, Dickie, who reminds us all of Beaker from the Muppet Show; his college roommate, Singh, a slight Indian gentleman in a full turban; and one of the partners from Cliff's firm, a surprisingly handsome fellow named Charlie. Lang's side is no better. In addition to her sister is her sister-in-law April, a sort of squarely built gal with a terrible perm, her best friend Lois, who you might assume was eight months pregnant if she weren't in her mid-fifties, and her niece Chalcy, a sullen fifteen-year-old with braces, limp greasy hair, and Coke-bottle glasses. These ravishing creatures are decked out in taffeta of an iridescent teal, in a style that flatters none of them.

But all bitchiness aside, Lang is genuinely radiant, Cliff is beaming, and the two of them kissed so passionately at the end of the ceremony that we all burst into applause and catcalls.

"You can't be serious," Hillary says around a mouthful of lamb chop. "The Bears haven't had much of an offense in years. They keep winning on the strength of their defense."

An avid football fan, whose first big splurge when she made junior partner was Bears season tickets, Hillary is arguing with Cliff's groomsman Charlie about the merits of the upcoming season. Charlie, originally from Madison, is a Packers fan who, to his credit, seems to be suppressing every urge to smack her. Actually, he looks sort of bemused, and maybe a little bewitched, and if I know Hillary, he should beware before he is beheaded.

"Well, I'm going to the Packers game this year," Charlie offers. "Some friends got a skybox, I assume it would offend your delicate sensibilities to join me? Give me the play-by-play live and in person?"

I personally find it amazing that he is bothering to ask her out, she has been borderline rude to him since we sat down for dinner.

"I have season tickets," Hillary says coldly. "Not a skybox, but tenth row at the fifty yard line will have to do." I kick her under the table, while Naomi glares at her from across the way. "But, um, thanks for the offer," she finishes weakly.

"Well, maybe you'll come up and say hello at halftime, that is usually when the dessert cart shows up." This guy is unbelievable; he is either a glutton for punishment or a total idiot. Hillary couldn't be more indifferent to him.

"Maybe." Hillary excuses herself and makes a break for the bathroom, dragging me with her.

"What a tool!" she says when we are safely out of earshot.

"I thought he was nice." I can't help it; I did think he was nice. But it is never fun to tell Hillary what she doesn't want to hear.

"Oh, please!" she starts in. "All that business about his big case, like I care. What an ego. Mr. Partner. Whatever!"

"Um, Hil . . ." She is going to hate this. "He didn't say anything about his big case or being partner. That was Cliff singing his praises when he came by the table. All he did was ask you about yourself and invite you to a skybox at Soldier Field for the biggest game of the year. And because you are stubborn and have taken it into your head to dislike him, you're going to be watching the Packers game in forty-below windchill instead of from a heated skybox. I'm not saying, but I'm just saying . . ."

"I'll be fine in my seats, thank you, and I'm not interested in him, period. Let's drop it." And just like that, conversation over.

Oy. I never understand Hillary and her taste in men. This guy is really cute, has been very attentive, and is a partner in Cliff's firm, so he's obviously smart and successful. What more does this woman want?

We freshen our lip gloss and return to the table. Naomi glares at Hillary in her "you didn't need to be rude, young lady" look, and Hillary glares back in her "butt out Ms. Nosey Parker and don't play Mommy with me" look, and I take the uncomfortable opportunity to finish my wine. Across the room I can see Charlie asking Lang's niece to dance, much to her obvious delight. Hillary doesn't seem to notice.

My message light is blinking when I get home from the wedding.

"Hey, Lily, this is Ron Schwartz. It's been a while, thought I would check in with you and see if I could cash in the rain check on dinner. Saw the show last week, and I think it was great. Give me a call. Bye."

Oh, lordy. Package Boy returns. I suppose I am going to have to call him back. Just when I had totally forgotten about him. Okay, just when I was pretty sure he had forgotten about me. I make a note in my BlackBerry to call him back tomorrow, change out of my wedding finery, and into my bathrobe to go over my notes for next week's shoot.

Just before midnight I do a final check of my design boards for a meeting with a potential new client tomorrow. My first show-related gig. The client, Pam, is recently engaged, and her fiancé is moving into her place. She saw the pilot and figured since the theme of the show is making the opposite sex at ease in your space, having me redo her bedroom, living room, and home office to make him feel at home would be a great gift. She has a very cool town house in Roscoe Village, and I think she will like the design plan I'm presenting to her tomorrow.

I finish up, pull the finish samples and fabric swatches, make my evening toilette, check the locks, and climb into bed. I think about Package Boy. He does earn points for persistence. Who knows, maybe he could actually be dateable. Then again, maybe he just called because the show is getting some buzz and he thinks it would be cool to be connected to a television personality.

I can't believe I just referred to myself as a television personality. Oy.

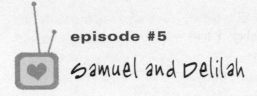

episode #5

Samuel and Delilah

Bravo *Wednesday July 5* 8PM–9PM

SWAP/MEET Delilah and Samuel

Local Chicago celebrities step up to the plate, with White Sox rookie Samuel Diaz-Perez and WGN reporter Delilah Quinn offering up their homes to the *Swap/Meet* crew. Highlights include carpenter Jake Kersten's one-of-a-kind baseball bat coffee table, and a hair-raising salon experience with stylist Jou DuFresne.

We are very behind. Enormously behind. Samuel Diaz-Perez, who is very handsome, and obviously very talented on the base-ball diamond, is essentially a nonexistent part of this shoot. Between a constant barrage of cell phone calls, mostly executed in rapid-fire Spanish, flirting with Birdie, who has batted her eyelashes today like she is trying to rid herself of flies, and a huge rainstorm making things tricky in the carpentry tent outside, we are starting to worry about getting everything done.

Everyone is on edge, especially Paul, who has been six sheets to the wind since about ten this morning, and sniping at everyone in his clipped British way.

"Darlings, can we please, for the love of all that is holy, get this fucking painting done? It isn't the bloody Sistine Chapel." Deep swig from "coffee" cup. Nothing like a loving pep talk to get the production assistants moving.

"Psst, Lily?" Birdie motions me over to the bedroom where the makeup gal is touching up her already flawless face. I head over.

"Yeah, Birdie, what's up?"

"He asked me out!" Well, duh. We were all there. Mid-art project, purposely simple, just painting watercolors over a black-and-white blowup of flowers, sophisticated paint by numbers, Samuel mentioned that none of the flowers were as lovely as Birdie. Birdie blushed prettily. Then he asked if she was a baseball fan, and Birdie, who has been hardly able to put together a coherent sentence in the twelve weeks we have been working together, replied that indeed she was, and that she was mightily impressed with the Sox this season, rattling off a series of stats and opinions that would make Bob Costas sound like a food critic.

Raoul, the lighting guy, was so surprised that he lost control of the white Foamcore board he was holding up behind her to brighten the space, which promptly clonked Birdie on the back of the head. Considering the four-inch stilettos she was wearing, not to mention the weight of her prow, she began to topple forward, caught deftly like a fly ball on a cloudy day by Samuel. He took the opportunity of having her in his arms to invite her to the first game of the coveted Sox/Cubs crosstown series.

"Really, with the hitting, really?" Bob said to Raoul while Samuel and Birdie gazed longingly at each other.

"I know he did, Bird, you must be really excited!" I make an attempt at enthusiasm.

Birdie sighs dramatically. Well, as dramatically as one can sigh while their lip gloss is being touched up. "He is just so sweet."

"Well, he seems to really like you, too; I'm sure that you guys will have a great time." And in the meantime, maybe we could FINISH THIS FUCKING SHOOT?

"Thanks, Lily, you're such a good friend."

Friend? Birdie thinks of me as a friend? I'm suddenly a little embarrassed by my propensity for making fun of her with Bryan, and for referring to her as birdbrain to Naomi and Hillary, who always ask for the "Audubon Blooper Report" after we wrap a shoot. After all, it isn't her fault if she isn't as naturally bright as some other people. And she has never been anything but sweet to me. I make a mental note to be nicer to her, and to try and stop denigrating her behind her back. This decision makes me feel all warm and fuzzy and evolved and stuff.

video diary confession:

"Okay, so this has been a pretty good day so far. Things are moving right along, and Samuel has been pretty good overall. Now I do have to go on record and say that as a third generation Northsider, I'm a Cubs fan all the way. But as a Chicagoan, I'm glad whenever any one of our teams has any sort of success, and if this slugger is helping the overall cause, then I think that is pretty great. But if he screws up my carpet, I'm going to send him back to the minors! Speaking of which, I'd better go check on the progress . . ."

"Okay, Lily, we're speeding. And, action," Bob calls out.

I head through the door into Delilah's home office, which had been the single most disorganized space I had ever seen, boxes of files everywhere. Samuel and Birdie are laying down carpet tiles over the concrete floor we found when we pulled up the old carpet. Genius product, easy to use, and surprisingly chic, not to mention pretty reasonably priced. Of course, I have chosen three colors, a deep green, a lighter sage, and a sort of stony gray. And in light of the installation crew, went with a random pattern, ergo, impossible to screw up. Birdie and Samuel have been laying them down and making goo-goo eyes at each other for about fifteen minutes, and to my delight, they have finished about a third of the room. The crew follows me in as I put on my official "positive check-in" face.

"Hey guys!" I say. "Wow! This is really looking terrific." Which it actually is.

"Thanks, sugar," says Birdie. "These lil ol' squares are so easy to use, even a silly gal like me can't get it wrong!"

I'm beginning to wonder if Birdie has been slipping ecstasy into my green tea, as, for the second time today, I'm sort of totally smitten with her. Then again I'm frequently predisposed to be negatively prejudicial about the preternaturally beautiful, especially if they have difficulty presiding over the assembly of prefabricated furniture. But at least I'm reasonably good about allowing those prejudices to be swayed.

"I am for certain enjoying them," chimes in Samuel. "Perhaps there is hoping they will be also in use in my home, is it not?"

I wag my finger at him. "You know the rules, slugger, no clues about what is going on over at your place! But I'm glad you are both enjoying yourself. These carpet tiles are a great alternative to installed carpeting, especially for people in rentals. When you are ready to move, the floor can come with you. They can go in over existing carpet, hardwood floor, linoleum, or as we are doing here, concrete. And if you get a stain on one, you can take it up and clean it or replace it. Great if you entertain a lot, have kids, or are just klutzy like me!" I deliver this last bit with a sly wink to the camera, and get the thumbs-up from Bob, and a big grin from Paul.

"We got it, Lily, thanks." The crew leaves to head out to the land of carpentry, where Curt is hopefully finishing the bookshelves for the office. I have three PA's working on getting all of Delilah's stuff into handy boxes, labeling each with one of those newfangled label makers. I sort of lost my mind at The Container Store, but the end result is going to be an office that should inspire Delilah to excellence in reporting. Or at least make it easier to balance her checkbook.

"Really, with the organization explosion, really?" was Bob's reaction as the seventh huge blue and white bag came in the door.

Once the bookshelves are done, we just have to prime and paint (back to MDF for us) and get them installed in the room. If Curt finishes them soon, we may be able to get them in tonight.

"Birdie, love?" Paul walks into the room.

"Yeah, sugar?" Birdie rises from the floor, legs telescoping upwards far more gracefully than I ever would have been able to manage.

"Darling, how did the end of day wrap-up bit at dear old Samuel's flat go?" Paul is speaking sweet, but his eyes have fire in them.

"Oh, my." Birdie looks crestfallen.

Paul continues. " 'Oh, my, it went so very well,' is that what you mean to say, *sugar*?" Paul's voice is dripping with sarcasm. "Or did you mean to say, 'Oh, my, I FUCKING DIDN'T GO OVER THERE!' "

Uh. Oh.

"Paul, I just got caught up over here . . . and I . . . I mean . . ."

"You mean that when Tommy took the van over, you *said* you would be right behind him in the Hybrid, and then never bothered to actually LEAVE. Is that right?"

Grand Honda donated an Accord Hybrid for us to use to shuttle back and forth between sites, and to go on the occasional off-site shopping spree, since there'd be plenty of on-air coverage for them.

"Paul, honey, I know you are angry with me, but I didn't do it on purpose . . ."

"Of course you didn't, you stupid cow, you'd have to have more than four brain cells in order to be malicious. You were just being you, such a delightful thing to look at, pity you cannot get the SIMPLEST THING RIGHT!"

I'm flabbergasted. Paul is clearly drunk, bitterly mean, and poor Birdie has tears welling up in her baby blues. Samuel Diaz-Perez gets up from the floor, walks over to Birdie, hands her a handkerchief from his pocket, turns around, and faces Paul.

"You are a very small little man, Mr. Brownnoser. And you should be making the apology to Miss Birdie for your conduct, which no gentleman would have allowed to happen." I try not to snicker at Paul being called Brownnoser.

"You know what, my fine ball-playing bastard? Fuck off."

Samuel Diaz-Perez looks genuinely remorseful as he punches Paul in the jaw. Paul goes down like a sack of potatoes; Ginny, his assistant, rushes in, while the rest of the crew scatters. Samuel escorts a shaking Birdie to Delilah's bedroom and closes the door.

"Hey." Curt comes over to the craft service table, where I'm eating my fifth brownie.

Lily's Rule #12: Chocolate cures most ills. Especially when one has PMS.

"Hey."

"Your shelves are in, they look great," Curt informs me.

"Thanks, Curt. That's one thing that has gone right today." I'm cranky. Blue. More shaken up by the events of the afternoon than I probably have a right to be. The monthly munchies aren't helping either, hence the brownies and the fact that I'm officially going to be seen on TV in my fat pants.

"Heard it got wild and woolly in here. Did you see the deed?"

"The punch? You betcha. Quite a right hook this boy has on him. If he doesn't make it in the majors he should try boxing." I know I'm being kind of snippy, but at this moment I really don't care.

"Heard Master Paul was asking for it."

"That he was, the little shit." I reach for brownie number six. "Called Birdie stupid and yelled at her for forgetting to go over to do the end of Day One wrap-up at Samuel's place."

"Well, she isn't exactly the brightest bulb in the marquee." Curt chuckles.

"Which isn't exactly her fault." I jump in, defending my new ally. "And if she hadn't been flirting with Samuel, he never would have gotten so mad at her."

"Or so tanked."

"That, too," I mumble, mouth full of brownie.

"You're her great supporter all of a sudden?" Curt asks,

snagging the last lone bit of chocolatey goodness off the platter before I devour it.

"I just feel bad, is all."

"Tell you what. Come check out my beautiful handiwork, and then we can go meet up with the rest of the crew for a drink. I think everyone is headed out to howl at the moon."

"I don't think I'm up for howling tonight. Early morning tomorrow."

"I didn't mean we were going to go wild; it's a bar." Curt laughs at me. "Howl at the Moon. Dueling piano jockeys taking requests, and sing-alongs. Both crews are going, let off some steam, have a couple beers, what do you say?"

"Do you think they know any Journey?" I ask.

"Let's find out."

As it turns out, they know Journey and a lot more. By the time Curt and I arrive, the gang from Delilah's has already taken over a section of the room near the dance floor. Buckets of iced long-necks are on the tables, and Curt snags me one. We clink bottles, and I take a deep swig of the icy brew thinking that it is the most refreshing beverage in the world. Over in the far corner, Jake is canoodling with a redhead in huge sunglasses and a baseball cap that bears a striking resemblance to Jake's sacred NYPD hat. I nudge Liam, the sound guy for the "red team" as Ashleigh and Jake's crew are known. Curt and I are the "blue team."

"Who's the new victim?" I ask, gesturing with my chin at Jake and his lady.

"Don't ask," Liam says. "He's lucky if he doesn't get fired for this shit one of these days."

"Why fired? Is she a producer's daughter or wife or something?"

"Doesn't she look familiar to you?" Liam asks, head tilted.

I look again. Cap, bright red hair, big glasses, small mole to left of . . .

It's DELILAH! I'd recognize that mole anywhere, I'm always fixated on it when she delivers me my nightly news. Liam notices the recognition register on my face.

"See what I mean?" he asks, smiling.

"Wow," I say. "Love must be in the air today. Birdie and Samuel were a little less physical, but no less interested."

"Must be." Liam finishes his beer, and grabs us two more from the nearest bucket. What the hell. I deserve a night out. Besides, it's just beer.

"So now I cooooommmme to youuuuuu . . . with ooooooopen aaaaaarms. Nooothing to hiiide, belieeeeeeve what I saaaayyyyy . . ." I have such a good voice. Really. I mean, listen to me, poor Steve Perry, he couldn't sing like me, no way, no how . . . hey! Stupid bouncer. That's my MICROPHONE!!!!

I'm being escorted, not so gently I might add, off of the little stage. My crew boos loudly at my dismissal.

"C'mon kiddo, time to go." Curt gently takes possession of me from the disgruntled bouncer.

"Hey, I'm having fun, Cuuuurrrt. Don't be a poopy parter. A partly pooper. A . . ."

"Yeah, I know, I'm a wet blanket. Still, I think we should get you home."

There is a blast of cool breeze on my face, and I sort of register that sly Curt has gotten me all the way across the bar and out the door.

"You are Sneaky McStealthy, Curtis my man. Look at me all

outside, you know, and all." Curt is waving his hand in the air like he just don't care. This apparently attracts a taxi of the yellow variety, which he suspects I would like to ride in.

"Take her to Dearborn and Maple. Eleven twenty-two." Curt bundles me into the cab, hands the driver a twenty, kisses my hand, and tells me to drink. Or bathe. Or something with water.

My keys do not like to work. They are all rubbery and having problems getting in the lock. It does appear to help when I stop trying to use my mailbox key and use the door key instead. My shoes seem to like the kitchen, so I leave them in the crisper drawer in the refrigerator, because I think it will be refreshing for them after such a long day. I see my machine light is blinking.

I sing myself over to the console. "Popuuuular . . . I'm so fricking popuuuullllar. I'm the cat's meow, I'm the, something that rhymes with meowwwww . . ." I goddamn love my voice tonight, fuck that bouncer, those people LOVED me.

Click. "Hey, it's Naomi. Hope we're still on for dinner Sunday, call me." Naomi. Lovely Naomi. Lovely muff-diving Naomi. La di da di da . . .

Click. "Hi, Lily, it's Ron. Hope you're well. Wondering if we can finally have that dinner? Maybe Friday night? Give me a call, seven seven three-five five five-one four zero four."

Hmmmm. Package Boy strikes again. Well, if he wants me, he can have me. I decide to call.

"Hello?" Someone sounds sleepy.

"Helllllo, you."

"Who is this?" Mr. Cranky-pants.

"It's me." Silly rabbit.

"Me, who?"

What a buffoon. "Me. Lila."

"Lily?"

Duh. "That's what I said."

"Lily, it's after midnight."

"And we're gonna let it all hannngg dowwwwwwn . . ."

"Are you singing Eric Clapton?"

"I'm taking requests!"

"Can I request that you not call me after midnight on a week-day?" He does not sound so very amused, my little box man.

"Touchy. Wanna come over and kiss me?"

"Lily, you sound like maybe you've been drinking a bit."

"Bottle of red. Bottle of whiiiiite . . ." Billy Joel is either entirely overrated or underrated and I can never remember which.

"Lily, I'm hanging up now." Which he does.

Fuck him. Fuck him and his package. FUCK HIM!

FUCK ME!

Oh. My. God.

My head. It is made of Jell-O. My Jell-O head is all sloshy and my brain bumps into it on the inside and makes bright sparks of pain behind my eyes. I wonder if five Advil was too many? Or not enough? My mouth is all fuzzy and I know I should have some OJ, but my refrigerator smelled like feet for some reason, which almost made me barf, so I'll have to wait and get it at craft service. All I know is that they'd better have bacon or I'm in big trouble. Mmm. Bacon. Bacony goodness. Meat candy.

And maybe a Coke.

It is going to be a very, very long day.

It took almost two days to recover. The second day I met the girls for lunch.

"Cheers," Hillary says, raising her iced tea glass to me and Naomi.

"Aww, shucks," I say. " 'Tweren't nothin'."

"Now, don't be modest, sweetie." Naomi smiles at me. "This is a very big accomplishment."

We got a small piece in *People* magazine, sort of a "If you're not watching this, you should be" sort of thing. I mean, we're up against *Law & Order*, so I don't know that we'll ever be the next huge hit, but apparently our numbers so far are good, and there has started to be some attention being paid. I even got recognized at the White Hen the other day.

"You're that designer chick!" remarked the clearly stoned twenty-something who was buying Red Bull and Corn Nuts. Breakfast of Champions.

"Yes, I am," I replied, humbly, I thought.

"Man, that episode last week was WACK!" I'm entirely clueless as to whether that is a good or a bad thing. "You totally fucked that girl's place!"

Ah. Yes. The now infamous Episode #3. Forget wishing for fame, chances are you'll be famous for something embarrassing. Just think Monica, Kato, and Pee-wee Herman. I'm destined to be defamed as the designer who destroyed the décor with defecations.

Hillary thought it was hysterical. Naomi said she could see how beautiful it would have been.

"So, my little famous friend," Hillary says, digging into her salad at The Atwood Café, where we are lunching in celebration of my making it into *People*. "Why do you suppose my pal Dave is up my tushie in a snit once again?"

Uh, oh. I'd almost managed to repress the awful drunk-dialing of Ron, and lord knows he hasn't called again since then. And I'm too mortified to call him again.

"Um . . ." I begin, hesitant to share the gruesome details when I have such a pretty burger glistening up at me. "Okay, I sort of called Ron back a little late in the evening and made an ass of myself."

"I heard there was singing involved, Lily; is that indeed true?" Hillary is fucking loving this, the ho.

"Yes, there may have been a bit of crooning," I admit reluctantly.

"Oh, Lily. How drunk were you?" Naomi asks.

"Oh, Naomi. I'd had maybe five beers. And all I had eaten all day was brownies." As if this is an excuse, which clearly, it isn't.

"I also hear there was a proposition made," Hillary quips.

"LILY!" Naomi drops her fork. "Did you make a drunk booty call? On a TUESDAY?" Her shock is a put-on, she is getting into the act with Hillary like the subtle pro she is.

"All right, look, you bitches. I got home drunk. He had left a message. Being somewhat without a barometer of good taste at the time, I called him back. Made a total idiot of myself, sang to him, invited him over to kiss me, at which point he hung up on me and has not called me since. So you can tell your friend Dave, who I happen to know once took all his clothes off at The Village Tap for no apparent reason except he was a little warm, that if his buddy the box boy couldn't see past one little tipsy mistake, then he wasn't worth my time anyway, and now I've saved him the price of dinner!" I pick up my burger and take a triumphant bite. "So there!" I say, trying not to spit beef morsels across the table.

"You've got ketchup on your chin, dearheart." Hillary smirks.

Naomi motions to the left side of her chin as I chase the offending condiment with my napkin.

The three of us laugh for a good long time.

 PETA, Paul, and Gary

When I get to the offices at 1000 West Washington for the afternoon production meeting, I'm shocked to see some sort of
demonstration going on. When I get closer, I notice that it is People for the Ethical Treatment of Animals, the notorious PETA,
and that their signs have blurry blown-up photos of Ashleigh's
design for Rick the vegan, the one with all the taxidermy. There
are a couple of local camera trucks outside, as well as some pho-
tographers.

I decide to avoid the mess on the sidewalk by sneaking up the
parking ramp to the second level and then I head inside. The conference room is abuzz. Ashleigh is sitting in a corner, obviously
upset and being consoled by Jou and Paul. Everyone is talking
about what is going to happen.

"Let's settle down, shall we, ducklings?" Paul begins. "Now, I
know that this sort of thing is upsetting to all of us, but the show
must go on. And at the end of the day, it will be fabulous publicity for the show. The network has decided to give us a two-hour

slot next week, and they are going to rerun Episode #3 before we premiere the new one. I think our ratings are about to go up, chickens!"

We are suddenly all kinds of poultry, an irony not lost on me, in light of the current predicament.

Paul continues, "I'm going down in a moment to make a statement to the press and the protesters, and I'd like both sets of team leaders flanking me when I do. Solidarity and all that, darlings."

This meant that Curt, Bryan, and I would be on one side, and Ashleigh, Jake, and Jou would be on the other side. I am so not prepared to be on television today. It is humid out, so I have my hair in these two silly braids like Pippi Longstocking. Didn't feel like putting in the contacts, not to mention makeup. I am too ugly to be on television today. So, I raise my hand.

"Um, Paul? Do you think we all need to be there? I mean, shouldn't it be just Ashleigh's team? After all, they are protesting her room."

"Not just mine, sweetheart." Ashleigh stands up in her corner. "There were several signs about your room being dangerous for that cat. Apparently they don't just care about the dead animals. They like the live ones, too!" God, that woman makes my ass twitch.

"Fine," I say. What else can I do?

Turns out, my look was the least of the issues covered at the little press conference.

Paul, who resorted to even more of his Dutch courage than usual, introduced us all to the PETA people as humans worth treating ethically. This, they did not find amusing. Then he

explained that all the animals used on the show had been purchased from a restaurant, and none were freshly made for the
show. Equally dumb maneuver. One of the PETA folks called
Paul an accessory to murder, at which point he asked if the
stuffed animals might not have died of natural causes before
their taxidermy fate.

That is when the fur began to fly, so to speak.

Ashleigh stepped forward and raised her hands like Evita on
the balcony.

"Please, please. I cannot believe you people are taking this so
personally. It was a mistake, an error in judgment, and it certainly
will not be repeated!" The crowd quieted. "Besides," she continued, "it isn't as if any animals were harmed in the shooting of this
episode."

Crap. Here comes . . .

"What about Lucy?" "Poor Lucy!" The chants got louder. Just
as I was stepping forward to defend myself, Curt grabbed my elbow. Paul began shouting.

"Listen, you grubby lot of wankers. You massacre tons of
chickpeas for your hummus-laden lifestyle, and no one protests
you at your dinner. Now we've been as patient as we are planning
on being with you, but I recommend that you take your petty little cause and FUCK OFF!"

I never really knew that whole "deafening silence" feeling until that very moment. Then, the uproar, and the crowd surged
forward violently. Curt and Jake shoved the rest of us back inside,
and we hightailed it upstairs to the conference room.

"Hey, Bry?" I whisper to him. "You think we're cancelled?"

We've all been called in for an emergency meeting.

"I doubt it, hon, they wouldn't want to tell us to our faces. They'd call and leave messages for sure."

"So what do you think is cooking?"

"I dunno, but I hope it's not my ass!"

We chuckle quietly as a series of blue suits enter the room. I recognize three of them as the bigwigs from Bravo and BBC. The fourth, who happens to be an extraordinarily handsome fellow, I have never seen before.

"Really, with the show of power, really!" Bob says softly.

Suit number one begins.

"We regret to inform you that Paul Brownmiller is taking an indefinite leave of absence to receive treatment for alcoholism. We know that some of you are aware that he has been struggling with this disease, and hope that you agree that his need for assistance has to take precedence for him right now. He sends his best to you all, along with his apologies for having to leave in the middle of our first season together."

Suit number two chimes in.

"We want to be very clear that we are supporting Paul in his recovery. And if any of you need to talk to someone about your feelings regarding this matter, we will be happy to arrange for a counseling session for you."

But what's behind suit number three?

"Additionally, if any of you are currently struggling with addictions, we encourage you to come to us so that we can get you the assistance you need as well. We think of this as a little family, and we want everyone as happy and healthy as possible."

Back to suit number one . . .

"While Paul is completing his rehabilitation, we have brought in Gary Blake to take over as series producer. Gary has been with us for years and was at the helm of *In My Kitchen* with Ishbel

Smythe-Jonson, and did our first two seasons of *Swap/Meet* back in the UK. We know he is the right person to be at the helm in Paul's absence, and hope that you will all welcome him to the team. Gary, would you like to say a few words?"

Gary steps forward. He is honest-to-God breathtaking. Tall, lithe, dark wavy hair shot with silver so that it literally sparkles. Square jaw, green-gray eyes, high cheekbones, full, perfectly shaped lips, and a fucking CLEFT CHIN. I mean, if George Clooney and Cary Grant had a kid . . .

"Thank you gentlemen, I appreciate your confidence in me." His voice is smoky sweet and low with a smooth British accent, and I suddenly have an aching heaviness in my nether regions that is usually reserved for Harrison Ford. Or maybe I just have to pee. But, as all the hair on the back of my neck is standing on end, I think I'm just really, really attracted to this guy.

He's still talking, and I'm not particularly paying any attention until I hear my name mentioned.

Uh. Oh.

"Um . . ." I say, flummoxed as to why he has uttered my name and if I'm supposed to be responding. "Of course?"

"See!" Gary continues, obviously thrilled. Thank God. "Lily gets it. We have a tremendous product, and we all need to focus on getting it into the hands of the consumer."

Sigh. I'm right. He knows how right I am. Maybe he will want to explain it to me over breakfast. Shit. There's my name again.

"Um . . . absolutely?" I venture.

"Lily, you're perfect!" Gary gushes. I have no fucking idea what I've just agreed to. But anything that will make that man smile that smile at me and call me perfect can't be bad.

The meeting wraps up quickly, the next production meeting is scheduled for tomorrow afternoon, and Bryan and I make plans to have dinner after. I start to head out, but Gary asks to see me. I follow his broad shoulders down the hall to Paul's old office.

My phone rings at nine PM. It interrupts my nap.

"H' lo?" I mumble.

"Lily, this is Gary."

YUM.

"Hey, what's up?" I mean other than me. We'd chatted earlier in his office for what felt like ten minutes and turned out to be two hours. Just talking about nothing in particular, like the conversation you might have with the friend of a friend if you happened to have parked on the same couch at a party. But there was something in the eye contact. At least, I wanted there to be. But one never knows if such things are for real or just wishful thinking.

"I just got back to the hotel. Dreary dinner, but great restaurant recommendation. So I wanted to thank you for providing me with a decent meal, even if the company far paled in comparison to this afternoon."

I'm honest-to-God blushing in my own living room.

"Well, I'm glad you liked it. Santorini is my favorite of all the Greektown restaurants."

"You were right, the grilled octopus was perfect, not rubbery at all." I could listen to this voice read out of a phone book for two hours and not be bored.

"Glad to hear it." He likes me. I can totally tell that he likes me. I have that rare and perfect knowledge that this conversation will gently lead to some sort of suggestion about getting together tonight, and I LOVE THAT I KNOW IT.

"How's your evening?" He's calm, and very casual.

"Okay," I reply, equally casual. "Stuffy."

He chuckles. "MY evening was stuffy, all those execs talking budget at me. Why is your evening stuffy?"

And this is where we ensure that the aforementioned suggestion has ample support on my end. "My air is on the fritz. Something wrong with the ventilation system. The maintenance guys are working on it." While I sit here and my hair frizzes.

"That is awful. What are you going to do?"

"Hope they fix it, I guess."

"I mean for the rest of the evening, are you just going to sit there? In the stuffiness?"

"Well, that's not all . . ." I say.

"What else?" he asks.

"I'm going to sit here and turn into a hedgerow." I love being able to use strange Briticisms with him. Hedgerow sounds so much cooler than shrubbery.

He laughs. "How's that exactly?"

"My hair. It is, at this moment, attempting to become a topiary."

"I see. Well, then, might I suggest an idea?"

"Shoot."

"Why don't you come here? I was going to order an eighteen-dollar in-room movie, and my air is set on Arctic Blast."

Ah, the booty call.

I should not do this. I should not sleep with my new interim temporary producer even if he is the most gorgeous man I have ever seen close up. I should not sleep with the man who stands between me and DIY stardom. Then again, I never really wanted DIY stardom, and if the show was cancelled tomorrow I would have socked away a little nest egg and still have my regular design business. . . .

"Okay, what room?" I hear myself say.

"Seven hundred and eight. See you soon."

Was it Jerry Seinfeld who did the bit about Night Guy and Morning Guy? Night Guy making decisions that Morning Guy doesn't approve of. Night Guy gets drunk, Morning Guy gets the hangover, that sort of thing? Well, Night Girl apparently decided that the Wyndham was a better option than the couch. So, Night Girl gets up, jumps in the shower, shaves legs and pits, gets out, slathers on the expensive Fresh lotion and spritzes the good perfume, then purposely gets into her most elegant cotton lounge pants and T-shirt. Just in case he is only offering air conditioning. Then she grabs a strip of four condoms out of the condom box on the nightstand. Just in case he isn't.

Gary answers the door wearing white drawstring pants of that sort of linen that feels like raw silk and seems to be favored by Hollywood types who marry barefoot on beaches in Saint Barth's. On top, a French blue button-down shirt, opened three buttons, cuffs rolled up. He smiles at me.

"Welcome to the North Pole!"

It takes every ounce of strength in my body not to look at his crotch.

Instead I take a quick breath, look him straight in the face, and reply, "I appreciate the invite. And more importantly, my hair appreciates it." I point to my head, where my curls, which I had already taken down from their barrettes at home, are about one-point-four-two humidity percentage points away from Jew-fro.

Gary reaches over and I swear to god, RUMPLES my hair. "I think your hair is amazing." I've never been much on rumpling, but I am starting to reconsider my position. "Shall we watch a movie?"

"Sure."

Gary climbs onto the bed, which has already been turned down for the evening. I don't know why this surprises me, there really isn't another place to watch from. Then again, the whole thing is surreal, especially in how easy and casual it seems. It feels like we both know that there is going to be sex, but no anxiousness, no games. This sort of thing never happens to me. At least not sober. I climb onto the bed next to him, and he starts flipping through the menu.

"Okay, we have the Renée Zellweger option, the Will Smith option, the Tom Cruise option, or the artsy Cate Blanchett option."

I feel like this is a test. If I pick Renée, he will think I'm fluffy. If I pick Cate, who is my actual first choice of the four, he will think I am trying to impress him. If I pick Tom, he may think I have a crush. Will seems like the safest choice.

"Will Smith?" I offer.

"Perfect, haven't seen it yet, but I loved his last one." For the second time today, I'm perfect. In my frump-gear and frizz, with no makeup and my ass at maximum capacity, I'm perfect. Life is so very fine. Gary hits the "Start Movie" button on the remote, and we are duly warned that he is being immediately charged $15.99 for the movie and that if he changes channels he will not be able to return to the film.

Before the opening credits are over, I'm leaning on the headboard beside him. By the time Will makes his first "guys are dumb" joke, Gary has slithered his arm behind me. By the time Will meets the heroine for the first time, I have shifted so that I'm leaning back against Gary, and his arm is draped more around my waist, his hand kneading my hip gently. By the time Will throws his first punch, Gary is nuzzling my head with his chin.

My body is all atingle. My nipples are hard, my palms are sweating, my clit is throbbing and jumping up and down in my pants as if it wants to get out where it could see the movie. When Will kisses the heroine for the first time, I inadvertently sigh. Gary chuckles.

"You girls are suckers for a kissing scene."

"That's because there are so many bad kissers in the world, it makes us happy to see it done well on screen."

"Are there really a lot of bad kissers out there?" Gary shifts behind me, and the movement sort of pulls me half around, so now I'm facing him. The blue-green flickering light of the television is very flattering to his evening whiskers and askew hair.

"Yes," I reply, lifting my chin up just slightly. "An awful lot of bad kissers."

"Poor baby," Gary says, reaching one hand forward and tucking a wayward curl around my ear. Then he leans forward, and . . .

Ahhhhhh.

Gary is not a bad kisser.

Gary is a divine kisser.

Gary is possibly the best kisser in the history of kissing. Gary's kissing skills appear to be matched by the deftness of his hands, which have found the perfect way to caress me. My clothes seem to have melted off, I don't really remember getting naked. But I am noticing that Gary is now divesting himself of his . . . sweet LORD. This is a very handsome beast. A definite COS, but no twists, no turns, the head is on straight, and Jay Leno's chin isn't visible anywhere.

Gary suddenly stops, lowers his head, and exclaims sheepishly, "Um, I don't suppose you brought condoms with you? I'm sort of unprepared."

Have I mentioned how much I LOVE Night Girl?

"My bag is by the chair."

Gary hops off the bed and grabs my purse, then looks back at me.

"Rear pocket," I direct him.

He feels around in the back pocket of my bag, coming up with the condoms.

"Four?" he says, smirking.

"I'm an ambitious girl."

"Well, we'd better get to work then." Gary jumps back on the bed, grabs me in a mad clutch, kissing all over my face and neck. He makes me laugh. A lot.

And then he makes me stop laughing.

Gary isn't the best lover I have ever had, but he is one of the most fun. There is playing and talking and lots of yummy kissing, one small but very serviceable orgasm, pretty good for a first time with someone new, and we manage to use three of the condoms before throwing in the towel around five in the morning.

"Shall I get a wake-up call?" he asks after we agree that we are duly spent.

"You'd better. What time are you meeting the execs for your breakfast meeting?"

"Eight-thirty. In the lobby."

"So I'd better be long gone by eight, just to be safe. How about seven-thirty, in case my car takes some time to come back from the valet."

"Smart bird you are." Gary picks up the bedside phone, and I sneak off to the bathroom while his back is turned. No need for him to see my flabby white ass in his post-coital bliss. I steal a fingerful of his whitening toothpaste and pee with the water running. And yes, I am aware that the man just spent twenty-four minutes with his face planted in my crotch, but listening to me pee seems awfully intimate for someone I just met this afternoon. Go figure.

I return to the bedroom to find that Gary has smoothed out the bed linens and fluffed the flattened pillows. He is standing naked and beautiful beside the bed. He walks over to me, kisses me lightly on the lips, whispers, "Mmm, minty," and disappears into the bathroom to make his own evening toilette. I climb into the bed and lie on my back, grinning like an idiot. Night Girl and Morning Girl tend to just overlap now and again at this time of day. They are arguing.

"*That was fan-fucking-tastic! I feel so delish,*" says Night Girl.

"*You idiot, he is your new PRODUCER!*" whines Morning Girl. "*Are you INSANE?*"

"*Shut up, you twit, how much FUN was that?*" snipes Night Girl.

"*Fun tonight, mortifying tomorrow, and I get to deal with the aftermath.*" Morning Girl is very pouty.

The flush, that awful hotel eardrum-shattering vacu-flush, finally shuts them both up. Gary appears, in his easy nakedness, and climbs into bed beside me, pulling me close to him. He kisses me.

"I don't make this a habit you know . . ." he begins.

"I know. Me either. We shouldn't analyze it. Let's just try and get an hour of sleep." I don't want to think, I just want to be here now.

"You're right. Good girl. Sleep."

He kisses my forehead, squeezes me close, and I close my eyes.

I wake at seven. Gary is beautiful in his sleep. Gary is probably beautiful trying to squeeze off a difficult shit. I hate to wake him. But even Morning Girl agrees that this is an opportunity not to be wasted. I slide my hand around his waist to find the not-unexpected but most welcome morning wood. I grasp it gently. Gary smiles in his sleep.

"Couldn't stand the idea of not using that last condom, huh?" He opens one eye and looks at me. I grin back at him.

"You have thirty minutes with me, Mr. Man. What are you going to do with them?"

Gary rolls over, trapping me underneath him, and kisses me hard.

"Toss me that condom and I'll show you."

Which he does. With enough time to spare to help me along to a lovely little orgasm of my own. We are panting and sweaty when the wake-up call comes.

I get up, use the bathroom, get dressed. Gary rises from the bed and hugs me.

"This was great. Thanks for a wonderful and unexpected night."

"Back at 'cha." I'm a little sheepish, but trying to be worldly.

"See you at the meeting, then."

"Absolutely."

I walk to the door and open it. Gary taps my shoulder, and I turn around. He kisses me again. Behind me there is a rustling noise. I pull back, look behind me. There, in the hallway, are two women in their mid- to late-thirties, each dragging a suitcase and a little girl of seven or eight, the kids schlepping American Girl bags bigger than they are. They are moving very quickly.

"Guess I should have put pants on to kiss you good-bye, huh?" Gary says.

I look down. Dangly bits everywhere. Good Lord, I have contributed to the early sexual education of two small children. Gary and I laugh.

"I'd really better go now, see you later . . ." Gary winks, and goes back inside. I begin the long walk down the hall to the elevator.

"Get home safe!" I hear behind me, turning to see Gary now smack in the middle of the hallway in front of his room, waving good-bye to me with one hand in the air over his head and the other waving his penis at me.

Oh. My.

At the elevator I catch a look of myself in the mirror. It's not good. I have the worst case of ho-hair that I've ever seen. And whisker burn on my chin. And mascara raccoon eyes. And my clothes look as if they have been balled up on the floor all night. Which they have. It would not take a fortune-teller to formulate that I have packed a fortnight of fortuitous fornicating into the past eight hours. I descend to the lobby, hold my ho-hair high, and begin the walk of shame. Luckily, seven-forty AM on a Tuesday is not a busy time at the Wyndham. I approach the valet desk, where a Latina of stately proportions is conversing with an African-American bellman.

I hand her my valet ticket.

"What room, please." She looks at me.

"No room," I reply, handing her my credit card. "I'm going to pay directly."

"Are you checking out today?" she inquires.

"I'm not a registered guest." Boy does THAT sound bad. She grins.

"Not a registered guest," pipes in the bellman, "but an overnight guest!" He is smiling widely.

"Ain't nothin' wrong with that!" She nods at me, swiping my card. "That'll be thirty-nine dollars. Honey, I would have charged it to his room!"

Oh. My. Goodness.

"Did you have a nice stay at the Wyndham?" My wicked little bellman asks me with a knowing cadence. I decide to name it and claim it.

"I did indeed." He winks at me.

"Good for you, girl. Sign here." She hands me my credit card slip, which I sign quickly. "Your car will be up in a minute, right out those doors."

"Thank you."

"We hope to see you back again for a visit real soon!" the bellman says, still smiling conspiratorially at me. "Thanks for choosing the Wyndham!"

I slink out the door, putting my slutty self on display for anyone in the vicinity of Erie and Saint Clair. Besides a couple of sidelong glances from Northwestern doctors in their scrubs, I manage to get my car without further shame or incident and head home to power nap before today's production meeting.

The fact that Gary will be there is not a thought I am willing to entertain on so little sleep.

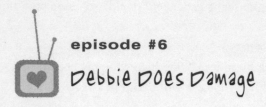

episode #6

Debbie Does Damage

Bravo *Wednesday July 12* 8PM–9PM

SWAP/MEET **Barton and Deborah**

Don't miss the surprise ending of this episode, where an accident-prone girl threatens to tear the set apart, and a straight-laced shoe salesman reveals a dark secret. You have to see it to believe it. Designers Lily Allen and Ashleigh Benning keep their cool, while carpenters Jake Kersten and Curt Hinman try not to misuse their power tools on the homeowners.

"You seem to be doing very well, all things considered," Hillary says to me over the sound of traffic. She is driving to Madison for a case, and I'm updating her on the Gary situation on my way to the shoot, which has turned out to be no situation at all.

"I guess, I mean, I didn't want it to be a big deal, and I certainly didn't want it to impact the work. But there has been

NOTHING since last week. No invites to hang out, not even a wink. It's like it NEVER HAPPENED!"

"But you said that was what you wanted. I mean, when you called me, you said, and I quote, 'It was a perfect night because it was what it was, no bullshit, no expectations, just a fun night.' I mean, that's what you got and now you're mad?"

"You're right. I know you're right." She is, too.

"You just wanted to be able to have the 'I know you ache for me, but we cannot be together, we'll always have Paris' conversation."

"I do not!" But I kind of do.

"You do so! Don't deny it. You wanted him to be all hot and bothered for you so that you could turn him down because you work together. Classic commitment-phobe behavior, Ms. Allen. You are scared to death of anything real, so you indulge your natural desires when you can, and never give anything a chance to develop." Hillary is so fucking smug when she is analyzing me.

"I think that is a little harsh, don't you? I was with Josh for eight months, and he's the one who needed space, not me." Didn't I just HAVE this conversation? Oh, wait, that was with Naomi. Now I'm getting part two of the dating lecture.

"Josh was as boring as a box of hair. You were never going to marry him, he was just convenient. He never got in your way, never asked you for more time or emotion than you were willing to give and didn't challenge you at all. Easy boyfriend choice, practically no boyfriend at all. Just a lump to have sex with once a week and pay for dinner. Look at Ron. He's a great guy, into you, good boyfriend material and you messed it up on purpose. Never gave him a chance."

"Hey, that's mean. And who are you to talk? You've got your

little fuck-buddy Chandler dangling on a string waiting for you to participate in an actual relationship with him, but Hillary doesn't do anything that might require thinking of another person first, huh?" Hillary's a good friend, but she has a dark streak in her that can be wicked. And I've never been one to take it placidly.

"We aren't talking about me. I know I'm fucked up about guys. We are talking about you, and you seem to think there is nothing wrong with you. Truth hurts, kiddo. You know I love you, but your relationships are totally pathological. Ask Naomi, she'll back me up."

"I've already had the Naomi end of this diatribe, thank you. You know what, I'm almost at work, and I'm going to go before this turns even uglier. I'll talk to you when you get back from Madison." She's really hurting my feelings.

"Whatever, if you have time." Her words are like little daggers.

"What's THAT supposed to mean?"

"You blew off breakfast because you fucked your producer. Forgivable. You blew off our lunch with Naomi because a client was feeling neglected. Fine. You cancelled on Naomi and Alice's dinner party because you had to finish some design boards, not okay. Naomi was really hurt. You should have come for dinner and left early if you were under the gun. But you just glibly backed out. Let me tell you something: you can't just be a friend when it is convenient for you. I don't care if your show is doing well and if you've started to see a bump in your private client base, work is work and friendship is friendship and your priorities had better get together quickly, because as much as I love you, you are pissing me off to no end these days."

This makes the biggest lump in my throat. I try to answer her around it. "I didn't know you felt that way about me."

"I adore you. But you are in a place right now that makes it hard to like you. Call Naomi. Make amends for bailing on her. We'll all cool off and deal with this next week when I'm back. I'll talk to you later."

Hillary doesn't wait for me to say good-bye, she just hangs up. Tears prick my eyes. I shake them off. She's probably just having a bad day; she's notorious for taking that shit out on me. I'll probably have flowers or cookies waiting for me when I get home.

"Okay, folks, let's get ready, we'll do the front door meet-and-greet in ten minutes." Bob half-shouts this at those of us who are milling around in the driveway of Barton's traditional Chicago bungalow and then turns back into conversation with Gary. I'm hanging back at the carpentry tent with Curt, wanting to keep a fair distance from Gary.

"These plans look pretty cool: our first kitchen," Curt says, looking over my drawings for the new cabinet fronts I have designed.

"Thanks." I'm so not feeling chatty. Hillary's vitriol from this morning is still bothering me, and the more I watch Gary and his total ignoring of the fact we slept together, the more pissed off I get at him. Curt just keeps talking.

"And I couldn't be happier that I'm off the hook in the living room except for the coffee table. I can't remember the last time you gave me so little to do. It's not even my birthday."

"Yeah, well, don't get used to it. We'll be back to our old habits by the next show. You just got lucky that we don't have time to rip out the living room built-in and start from scratch." The words seem flip enough, but I can hear that my tone shows how not into this whole thing I am.

"You want to fill me in on this mood of yours? Being a guy, I would normally assume that you were on the rag, but since I remember the great brownie debacle was only two weeks ago, I know it has to be something else."

The mere fact of Curt knowing my menstrual cycle makes me laugh.

"Do you put little red dots on your calendar for me?"

"Hey, there are nail guns and power drills out here just lying around. A guy with any sense of self-preservation will keep a good handle on the women in his life and their schedules."

"Oh, Curtis, am I a woman in your life?" I'm teasing him, but something about it feels sort of sweet.

"My little peach crumb, you are the only woman in my life. Other than Mom and Aunt Ella. Talk to me. What the hell is up with you today? You're all wonky."

"I had a fight with Hillary."

"Is she the lawyer or the lesbian?"

"The lawyer."

"Did she borrow your new sweater without asking and stain it? Accept a date with a boy you like? What?" Curt really can be a doofus sometimes.

"Do you get all your ideas about girl problems from *Brady Bunch* reruns?"

"Yeah, mostly."

"She yelled at me. She said I was being a bad friend. She said that since the show started airing and I have the shooting schedule on top of my normal design stuff, that I have been unavailable to my friends and selfish about spending time with them. Oh, and I'm apparently afraid of commitment and sabotage all my relationships with men on purpose."

"Was she right?" Curt asks.

"What do you mean?" I can't believe he just said that.

"I mean, was she right? Are you blowing off your friends and using work as the excuse? Are you avoiding real relationships with guys by doing stupid shit like sleeping with your producer?"

Talk about a secret reveal.

"What the fuck are you talking about?"

"Lower your voice, princess, I don't think anyone else knows. But I saw you leaving the Wyndham at an ungodly early hour last week, and from the state of your hair, I doubt that you had been up all night filling our new guy in on innovations in design. Plus, for the most outgoing person on the crew, you seem to have about four words of conversation with him whenever you are in a room together, and only about business."

"What the hell were you doing lurking around the Wyndham at seven-thirty in the morning?"

"My best friend and his wife had just had a baby over at Prentice. I was driving by on my way to the parking lot to see the little bugger before work."

"Curt, you can't tell anyone, okay, it was a really big mistake, and it hasn't happened again, and it won't be happening again, and I . . ." Curt puts a hand on my arm.

"Hey, you're a grown woman, and what you do with your private life is none of my business. I don't get why you would do it, but it isn't my place to know. What I do know is that if your oldest and dearest friends think you are being a shit, then you probably are being a shit, and you might want to accept that they are sharing that information out of love and concern, and you should check yourself before playing the victim."

"Okay, people, let's get set up, Lily, Birdie, over here please,"

Gary calls us all over to get the day started. Curt looks at me and smiles.

"Hey, let's grab a beer after work and you can cry on my shoulder."

I shake my head. "Can't, thanks. I have three new clients, and they all need to see design ideas next week."

"Okay, if you have *work* to do." The emphasis is not lost on me.

"*Et tu*, Curtis?" Just what I need, another so-called friend on my case. I know I'm being bitchy to him because I'm mortified that he knows about me and Gary, but somehow I can't seem to fix my tone or attitude.

I walk over to the front door, wait for my cue from the director, and ring the bell.

"Look out!" I yell, too late, as Debbie, the homeowner from hell, takes a step backward, knocking into the ladder behind her, sending the paint tray that had been on top of the ladder careening end over end, spraying an arc of blue paint over Barton's new cabinet fronts, freshly stained, which Curt had just finished installing.

"Oops!" Debbie giggles. "Think Barton would like the Jackson Pollock look?"

I'm going to fucking kill her. The day has been one endless stream of accidents. And not the typical glitchy accidents that make for interesting television. The kind of accidents that come dangerously close to sending people to the hospital or sending me to a padded cell somewhere.

First, she took it upon herself to open the cardboard crate containing Barton's new stainless steel refrigerator by running a box cutter straight down the middle instead of at the seams, scoring a lovely shiny scratch down the front of both the fridge and freezer doors. Cannot be fixed, replaced, or ignored.

Then she thought she'd help out while we were setting up a living room shot, and while trying to tape some carpet remnants over a grouping of cables, yanked on a large black cord, accidentally knocked over a light tree, which nearly took off Reg the sound guy's head before crashing to the floor in a shower of sparks and exploding glass.

She threw out all the hardware from the cabinets and drawers, requiring that two production assistants spend over an hour Dumpster-diving to retrieve them.

At lunch she tripped carrying a tall glass of chocolate milk, which inconveniently showered the entire craft service table, rendering everything on the buffet moist and chocolatey, which is not what you really look for in spaghetti marinara and garlic bread.

Curt originally flat-out refused to work with her, but Gary convinced him that it could just be a demonstration segment. Bad idea. While jigging the final piece of scrollwork that he had designed to be the base of the coffee table, and which he had spent nearly two hours working on, Debbie leaned over close to his ear, and then sneezed loudly and abruptly. Curt's hand slipped with the saw, ruining the piece.

"Really, with the sneezing, really?" Bob said.

After each of these incidents, Debbie has giggled merrily and said, "Ooops!" Half the crew is ready to walk, and it is only the afternoon of Day One. Reg is calling her Hurricane Debbie. Gary doesn't have a strand of his fabulous hair out of place, which is amazing considering the havoc she is wreaking with his show. And I wouldn't trust Curt around her with a nail gun.

video diary confession:

*"Okay, I've just about had it. I'm literally up to here with Debbie. I'm be-
ginning to wonder if any of us are going to get out alive. I mean, my very
first show was with a guy who we all thought was pretty inept, but at least
he wasn't dangerous. I feel like I'm petting a black cat under a metal ladder in an electrical storm on Friday the 13th. And don't get me wrong, I
think the accident-prone deserve new rooms and makeovers and dates as
much as anyone, but I'm starting to think that they should get them on a
different show. I'm going back out there, but if Debbie kills me before the
show is over I just want to tell my family and friends that I love them, and
that I'm sorry for everything bad I ever did. Wish me luck . . ."*

Even Birdie, that perma-ray of sunshine, takes a moment to
pull me aside when she returns from doing a segment with Barton
over at Debbie's condo.

"I swear, this show may just be the end of me!" she drawls,
flopping beside me on the floor of the living room, where I'm as-
sembling some picture frames.

"You and me both. What's going on at the other house?"

"Not much better than things here. That child left every
drawer and cabinet in her place crammed with junk! I mean, bat-
teries and plastic bags and paper clips and old takeout menus, and
pizza boxes, and goodness knows what all. The crew went to
move the bed out of the bedroom to paint the walls, and found
that underneath was like one big pile of garbage! Totally gross.
They ended up literally shoveling it into boxes. I swear, did you
ever in your life? And this Barton guy is weird. Turns out he is a
shoe salesman because he has some sort of fetish thing, so he
keeps disappearing, and we find him in her closet sniffing her
shoes!" Birdie laughs. "I swear Ashleigh is about to lose her cool.

We had to reshoot two different segments because she swore on camera! Called Debbie the c-word and referred to Barton as a fucking foot-pervert imbecile!"

"I guess it will be entertaining for the folks at home, but I, for one, can't wait until tomorrow is done." At this point I don't even care how it all looks in the end, I just want it to be over.

"I know. Sam is out of town, but he gets back tomorrow night, so I'm just counting the minutes!"

Birdie and Samuel Diaz Perez have become quite the item, making her sort of even more sickening to be around, but generating great press for the show. The Latin slugger and his blond bombshell, their smiling pictures are all over the local and national press . . . testing hand lotion at L'Occitane, getting side by side pedicures at Polish, signing autographs at the Lincoln Park Zoo.

"Looks like things are going well for you guys, I think that's great, Bird."

"And his batting average has never been higher! The team is calling me their good luck charm. I think the Sox might just go all the way this year."

"Birdie, if you're going to be a Chicagoan, you have to learn one important rule. Don't EVER imply that this might be any of the teams' year. Not any of them. For any reason. It's a recipe for heartache."

Birdie laughs it off. "Well, I'd better check in with Gary and warn him about the end of Day One wrap-up."

"Warn him why?"

"Silly, you know I'm such a ninny it always takes me an hour. He'd better get ready to start soon or we'll lose the light on the porch!"

Sometimes her self-awareness astounds me.

We get through the rest of the day, and I get home exhausted and frustrated. There are no flowers or cookies waiting for me, and no message from Hillary apologizing. She is probably all tied up in Madison, and tomorrow I'll get my delivery and phone call. I heat up a Lean Cuisine, work on the designs for the new clients, and right before bed realize that I have forgotten to call Naomi. I'll have to catch her tomorrow. Besides, I'm sure that Hillary is exaggerating about her being upset.

"You have beautiful feet," Barton whispers creepily in my ear. We are waiting outside his place to do the reveal. He now has a very blue kitchen, since we couldn't save the stained cabinets after Debbie's paint splatter, so we had to just paint them over. The fridge is still better than his old one, but when he moves the colorful magnets around, he's going to notice the scratch. His living room turned out pretty great. Curt even managed to redo the scrollwork base of the coffee table. And other than the original 1970's horror of a light fixture still being in place (Debbie accidentally crashed into me as I was coming around the corner carrying the new one in to be installed) and three of the picture frames missing their glass (Debbie swiped them right off the table with the Swiffer handle while she was helping us clean the floor), I'm reasonably proud.

And wishing I hadn't worn the strappy sandals.

"All right, you can go in," Bob calls out.

I lead Barton into his living room first, where he exclaims over everything, and is really very kind about quickly masking his disappointment in the light fixture, which he had vociferously slammed on his application video. I highlight Curt's table, drawing his attention to the detail work, and he's duly impressed. We move on to the kitchen, where Barton is a little quieter in his praise.

"It's, um, very blue," he says.

"Yes, it is." I shake my head. "See, originally the blue was for the ceiling and accent wall. The cabinets were stained a dark cherry. But as you know, the challenge of this show is as much about the time pressure as anything else, and there was an accident that you'll see when the show airs that required a creative use of the paint. But if you'd prefer the look of the wood, you can easily strip the cabinet fronts down again and restain."

Bob nods and smiles at me. Barton is really happy about the refrigerator, seems thrilled with the new solid surface countertops, and nearly jumps for joy checking out the cool undermount sink and funky faucet. I think we're forgiven for the blue cabinetry.

Barton's friends arrive, a very motley crew that makes me think that there won't be much trading of digits at the party tonight. They all seem to like the place.

We head over to Rockit, where the party is already in full swing. They are getting set up to film the "homeowners' first meeting" segment, and I grab myself a glass of red wine off a passing tray. I turn to see who's got room at their table for me, just in time for Debbie to plow into me, dumping my whole glass down my front, and her drink, something biliously blue and smelling of pineapple, smack into my face. I wipe my stinging eyes.

Debbie giggles uproariously. "Ooops!" she exclaims.

A cocktail waitress rushes over with a couple of bar rags. I'm totally drenched, my hair is already starting to clump together in sticky dreadlocks, my outfit is completely ruined. It is at this moment that a camera appears in my face. I don't look up.

"C'mon, guys, give me a fucking break, would you?"

"They can't," I hear Debbie say. I look up. The guys behind the camera aren't my crew. "You've been *Spanked!*"

Goddammit. Goddammit all to hell. Bravo's new reality prank show. Doing some perfect crossover promotion. Debbie is laughing.

"Great," I say, then elbow my way off camera, toward the bathroom, muttering. Fucking prank show, nearly ruined my rooms, made me look like an ass.

Gary grabs my arm just as I get to the hallway where the bathrooms are. He tries to block my way and guide me back toward the cameras. "Don't be such a spoilsport, this is great TV!"

A lightbulb goes off over my head. That bastard. "You knew."

"Of course I knew, it was my idea! I couldn't believe no one at the network had thought of it."

"She went too far, Gary; someone could have gotten hurt! She nearly decapitated Reg!" I'm so pissed.

"She was fine, we were really careful to set stuff up for her. It's going to be hilarious! They're going to run our episode first, with a fake end segment. And then *Spanked!* will run right after with the real ending. Brilliant!"

"Fuck you, Gary." I start to move toward the bathroom. He steps in front of me.

"Don't make this about last week." His eyes are very cold.

"Gary, I could give a FUCK about last week. Last week was a blip on my radar. Last week was completely and utterly inconsequential, not terribly interesting, and I haven't given it three seconds thought since it happened."

Okay, this is a major series of lies, but I won't give him the satisfaction of knowing he hurt my feelings. I can feel a rant coming on. So I let 'er rip.

"What I care about is that on your first episode, you set us all up. Curt is lucky he didn't cut off a finger or two when she sneezed in his ear, ever think of that? Any one of us could have lost an eye to a flying shard of glass, she broke so much crap. And since I assume that Barton, strange as he is, was a real participant, he got lesser rooms from us, not to mention no real shot at meeting anyone tonight, since her end was all rigged."

Gary starts to say something, then stops. I keep going, barely noticing that a small crowd is gathering. "This is a family, Mr. New Producer. A very strange, occasionally dysfunctional, but ultimately supportive family. You have to be able to trust the people you work with, you have to be sure they are on your side. Paul may have been half in the bag most of the time, but at least we could trust him. How the FUCK are we supposed to trust you knowing that the FIRST thing you did on our behalf was at best, make us look like idiots, and at worst, actually put us all in physical danger.

"We aren't supposed to be shocking, we're supposed to try and help make people's lives better. We are supposed to make their homes homier, we are supposed to help them look as good as they possibly can, and we are supposed to introduce them to a new group of people. What people are going to ask us to do those things for them if they have to wonder if they are going to be a part of some fucking RATINGS scam in the process?"

There is dead silence. And then a lone pair of hands clapping. I look behind me. It's Curt. Then Reg joins him. Pretty soon, the whole cast and crew of *Swap/Meet* is applauding me quietly, while Barton and his friends talk to each other across the room, and Debbie and her crew film in the opposite corner. Gary looks up at us.

"Good work everyone. I hope when you see how this episode works in terms of press and promotion that you will understand why I did it. In the meantime, I'm sorry if you are put out. It wasn't my intention. Enjoy the rest of the party. I'll see you all at the production meeting Wednesday." He excuses himself through the middle of the crowd and disappears. I turn and head into the ladies room. The door opens, and of all people, Ashleigh is standing with me.

"That was a nice thing you said out there," she says, checking out her lipstick.

"Thanks. I just thought what he did was really shitty."

"Well, it is sweet that you feel so warm and fuzzy about this show, but a piece of advice. This isn't about family. We didn't take this show on to make new friends. We are all here to make money, and that means ratings and press. So the next time you want to play Norma Rae, I'd suggest you think twice, because without someone like Gary figuring out how to get us in the spotlight, we can all be cuddly with each other in the has-been lane at unemployment. 'Kay, sweetie?"

Ashleigh smiles at me with her blinding caps and her immobile BOTOXed forehead. "Great." Then she swishes out of the bathroom again. I clean myself up as best I can and head out. Curt grabs me and pulls me back down the hall.

"What?" I ask him.

"Debbie's crew, they are set up to get footage of you coming back through the party. I found a back way." He drags me down the hall, into the kitchen, and out into the alley.

"My hero!"

"My favorite damsel in distress."

"Thanks for having my back."

"Thanks for being worried about my fingers."

"You're welcome." Curt flags a cab.

"You okay getting home?" he asks me.

"Yeah, fine, you wanna come?"

"You mean to your place?" He looks really uncomfortable.

"Not like THAT, you moron, I just mean, come over, hang out, have a beer or something."

"Yeah, okay, I guess."

We get in the cab and head over to my apartment. He praises my place, admires the finish and detail work on my grandmother's four-poster bed and dresser, and once I'm perched on the sofa, settles on the ottoman across from me.

"Can I ask you something?" I start.

"Yeah." He looks a little like he might be worried I'm trying to ambush him.

"How come you were so mean and cold to me for the first six weeks and now you're so nice?"

He sighs, runs his hand through his hair, and takes a swig of beer. "Look, some of it was my own baggage, some of it was misinformation, and some of it was lousy timing. Let's just say that once I saw the kind of person you really are, I needed to relate to you differently."

"Yeah, I'm going to need more than that, Mr. Hinman. You're very close-mouthed about your past, and I know that I'm a little too open about my personal life, but you keep everything so close to the vest I feel like you know me and I don't really know you. And I want to know you, Curt, I really do."

Curt smiles at me. "That's very sweet, kiddo. All right, you have to promise not to analyze me. I'm not one of your girlfriends, okay?"

I smile back at him, feeling like I'm about to be given the password into the inner sanctum. "Deal."

"Okay, first off, you should know that this is my sixth show in five years. The first four I was off-camera carpenter on shows where the on-air guy was an idiot with a pretty face who got the public credit for my work. I thought it'd be an easy switch to on-air work, and padded my resume to land the last gig, which was sort of a hipper version of *New Yankee Workshop*. All me, all the time. We filmed four episodes, none of which aired, and I know that I was really awful. Bob directed that one, and pulled some strings for me with BBC to get me this gig. So I came in feeling a little like a failure, and wondering how many people knew it." Curt polishes off his beer, and I fetch him another while he keeps talking.

"That's the baggage part, I had a lot to prove on this show, and I think I was worried about you making me look bad. Especially after what I'd heard about you."

What?!?! "What do you mean, what you'd heard about me?"

"Okay, you're gonna be mad."

"I'm mad already, now tell me who I'm mad at and why!" What the hell could he have heard about me?

"I got to the first meeting early. Ashleigh was the only person there. She introduced herself and we got to chatting. I asked if she knew you, and she essentially told me you were a hack and a diva, that you got the job because you were fucking one of Paul's golfing cronies, and that she had gotten at least six jobs fixing your bad work. And then the first thing you did was give me plans with no materials breakdown, so I thought she was right." Curt ducks like I'm going to bean him with my beer bottle.

"That. Fucking. CUNT!!!"

"Yeah, I know." Curt grimaces. "Look, I know now that it isn't true. You told me how you got the gig, and Bryan filled me in on you being the one to fix HER work. I know I should have waited to form my own opinion, but you know, mea culpa, now I love you!" He bats his eyelashes at me, looking ridiculous.

I can't help but laugh. "Well, I'm going to try and be Zen about it. Ashleigh has to wake up every morning and be her."

"And she has to sleep with her eyes open from all the BOTOX and surgery!" Curt pipes in.

"Okay, mister, that's two out of three, baggage and misinformation, what about timing?"

"Here." Curt hands me his wallet, open to a picture. I take it from his hand. It is a picture of him with a woman that could be my sister, we look so much alike.

"Holy Doppelganger, Batman! Who is she?"

"My ex-girlfriend. Left me for another guy the weekend before we started filming. You can imagine how inclined I was to work with her frigging twin. Forgive me?"

"Of course. That really sucks. I'm sorry about all of it."

"Me, too. And thank you for being so much smarter and nicer than me. You're really a great girl, and I'm glad I was at least smart enough to recognize it eventually." He winks at me.

"So am I." I smile back.

"My turn to play inquisitor, Missy."

"Okay. What do you want to know?" But I'm pretty sure I know what he's going to ask.

"Gary? I thought I'd have to worry about Jake, and by the way, your obvious distain of him is one of the things that originally endeared you to me. But GARY? I mean, on the FIRST DAY? What were you thinking?"

Oy.

I fill him in on what happened, as well as Naomi and Hillary's concerns about my dating pathology, Chuck and my dad, not to mention my mortification at the situation as it stands. He's a good listener. When I finish he looks at me seriously.

"I think you're going to be okay, and as long as you keep a low

profile with the Britiot and make sure Ashleigh doesn't get hold
of that info, stuff at the show will be fine. I'll have your back
there. I'm the wrong guy to give dating advice, but I'll repeat
what I said earlier . . . if your best friends are offering cautionary
opinions, especially when they have nothing to gain by interfer-
ing but your wrath, you should take a hard look at what they are
saying."

"I'll think about it." I hate when everyone I like and respect
gangs up on me.

"Good. I should get home." Curt stands and stretches. His
shirt comes loose and I notice a very nice abdomen he's been hiding under those flannel shirts.

He catches me checking him out. "Hey, don't you have enough
trouble on the set? I'm not a piece of meat to be next on the menu
for your voracious appetite!"

I laugh. "Just because I appreciate your form doesn't mean I'm
longing for your affection, Tiger. Your virtue is safe with me."
Which it is. I definitely think he has a lovely look to him, but it
feels more like art appreciation than lust.

"Glad to hear it."

I walk him to the door.

"Thanks for inviting me over, it feels really good to come
clean about all that stuff."

"Thanks for coming, and for being so honest." I lean over and
kiss Curt's cheek. "See you Wednesday."

"Bye, kiddo. See you Wednesday."

Curt leaves and while I'm cleaning up the beer bottles, I real-
ize that there were still no flowers or cookies when I got home.
There are also no messages on my machine from either Naomi or
Hillary. I really want to call them both to tell them how crappy

my day was, and how great my talk with Curt was, but I can't bring myself to pick up the phone. Instead I take a hot bath, get into my big fluffy chenille bathrobe, and work on the design boards for the next episode.

The Bitches of Eastwick

Lily's Rule #41: Never, EVER get directly involved in your friend's breakups or reconciliations. NEVER.

I'm in hell. My whole do-the-right-thing-don't-take-sides-support-everyone attitude has landed me in the circle of hell that Dante apparently forgot. The circle of hell called "Being in the middle of two gay men trying to save their marriage."

Bryan and Jou are making me into a crazy person. They eventually decided, on my advice, to indeed go into therapy with Naomi's pal to try and salvage the relationship. I didn't realize when I made this suggestion that I would thereby become the recipient of eighty thousand daily phone calls from BOTH sides of the equation to discuss their progress, setbacks, and progress again. If they don't finish their therapy soon, I'm going to have to seek some of my own.

At the production meeting this morning, they flanked me on either side and kept writing me notes while Ashleigh rambled on and on about her private meetings with Gary, and her ideas for special episodes.

Jou finally admitted that he still holds a lot of anger about his childhood! Bryan scribbles on the bottom of his notepad and nudges me.

Yesterday Dr. Clarence suggested that it was time for Bryan to acknowledge me with his parents in ways that he usually avoids!!!! Jou pushes a Post-it note over.

"If I'm not interrupting you!" Ashleigh snipes loudly, and every head in the room looks over at the three of us.

Gary glares at me pointedly. Fucker.

For the first time maybe ever, I'm actually looking forward to my workout later. I think the combination of stress-relieving physical activity and the support of Hillary and Naomi will be just the ticket.

"Lily, if you're ready?" Gary says coldly.

"Of course, Gary." Whatever.

"Great, thanks," Gary continues, turning his gaze to the rest of the room. "And thank you, Ashleigh, for sharing your ideas, and as we have been discussing the past two weeks, I'm very interested in the concept of keeping things fresh for our burgeoning audience. Which is why I am pleased to announce the details for the next three episodes."

Ginny, formerly Paul's Advil and Tums girl, now Gary's right hand, starts to hand out the brief on Episodes #7, 8, and 9. Gary continues to talk.

"We're committing to these three 'twist' episodes to follow up the momentum we believe we'll see after the two-hour *Spanked!* episode. If our numbers look good, we'll be suggesting future twist episodes as a part of the renegotiation package if we get picked up for next season. Number seven will be Natasha and Morris. The twist is that they were high school sweethearts who haven't seen each other in eighteen years. Number eight, we're calling the 'Starting Over' Episode: two single seniors, a divorcée and a widower, ready to jump back into the dating world. And finally number nine, I got approval to take you all on location, so we're off to sunny LA for a celebrity episode, for which we have landed Enzo Mangiafiore as our single guy, and Isadora Gregg as our single girl."

A frisson of electricity moves through the room. The two starred in this summer's unexpected blockbuster *Hit List*, a quirky take on the dueling guns for hire theme. They were both quickly catapulting into real stardom, and even I was excited about the prospect of meeting them.

"Who will be designing for Isadora?" asks Ashleigh, whose forehead is flushing pink. I assume this is because her forehead is the current location of the skin formerly known as her cheeks. She obviously has a thing for Enzo, and knows that whoever is designing for Isadora will be working with him for two days.

"Lily will," Gary says. Ashleigh looks pissed.

Bryan and Jou both elbow my ribs at the same time. I'm suspicious about why I'm getting this gift. I bet Enzo has some hellish reputation about being obnoxious or indifferently hygienic or something. No way is Gary being nice to me.

"And you didn't mention the names of the Swinging Seniors," Bryan says, cleverly changing the topic, because he knows if I'm working with Enzo, he's working with Enzo.

"Oh, yes, of course," Gary says, looking down at his notes. "Renee and Walter."

That's funny, 'cause Renee is my mom's name.

What a coincidence.

I flip open the brief. Episode #8, Walter and Renee. Renee Allen. Sixty-two. One bedroom apartment in DEERFIELD.

I am so fucked. Ashleigh is looking at me with delight, and I suddenly know that it was her idea to use my mom in this episode.

I put on a fake smile, and try not to think about throwing smug Gary and his perfect hair out the window, while mentally kicking Ashleigh in the head with my new BCBG stilettos.

I pull into the parking lot at HiFi, and notice the profound absence of Hillary's Audi. It's very unlike her to be late, but as she is in charge of picking up the car-less Naomi, perhaps they have hit a little midday Chicago traffic, more and more common these days as the gym is perilously close to the notorious Clybourn Corridor.

I head into the gym and hit the locker room to change. But by the time I have wiggled out of my jeans and blouse and struggled into the only sports bra I've been able to find that can immobilize my D-cup rack, I realize that Hillary and Naomi are really late. I check my phone. No messages. This is very unusual; Naomi for sure wouldn't have not called to say she was going to be late.

I head out to the main workout room, where Giorgio is waiting by the water cooler. He looks a little confused.

"Today is all about you, *principessa*," he says, handing me a towel.

"What do you mean?" I ask him.

"The ladies called, they will not be able to join us," he answers.

This sounds fishy.

"Miss Hillary is stuck in a deposition, and Miss Naomi feels a cold coming on," Giorgio continues.

I don't think I've ever worked out with just Giorgio before. Twice a week for two years, never before have there been less than two of us. And for sure Naomi hasn't missed any sessions due to impending illness; we have to practically tie her to the bed on workout days when she's spiking a fever and getting the chills.

I wonder if Hillary's right. I wonder if Naomi is really pissed at me for blowing her and Alice off. Giorgio and I decide to stay in the main room, since it's just the two of us, and we start my circuit on the elliptical machine.

"How did they sound when they called?" I ask.

"Hillary sounded busy, and Naomi sounded tired," he says, ratcheting up the tension two levels. On both the machine and in my head. "Why? Is something going on with you guys?"

"I dunno, maybe." I'm hesitant to share my concerns with Giorgio, especially about Hillary. I know he still has a thing for her, so if I tell him what she said, he'll take her side for sure. And frankly, I don't really need another person thinking I'm a shit. "I'm sure it's nothing."

"Don't want to talk about it?" I hop off the machine and we head over to the squat machine. He sets the weight while I step on.

I get my shoulders under the pads and release the safety. I look over at Giorgio and he nods to me to start. I squat down, and feel the resistance as I come back up.

"I just had a really rough day and I'm selfishly mad that they aren't here to listen to me bitch." A cop-out, but an easy one to take. I take a quick break after the first set.

"Tell Uncle Giorgio." He gestures for me to start the second set.

"Well, let's see . . . I slept with my new producer, who decided that the mature way to handle it is to ignore me. At the same time he made a business decision that made me very angry, and I decided that the mature way to handle that was to scold him like a child in front of everyone we both work with. My friends Bryan and Jou are in therapy on my suggestion, and keeping me constantly and ir-ritatingly in the loop about every detail of their progress."

I step off the machine and take a slug of water from my bottle. We walk over to the rowing machine and I sit down. "I'm swamped with new private clients, and trying to ensure that whenever this silly television business is over that I have kept my business success-ful so that I can support myself in my old age. I have no dating life and no promise of one anytime soon, and my mother, to whom I am a terrible reproductive disappointment, has been recruited to be a participant on my show, ensuring that she and I will spend two days attempting to work together and not reveal anything to one another on camera, which is not so different from our real rela-tionship. This brilliant idea is courtesy of Ashleigh, the lizard-bitch of the Gold Coast, who is bound and determined to sabotage me at work."

I let the weights drop loudly back down. A few other trainers and clients look over in our direction.

"Easy, killer, let's not take it out on the equipment, okay?" Giorgio adds another ten pounds to the stack. He hands me the handles again. I get back to it.

"And, yes, it's possible that Hillary and Naomi aren't so happy with my behavior of late, and I hate the idea of them being mad at me, but I also think they are being a mite touchy and could cut me a little slack in light of all the stuff they know I'm going through right now."

I grunt through the last five reps and let the weight down gen-tly this time. I'd hate to appear indecorous while inadequately in-toning the insupportable invisibility of my best friends in my time of injustice just because I may have inadvertently been insensitive.

"That seems like a lot to be dealing with. I have a recom-mendation for you." Giorgio hands me my towel and I wipe my forehead as we head back to the cardio wall and I jump on a treadmill.

"Yeah, what's that?"

"More exercise. Good for the stress level."

"G, according to you, more exercise is the answer to everything." I laugh.

"It IS!" he insists.

"I'll think about it," I say.

"It's all I ask."

We plow through the rest of the workout, keeping the conversation light and the sweating heavy. I shower and make an internal vow to call both Hillary and Naomi as soon as I get home. Well, as soon as I have called my mother to find out what the hell she was thinking saying yes to the show without discussing it with me first, and then talk her out of it. What a fun evening I have to look forward to.

And I have the sinking feeling that this is usually the part where the voice-over says, "But nothing could have prepared her for what dangers lurked ahead . . ."

"They said you had told someone how much you wished you could do something like this for me, and that's why they decided to go for it and surprise you," my mother says excitedly. "Really, sweetheart, I'm so flattered and excited to watch you work! Isn't is a lovely surprise?"

Gulp. Must officially suck this up. Mom is too happy to try and get out of it. "Of course I'm excited Mom, I just wish I was getting to design your room, and not Ashleigh, that's all."

"Well, dear, I asked about that, but they said that there was too much temptation for you to tell me what you were going to do, and that it would be better for us to be able to work together."

"Well, I suppose better for Ashleigh to design your room than to have to suffer her company for two days. I can always fix what she's done after the show!" I'm trying to gear up to be happy about this, even if it kills me.

"I just want to say that I am very touched that you would want to do this for me, and until I talked to that nice Gary I never thought about even wanting to potentially date again. But when he said that you worried about me, that you thought I put too much time into other people and not into myself, well, that was very sweet to hear, and I knew I had to say yes."

Gary. That sneaky FUCK. Those choice sentiments were uttered at approximately four in the morning the night of our shagfest. The fact that he would use them against my mother to convince her to do an episode that was ultimately about exploiting our relationship to garner an audience is absolutely disgusting. In fact, it is unbelievably unacceptable and unwarranted, although not uncharacteristic, that information uncovered while I was un-clothed could be unmercifully used so unjustly. I no longer feel re-motely bad about letting him have it in front of everyone on the staff.

Lily's Rule #71: At the end of the day, sometimes you have to go along to get along. So suck it up when you have to.

"Well, Mom, we'll have a grand old time, and you'll love working with Bryan."

"I'm actually getting excited about it. And you know, Ethan can't wait to see me on TV!"

Sigh. Of course he can't. "That's great."

"You know, dear, that Gary fellow sounded very nice. And he clearly thinks the world of you."

Oh shit. I know that intonation. That's a "Why aren't you dating?" hint if ever I heard one. "He's a good producer." It's the best I can do.

"He certainly seems passionate about it. You should have heard him talking about the show. He's very persuasive, isn't he?"

"Oh, yes, the original silver-tongued devil." Pity I'd let myself get so intimately acquainted with that silver tongue.

"I can't wait to meet him."

Oy. "Well, Mom, I have to go, but I just wanted to call and say how glad I am that you're going to do the show."

"I'm looking forward to it too, sweetheart. Talk to you later."

I call Hillary first.

"This is Hillary, leave a message." Beep.

"Hil, it's Lily. Just wanted to check in and catch up. Giorgio missed you today. And so did I. Call me, 'kay?"

Then Naomi. Alice answers, a little coldly, or maybe I'm just paranoid.

"Hey, Alice, how are you?"

"Fine, thanks. You?" she answers.

"I'm okay. Is she feeling better?"

"She's fine. She's at some JUF thing with Hillary, aren't you supposed to be there?"

Oh crap. Oh sweet hot stinky pile of crap.

I grab my BlackBerry. Six PM. JUF Young Leadership Division cocktail party at Mars Gallery. CRAP!

"Um, yeah, I was on my way, but I, um, forgot something at

home, and um, I thought if she hadn't left yet we could go to-gether."

"Hillary picked her up a half an hour ago."

"Okay, then, I'll, um, just see her there. Thanks, Alice."

"Sure."

Oh crap-a-doodle-doo.

I grab my purse and run out the door, heading for the garage. I look like shit, but there is no time to change if I'm going to make it. I drive like a bat out of hell to Fulton, parking two blocks away from the gallery. By the time I get upstairs it is nearly seven. I spot Hillary and Naomi across the room, chatting with some girls I recognize from my periodic attendance at these events. I start to head over, but I get waylaid by a pair of giggling twenty-somethings in nearly identical satiny sleeveless tops, dark jeans, and pointy black boots.

"OH. MY. GOD. I love your show!" Number One gushes.

"It's just the best!" Number Two chimes in.

"Is that Jake just the HOTTEST or what?" says Number One.

"Is he single?" Number Two asks.

I have to say, it's sort of flattering. I mean, they know all the details of the show, they love my work, they hate Ashleigh, they don't think the disastrous Episode #3 was my fault. In fact I'm re-ally getting into the attention when I suddenly feel the hair on the back of my neck stand up. I turn around and find Hillary and Naomi standing behind me.

"We're going," she says.

"Are you going to Thirsty's?" I ask.

"Yeah," Hillary says.

"Can I come?" Normally I would just assume I was included, but these days, who knows?

"If you want." Not exactly a rousing invitation.

"We're going to SushiSamba if you want to come with us!" says Number Two.

"Oh. My. God. Totally come with us! We're meeting our friends, and they're all fans, too!" says Number One.

"No really, I . . ." I can't imagine anything less appealing.

"By all means, go to SushiSamba with your fans." Hillary emphasizes the word *fans* as if it tastes bad to say. This sort of pisses me off. I mean, I may have been a little distracted lately, but they haven't exactly been as supportive as they might have been.

"Maybe I will." Which I won't.

"Excellent!" says Number One. Poor deluded girl.

"Fine," says Hillary.

"Hillary . . ." starts Naomi, then, seeing Hillary's glare, she stops.

"Okay, well, bye then. Talk to you later," I say.

"Bye." Hillary turns on her heel. Naomi kisses my cheek.

"Bye, Lily. Talk to you later." Then she hurries after Hillary.

I wait until they are well gone, make my apologies to my groupies, and head back out to my car. I drive over to Thirsty's and see them in the window. Alice has joined them. So have Chandler, Dave, and Ron. They are laughing. I feel like Stella Dallas.

I stop at the White Hen and buy a pack of Parliament Ultra Lights, a box of Mallomars, and a tube of Pringles Salt & Vinegar. At home, I climb into my sweats, open a bottle of pinot grigio, put my *Arrested Development* DVD on, and settle down for a gluttonous wallow.

episode #7
Morris and Natasha

Bravo *Wednesday July 19* 8PM–9PM

SWAP/MEET Natasha and Morris

Two former high school sweethearts get a surprise reunion on
this week's episode. But the surprise may be even more than the
Swap/Meet team is ready for. Highlights include a wall mural
project in Morris's place, a faux-copper ceiling in Natasha's, and
fireworks between designer Ashleigh Benning and homeowner
Natasha. Plus special style segments on finding the right glasses
for your face with Jou DuFresne, and proper skin care for men
with Bryan LeClerc.

"Okay, Lily, we're speeding. And, action!" Bob yells out. I lead
Morris into Natasha's kitchen.

"So, Morris, what do you think about the ceiling in here?" I ask
him, gesturing at the tragic popcorn drop ceiling with fluorescent

fixtures that poor Natasha has been saddled with in her 1970's Bucktown condo.

"I think it's really, really ugly?" Morris says obligingly, if a little hesitantly. So far, he's been good to work with. Not terribly comfortable in front of the camera, but not a klutz, a nice guy, with a quiet wit about him. A little incongruous, he's not bad looking, just very average. But the pictures I've seen of Natasha show her to be a genuine bombshell. I'm trying to imagine them as a couple. And frankly, I'm slightly concerned about the party when we reintroduce them. I mean, after all, the hope for the show was that they might rekindle their romance; but while I can totally see Morris wanting to hook up with Natasha, I'm having a tougher time seeing Natasha going for him.

"So let's look at the design I've done for the kitchen," I say, leading Morris over to the kitchen table to look at the design board I've put together. "We're going to keep the terra-cotta floor, because it's in great shape, and it would be too big a project to tackle in just the two days. And the cabinets are also in good shape, but the dark stain on the wood is a little dated, so we're going to paint them in a buttery yellow.

"On the upper cabinets we're going to cut out the recessed panels and replace them with glass inserts, and you and I are going to do a really fun frosted detail on them. The butcher block counters are going to get a sanding and re-sealing to bring them back to their original glory, and we're going to replace that old porcelain sink with a great undermount stainless double sink.

"Now, the appliances are all stainless, and new, so we don't have to do anything there, but this table set has got to go, so Curt is going to build a new table, which you'll be helping him with later, and we'll paint the frame of these chairs and reupholster the seats. But the project I'm most excited about is the ceiling. Take a look at this." I reach under the table and pull out what looks like an old copper ceiling tile with a beautiful patina.

"That's really cool, is it old copper?" Love Morris, perfect cue!

"Actually, while it looks like old copper, it isn't. Here feel it."

Morris reaches over and takes the tile from me. "Plastic?" he asks.

"Plastic," I say. "These are a great new product I found, a plastic replica of old-fashioned metal ceiling tiles. They come in twenty different styles and finishes, are about half the cost of metal tiles, and can be installed over plaster and drywall with simple adhesive, or, as we're going to do, used in existing drop panel ceilings like this one. They even come with this really cool matching tape that you stick directly to the drop ceiling frame to make it literally disappear into the rest of the ceiling."

Whew. Bob gives me a thumbs-up. I'm getting more and more comfortable with the "casual product explication" segments. It can be deadly to deliberately describe the decorative arts, and sometimes my declamations are definitively neither deft nor delightful, and instead are depressing in their detailed depictions.

Morris and I finish up in the kitchen, and then head into the very small back room, which lies between the master bedroom and the second bedroom. At the moment, the truly tiny eight-foot-by-eight-foot room is packed to the rafters with boxes, luggage, and Natasha's bike. Like many people cursed with a room too small to fit a grown-up bed, and even too small to be a comfortable office space, Natasha has mistaken it for a large closet, almost a huge junk drawer.

Usually the history of these rooms is a developer "extra," a bonus room that can be converted into a laundry room, a small nursery, or a walk-in closet. People purchasing these condos without the extra money to build out one of these options get your basic drywall and flooring, and it is up to the homeowners to use the space as they see fit. Normally, I would bring in a built-in custom system to make the perfect closet for any fashion-conscious girl. But in the interview materials from Natasha, I realized that more than anything, she needed a getaway private space. Someplace she could lock out the world. Her job as a child advocate is rewarding, but can get depressing, and I want to create a space for her to float away from all the ugliness she is confronted with through her work.

"I'm calling this the Womb," I tell Morris, once the camera crew is set up behind us in the hallway. "I want to create a space to shut out the world and get cozy." I tape up the design on the wall beside us. "We're doing a design I think of as Moroccan Library. We're bringing in this sleigh daybed instead of a traditional loveseat because it will be a more luxurious place to relax and read than a normal sofa. Plus it can serve as an extra bed for houseguests.

"We're going to paint the walls this deep cranberry red, which has a lot of blue in it. This is actually a soothing color, unlike red with a lot of orange in it, which is energizing.

"This wall will get a built-in wood shelving system. At the bottom, here, we're putting in a minifridge, and a cabinet which we're going to stock with little snacks. This shelf right over the fridge will be slightly deeper; it will house an electric teakettle on one end and a portable iPod docking sound system on the other end. The rest of the shelves will be for books. Here, over in the corner, we're going to mount a small combo TV/DVD/VCR unit from the ceiling. There are going to be tons of pillows, a great rug. This whole room is going to be about relaxation, reading, napping, and generally escaping from the pressures of the world."

"Wow. That's really cool," Morris says. Bob smiles and motions for the camera crew to stop filming. Birdie is on her way over from Morris's house, and we are going to work on frosting the cabinet door glass together before breaking for lunch. I run out to the land of carpentry to check in with Curt, who is working on the kitchen table. I asked him to do something in a simple mission or Arts and Crafts style so that it wouldn't be too fussy in the room. But I left the actual design up to him.

Once I get outside to the tent, I can see that the base of the table is almost finished, and I can tell how beautiful it's going to be already. Simple straight lines, with some openwork square details; Frank Lloyd Wright couldn't have done any better.

One of the camera guys is filming, and Curt is explaining his process while sanding down the table base. Gary motions for me to go over and talk to him. This isn't a planned segment, just some filler footage that the editors can use or not, depending on how much of the other stuff works well. The nice part about it not being at all scripted is that we can just relax and kibitz and not worry about crediting sponsors, or explaining techniques, or identifying unusual products.

"Hey there, design lady, what do you think of the table so far?" Curt asks as I approach, blowing the dust off the piece with the air hose for the nail gun.

"I was just admiring it from afar. It looks beautiful." I walk around the base to admire it from all angles. "Perfection, although I expected nothing less." Curt sprays me with a gust of air from the compressor. I whack him on the arm.

Gary rolls his eyes and taps the camera guy on the shoulder. "Let's go in and do a check-in with Morris; there's nothing going on out here."

They leave, and Curt shakes his head. "That prick is just asking for it."

"Asking for what?"

"Asking for me to plant my boot in his narrow white ass," Curt replies. "This is total bullshit."

"Whatever, it isn't that big a deal. If he wants to behave like a child, that is his business." I'm trying to take the high road.

"Kiddo, he's trying to cut you down to the bare minimum of footage. He's effectively pushing you out of the show by not filming you as much as he films everyone else, so that the editors have less of you to start with. Haven't you noticed how little non-segmented footage you are getting today?"

That son of a bitch. I hadn't really been thinking of it, but Curt is right, he has been shifting the cameramen away from me pretty quickly all morning. It never occurred to me that it would be purposeful.

"Excuse me, Curt, I think it's time for a quick video diary." Fucking Gary.

"Princess, don't do anything stupid." Curt looks worried.

"Not at all, I'm just going to make my producer step up. After all, didn't Ashleigh get some problems solved with her video diary?" Ashleigh had made some pointed comments in one of her video diary segments about how difficult she was finding it not having on-hand soft-goods people on every show. Sometimes in the middle of a show, she said, she might get inspired to change drapes, or recover a chair, and she felt like it was hampering her creativity to have to anticipate needing soft-goods assistance ahead of time. Actually what she did was cry on camera first, and then say some things about getting some "fucking seamstresses on set for a fucking change" when her plan to make drapes for Samuel out of Astro Turf didn't work and she needed a fix. Lucky for her, I had a good friend who often did freelance custom work for me who was available to come down to the site and whip up some new drapes, but it could have been a disaster. Of course, neither Ashleigh nor Gary bothered to thank me.

"Just be careful in there, the Britiot is still the boss till Paul finishes drying out." Curt smiles at me and then turns back to the table base. I head inside to the bedroom where the portable video recorder is set up on a tripod with a chair.

video diary confession:

"Okay, I'm just getting so excited about this particular show. I mean, think about how amazing it can be to reunite two people who were not only good friends, but romantically involved so long ago. Even if the romance doesn't get rekindled, just think about how wonderful it will be for them to see one another again, and to be reminded of a time when love was simpler, purer. . . . We found out from Morris's best friend that she and Morris broke up because they were headed off to opposite ends of the country to go to college and thought it was smartest to make a clean break. I mean (sniff), things are so hard these days (sniff), we're all so busy, and it can be so hard to meet people (wipe eyes), it is just so gratifying to be able to reconfirm the possibility of love. (Sniff) Morris seems like such a nice guy, I think Natasha will probably be really happy to see him. (Wipe eyes) I feel silly getting so emotional, I guess, it's just . . . sometimes you meet someone you think is truly extraordinary, but it's just the wrong time or situation, so you do something to end it so that you (sniff) don't have to risk your heart, but . . . I'm sorry . . . (wipe eyes) . . . I have to stop."

I sneak off to the bathroom before anyone sees me. I wash my face with cold water and hit my eyes with a little Visine. Thank God my freshman roommate at Brandeis was a drama major who taught me how to cry at will. If I know Gary, he'll read into my little confession that I'm pining for him and that my blowup at him after the *Spanked!* episode was really just misplaced frustration at feeling that I couldn't pursue a relationship with him. Guys like Gary always think that "this song is about you."

If I've played my cards right, Gary will see the footage tonight, and tomorrow will be kind and sweet, assuming he has broken my little heart, and his overweening ego will mean that more footage and better treatment will be on the way to assuage my pain. I head back out to tell Curt about what I've done, and he agrees that he will be vague, but drop hints to Gary if the opportunity arises.

Lily's Rule #112: It isn't anti-feminist to use feminine wiles against a guy if he's a self-absorbed asshole.

I wonder what's for lunch? All that fake crying has given me quite the appetite!

"Lily? Can I put a bug in your ear while you are being gilded?" Gary has wandered into the makeup area as I'm being touched up for Day Two. I cringe inwardly. The goddamned gilding jokes have been tired since I was a kid.

But I am bound and determined to get Gary back in my corner, so I ignore the stupid joke and reply. "Of course." Hmm, wonder what this could be about. I try not to smile while Tanya the makeup girl is touching up my lip gloss.

"So, here's what I'm thinking. Since we are going to be shooting a new promo to run in conjunction with the three "twist" episodes, how'd you like to do it instead of Birdie?" SCORE!

"Of course, Gary, if you think it will be good." I try to look lovestruck.

"You'll be brilliant. I'll have Bob go over the details with you later. But keep it our little secret for now, all right love? I have to figure out how to tell Ashleigh without her busting any stitches." Gary smiles at me with a conspiratorial air. Schmuck.

"It'll be our little secret. And you know how good I am at keeping secrets." I wink at him and smile.

He smiles back. "That's my girl." He leans over and kisses my temple. "Now Tanya, not too much makeup, darling, she's a natural beauty!"

I really wish he'd left off the kiss and compliment. I can't help but remember how much fun it was to sleep with him, what a good kisser he was, how exciting it was to have someone that gorgeous interested in me. I have to shake it off. There's work to be done.

But Curt is going to be so thrilled to hear that my plan is working, after all; a promo for three shows will get plenty of airtime. Plus Ashleigh will be so mad her forehead might actually move!

Thank God for the Jacuzzi tub. Everything hurts. Day Two is invariably a mess, and today was no exception. Unlike most shows where there is a built-in reveal that needs to happen at a certain time, we don't have that restriction. We do have to ostensibly finish on "Day Two," but both participants are at their hotels until the reveal on Day Four, and we have access on Day Three while the homeowners are getting their makeovers to shoot the "glamour shots," that is, both places totally perfect and lit for maximum beauty, to alternate with the "before" shots. The still photographer also shoots the apartment on Day Three to document the work and create an archive in case there is a *Swap/Meet* book one day.

Unfortunately, this means that Day Two can go as late as midnight, which today it almost did. There was just a lot of detail work to attend to, especially in the Womb, getting it just right. I'm so glad that I decided to take tomorrow off from going to the gym. I'd be no good anyway, as sore and tired as I am. And frankly, I'm still irritated that Hillary and Naomi are being so snarky with me. I know we'll get past it.

As with any good friends, real friends, true friends, periodically one of the three of us is on the outs with the other two.

With Naomi, it was about six months after she came out. She went through a period of what I called "growing pains" and what Hillary called "Superdyke Syndrome." It was more of an identity crisis, really. Naomi wasn't sure what kind of lesbian she should be. She wasn't butch enough to carry off the short hair or overalls or Timberland boots. She wasn't femme enough to be a true lipstick lesbian. And she wasn't crunchy enough to be a no-bra-wearing, non-leg-shaving Earth Mother. Not that she didn't experiment with all three, with varying degrees of success and commitment.

After months of secret conversations with me, ultimately Hillary was the one who told her to get over herself and just "be exactly who she was before" only trading out "trouser snake for fur taco." Hillary always was the poet among us. But she was also right. Once Naomi realized that she didn't have to change her whole persona, things were a lot easier and we were able to have a more solid relationship again.

Hillary's brief visit to the dark side happened right after she joined the law firm. Working an eighty-hour week, as many first year associates do, she completely shut off from us, choosing to spend what little free time she had with other lawyers, networking, building alliances, and generally becoming what I referred to as a Lawbot. We actually had to abduct her to Canyon Ranch Spa for four days just to knock some sense into her. But once again, she eventually saw the error of her ways, and that she would never survive without us. She mellowed out a bit and started accepting invitations again. And after she figured out that she could actually mingle her social groups, things fell into their current state of affairs.

And in both cases, we were right on the money. Naomi needed to own her uniqueness, and Hillary needed to have a life outside the firm, and we as friends needed to tell the person in denial, who was too close to really recognize her own pathology that, um, shit. Of course I was a part of the "we" both times, and now Naomi and Hillary are the "we," which sucks out loud. I hate being left out. And it's probably my turn to be in the hot seat, and they're probably right, and if they're right, I'm wrong.

I'm wrong. I fucking hate being wrong. I'm so much better at being right.

Stupid friends. Now I have to eat crow. I fucking hate eating crow. It's impossible to find a wine to match.

Sigh.

Well, I'll have to eat crow tomorrow, because it's too late to call them tonight, and I have no intention of getting out of this bathtub for at least an hour. The gym. Now I have to fucking go to the gym tomorrow, or they'll just be more pissed off. And I'll have to bring presents. Which means I have to get up to go shopping. So much for sleeping in and watching all the shows TiVo has been recording for me while I have been off making more television shows for TiVo to record. I love irony.

I get to HiFi early, laden with goodies, and wearing my most sincere apology face. Giorgio, my accomplice, lets me into our little private room to set up, and then heads back to the main gym to wait for Hillary and Naomi. He's going to tell them I called at the last minute to cancel.

I unload my treats. For Hillary, a great new bag to house her laptop and accessories, in a gorgeous taupe oriental silk, so pretty you'd never know it was a business bag. For Naomi, a pair of silver and navy Pumas, which she has been coveting forever, but wouldn't buy for herself. A homemade "mea culpa" card for each of them, expressing my deepest love, with one of my favorite pictures of the three of us on the front. We are probably about seven years old, all three of us naked as can be, skinny-dipping in a lake on a camping trip with Hillary's folks. We are floating on our backs, holding hands, like three mini-Ophelias. Inside the cards, gift certificates for Cheeky, Chicagoland's best lingerie store, and totally worth the drive to Highland Park for some new Hanky Panky thongs or the most perfect boobilicious bra.

I can hear them coming down the hall, and they sound pissed. Like angry bees humming. The door opens and Hillary stomps inside, Naomi right behind her. Giorgio winks at me over their heads, and leaves, closing the door behind them.

"Thought you weren't coming," Hillary says coldly.

"Hil . . ." Naomi starts.

"No, she's right to be icy. I've been very foolish." Hillary and Naomi exchange a meaningful glance. "I've been distant, inconsiderate, and selfish. I've blown you off, I've let you down, and I'm really really, really sorry. I promise to get my shit together."

"We just don't want you to turn into some A-list television diva," Hillary replies.

"What she means is that you have to think of this show as your current job and still be yourself. And you've always been pretty sensitive to other people, so when we see you behaving so differently, it concerns us," Naomi adds.

"I know, you guys, I do. I mean, I was pretty hacked off at how harsh you were, but I trust you both, and I love you both, and I know that if you are both concerned for me, then I have to pay closer attention to my own behavior."

"What do you think, Mimi, should we forgive her?" Hillary smirks at me.

"I don't know, Hillary, she's been so RUDE and self-absorbed." Naomi smiles.

"I brought presents . . ." I throw in.

"Forgiven!" Hillary says. "What'd you bring us?"

I give them their presents, which they love, hand Naomi a small box of Vosges caramels for Alice, and we get down to a serious round of hugs when the door opens again.

"Is it safe to come in?" asks Giorgio.

"Nope, We're leaving," says Hillary. "Sorry, George, you'll have to abuse us next time, we have some bonding we have to do."

Giorgio looks flummoxed. Hillary kisses his cheek, and he blushes.

"Come on, ladies, grab your booty. We're going to high tea at the Drake, on me," I say. When we were little girls Naomi's mom took us there once for a special treat. Something about the palm trees, the harpist, the little sandwiches and pastries, it's just magical. Throughout the years, we have always returned to celebrate successes or get over heartaches.

We head out, and back to the locker room so that Hillary and Naomi can change into their street clothes.

"Well, well, well," Marc says, when the three of us emerge. "Three beautiful women smiling for me."

"Smiling for ourselves, you vain little boy." Hillary mocks him. "But you can look if you like."

"You know you're my favorites." He flirts, flashing that wicked little grin.

"We know," I say. Then I lead my two best friends out the back door.

 Sensimilla and Sensibility

"OH. MY. GOD. IT'S FANTASTIC!!!!" Natasha shrieks when I open the door to the Womb. She loved her kitchen, especially the ceiling, which turned out truly spectacular. But I knew this would be the best part of the show, giving her a space to escape to.

I give her a tour around the tiny room, pointing out the little fridge, stocked with those adorable half-cans of pop, and half-bottles of wine. The cabinet next to it I've filled with an endless assortment of individual serving packages of every possible type of snack, from junk food like Pringles and mini-Oreos to more upscale treats like small jars of lemon artichoke pesto with slim breadsticks. The people at Argo Tea helped me get her set up with an electric kettle, and an individual size teapot with a removable steel mesh insert for loose tea. I bought every tea that had the words "calming," "relaxing," "mellow," or "decaffeinated" on it. Packets of sugar, sweetener, even those great individual serving honey tubes. And of course, a gorgeous set of two tea mugs.

The color, which took us no less than five coats to get the right depth and richness, glows with warmth. The daybed is lush with pillows and soft fabrics, a micro-chenille throw tossed over the edge. I want this room.

Natasha starts to tear up. "It's just so perfect, Lily, thank you so much."

"My pleasure, I'm so glad you like it!" I motion her over to sit with me on the daybed. "So, you think you'll be using this space?"

"I think I may never leave this room!" she gushes.

"Well, we're glad you like what we've done in your home. Do you think you are ready to meet the man who helped me get this done for you?" I've been prompted to try and see if we can get her to bring up Morris, and Ashleigh is doing the same with him. If we can't, we'll just use the standard reveal footage, but Gary is hoping that maybe one or both of them might wax poetic about their lost love.

"The way I feel right now, I could just kiss him!" She laughs.

"Well, who knows, maybe he'll be kissable." Bob makes a motion with his hand that sends me a message to really start digging. After all, we have her girlfriends waiting downstairs on the charter bus, and we can't keep them there forever. "So, tell me, how is it possible that you are still single, Natasha? I mean, you're gorgeous, smart. No Mr. Right yet?"

"Well, you know how it is, you devote yourself to your education and career and before you know it you are thirty-three and still living alone!" Don't I know it.

"Relationships are hard, that's for sure. I sometimes start wondering about all the guys I dated way back when and wondering where they are and what they are doing." Blatant, but it works.

"I know what you mean. I had a dream a few weeks ago about my high school boyfriend, isn't that weird?" BINGO!

"Tell me about him."

"His name was Andrew. I was madly in love with him."

Andrew? ANDREW? Who the fuck is Andrew? "Your high school boyfriend's name was Andrew?"

"Yep. We dated for two years, he was a year older than me. I spent my senior year in mourning. I do sometimes wonder what he is up to these days. Last I heard he was living in California.

This does not compute at all. I mean, Morris's friend said that he and Natasha were madly in love. Bob shrugs at me.

"So that was your only high school boyfriend?" I ask.

"Pretty much."

Is it possible we have the wrong Natasha? Did Morris make the whole thing up? Or is Morris's friend a jerk trying to set him up for humiliation? Whatever the case, we're going to have to find out later. Bob stops filming to set up for the friends to come upstairs. I zip into the bedroom to try and get hold of Gary, hoping that this isn't one of his idiotic ideas. I know he is watching the taping over at Morris's house, so I send him a text message to his BlackBerry.

G– Got Natasha to wax poetic about h.s. boyfriend, Andrew?!?!

I wait, and less than a minute later I get a reply.

L– Ashleigh couldn't get him to talk at all, the friends are all here, and he HATES the apartment.

I smile at this, I can't help the perverse pleasure I feel that Natasha loves her place and Morris hates his. Not that I don't feel bad for him. But if one designer has to be the moron, I do prefer that it is Ashleigh. I reply to Gary.

Poor Morris. Any clue about the mix-up here? I thought research got the skinny on the lost love angle from Morris's best bud who nominated him for the show?

Again, less than a minute elapses.

I have no idea. I know we confirmed that they went to the same high school and were in the same class. But it sounds like no one confirmed with any of Natasha's friends whether they were involved. Should be interesting.

Now I feel really badly for Morris. He has an ugly Ashleighed apartment, and the potential for some really embarrassing footage. I take a deep breath and reply again.

Could we cut the show to look like we are trying to reunite old high school classmates and not lovers? However it happened, it is going to be mortifying for him, and he already hates his apartment, couldn't we spare him?

The reply comes after a very long three minutes.

Is it important to you? I mean, important enough to make me whole for the Spanked! episode, even though it will be our highest rated show ever?

Well, duh?

Yes, Gary. That important.

I mutter a quick prayer under my breath.

Okay. For you. And for Morris, who seems a good bloke.

I hate that I'm liking him right now.

Thank you.

Bob calls me over to discuss the kitchen design with Natasha's girlfriends. My phone buzzes again.

You're welcome, beautiful. Come find me at the party so we can have a drink and talk about your new promo.

Oy. Gary being nice and human and drinking. This is potentially a bad idea. I'm going to need a backup plan.

"Really, with the Crackberry, really?" Bob says. I tell him to give me two minutes, I just have to use the bathroom. I sneak into Natasha's master bath and call Hillary.

"Hey, it's me. I don't have much time, and I think I need your help."

"Whassup?" she asks.

"How's your Dad stash?" Hillary's Dad, ever the hippie, grows his own weed in the basement. Whenever he gets a new batch, he gives Hillary a quarter-ounce or so to stick in her freezer for emergencies.

"Plentiful, he just gave me a sample of some fresh last week. The buds are enormous. Why? You need to get your buzz on?"

"Call Naomi and Alice, see if they are up for a stoner night. I'll stop and pick up munchies, and meet you at your place around nine."

"Why the urgency? Something wrong?" she asks.

"I need to have a definite plan, a place I have to be, people waiting for me tonight. Just trying to avoid any possibility of a judgment lapse. And call my cell at eight-thirty, just to be sure I'm on my way."

"You got it, I'll see you tonight and you can solve the mystery then."

"Love you."

"Love you back."

I turn the phone to silent so that it doesn't ring when I'm on camera. Thank God I have my girls back. I head on over to the kitchen to point out the ceiling for the umpteenth time.

I decide to leave my car and ride with the girls on the bus, to see if I can indulge my curiosity about where our info got mixed up. I never eschew a little escapade in espionage, especially if I can establish the reversal of an estrangement.

I track down the girl who was one of Natasha's sorority sisters, figuring she will be the likeliest to have some info about whether she and Morris even knew each other. Luckily the seat next to her on the bus is open.

"Hi, I'm Lily." I extend my hand to her. She grasps it.

"I'm Jenny," she says. "I really love what you did with Nat's apartment. It looks awesome!"

"Thanks. It was fun to do for her, I hope she enjoys it." Time for some subtle interrogation. "So, are you guys excited to meet some new single men?"

"Absolutely! We hardly ever get out these days. The bar scene is geared for twenty-somethings, and we're all tired of the Viagra Triangle." This is the corner of the Gold Coast where Rush and State meet, home of Gibson's, Hugo's, and Carmine's, a great spot to get a terrific dinner, but known for an overabundance of gentlemen of a certain age and their desire for young playmates.

"I know what you mean, Jenny, we're all in the same boat on that one!" I continue to pry. "Did she have problems with guys in college?"

"Well, at first she was still a little hung up on her high school boyfriend."

"Andrew?"

"Oh, she told you about him? Yeah. Very moody about him. But there had been another guy who was really sweet to her, kind of helped her get back some of her self-esteem, so after she settled in at school, she didn't have any problems with guys, just never found anyone good enough to stick with." Ah HA! Maybe that is the ticket, Morris was sweet to her, sweet on her, and even though the relationship didn't stick with her in the same way as this Andrew person, at least it is a function of two people having different perspectives on their relationship.

"Did she keep in touch with that guy? The one who helped her, I mean."

"Donald? Sure. They are still great friends, even though he is living in Portland." Crap. Donald. Who the fuck is DONALD? And where the heck does Morris come in? My career as a detective may be in serious jeopardy.

"Get OUT!" Hillary says, around a lungful of her dad's best cannabis.

I'm nicely buzzed, and pass the bowl over to Naomi, who takes a decent hit and lets Alice shotgun. Hillary and I groan out loud.

"Can I please finish my story, without the lesbian lovers interrupting me with icky smooching?" I'm trying to fill them in on the evening's excitement.

"Sorry," Naomi says sheepishly, leaning against Alice. "Do continue."

"Okay, so we get to L8 for the party, and Gary has Morris over in the corner. Now, he promised me that we were setting the whole thing up as just reuniting high school friends, since obviously the whole 'boyfriend/girlfriend' angle was off. So I bring over Natasha, who sticks her hand out to Morris and says it is nice to meet him and thanks for his hard work."

"She didn't recognize him?" Alice asks.

"Nope. But he recognized her. 'Nat?' he says. And she says 'Yes? I'm sorry, do I know you?' and his voice gets all weird and he says, 'It's me, Morris Golden.' And Natasha looks him up and down and says, 'Morris Golden?' and he says, 'From Lakeside High?' and she pauses for a minute, and says, 'You were in my freshman physics class, right?' and he says, 'English. We had to read the *Romeo and Juliet* balcony scene. And this is probably going to sound really stupid, but I had a huge crush on you and never really forgot you, and my friends thought that this might be a way to see you again. I hope you aren't mad.' So Natasha looks really puzzled for a minute, and then she smiles and gives him a big hug, and they go over to a corner to talk. And by the end of the night, she had accepted his offer of a date!"

"That is the most extraordinary thing I have ever heard," Hillary says. "Gary must have loved it, the prick, it's so Jerry Springer, great for ratings."

"Of course he did. Plus I still had to give him credit for not setting it up to embarrass Morris. The show went oddball on its own. I give Natasha the hugest credit, once she got over the surprise, she spent the night introducing Morris to everyone as a high school friend, and reminiscing about old times as if they had been really close. She was very cool about the whole thing." I reach my hand out to Hillary to snag the pipe. I take a deep drag, and after I finish my coughing fit, head over to get the garlic bagel chips off Hillary's counter.

"Hey, grab the pinwheels, too, wouldja?" Naomi calls over.

"And the dip!" adds Hillary.

I hold the bag of bagel chips in my teeth, grab the pinwheel cookies in one hand and the spinach artichoke dip in the other, and plop back on the couch.

"The best part of everything was that Natasha said she loved her place so much, and Morris said how much he liked working with me and . . ."

"And blah, blah, blah, Madame Ego, can we tone down the self-love a bit?" Hillary smacks me with a throw pillow.

"Okay. Fine. I get it." I start to laugh. Then Hillary starts to laugh. Naomi and Alice start giggling. Pretty soon we are all wiping our eyes and holding our sides. I am back in the bosom of my friends, high as a kite, full of crap food, and generally feeling fine.

episode #8

Mommie Nearest

Bravo *Wednesday July 26* 8PM–9PM

SWAP/MEET **Renee and Walter: Starting Over**

This week two sixty-something silver foxes try to get back in the dating game. A widower and a divorcée take on the *Swap/Meet* challenge to grab a second chance at a social life. Watch as designer Lily Allen works with her mother Renee on Walter's pad. Highlights include some mother / daughter bonding between the designer and her proud mom, and Ashleigh Benning bonding with Walter.

"Renee, you're perfect. That was great." Gary is gushing all over my mother, who alternates between telling everyone "funny" (read: mortifying) stories about my youth, and giving me pointed glances that seem to say, "Why can't you find a nice man like this handsome fellow?" If she only knew that within twelve hours of meeting him, we were performing bedroom acrobatics at the Wyndham. Probably better not to mention it. She'd only want to know what I did to screw it up, and why I wouldn't be having wonderful British grandchildren named Portia and Chauncy for her.

We've just finished the morning meet-and-greet scene, where my mother and I ostensibly meet on Walter's front porch and head in to look at the rooms. I'm going to be redoing his living room and bedroom, the two places he hasn't been able to bring himself to redecorate since his wife's death three years ago.

"You girls take a break for a few minutes, and then we'll do the design plan explanation in the living room once the crew is set up." Bob heads off to Walter's living room, a nightmare of huge floral pattern chintz and horrific Victorian reproduction wallpaper. Mom and I grab a couple bottles of water at craft service, which is set up in the kitchen, and I snag a chocolate chip cookie off the plate of goodies on the kitchen table.

"I made those for the crew," my mother says, in a voice that smacks of "Fourteen is the largest size they carry in the department stores before you have to shop in the big girls section. . . ." Because of course she stayed up all night baking for my colleagues, not that I've seen a homemade batch of cookies come my way since college.

"I'm *on* the crew, Mom," I say, in a voice that smacks of, "I know how big my ass is, fuck you very much, and as I am a grown-up, I will thank you to not tell me how to live my life." She smiles. I smile. It is going to be a long two days.

"How are you doing?" Curt asks me, over the whine of the rotating sander. He's building me a pair of new occasional tables to match the most perfect coffee table I found at an antique store after nearly two days of searching. Birdie and my mom are currently hot-gluing trim to a pair of lampshades for the bedroom, and getting along like a house afire. I think for a moment before answering him.

"I'm hanging in there," I say. "The tables look great, Curt, thanks. I know getting the detail to match was a pain, but I think it is really going to be spectacular."

"No worries, princess. Besides, you saved me from building yet another mind-numbing set of shelves by recycling those units you found in the basement, so I'm not crunched for time. Is Mommy behaving herself?"

"Of course, polite, interested in everyone and everything, showing off pictures of the wee cousins, and only saying the most complimentary things about Walter's house. This in spite of the fact that Walter's dearly departed wife clearly took all of her decorating inspiration directly out of a circa 1954 Sears Catalog."

"Now, now, now, not all of us have your eye for elegant sophistication, and if we did, you'd be out of a job." He winks at me.

Gary has come out of the house through the garage and winds his way over to the land of carpentry. He sidles up and puts an arm around my shoulders. "Your mother is a darling, she's *making* this show. Thank goodness, because Ashleigh is stalking Walter, who is managing to avoid her advances by the hair of his chinny chin chin, which is not only bad for her mood, but is also not making for scintillating television." I hate how good it feels to have his arm around me. Thank God Curt is here, keeping his gaze fixed on mine, giving me the strength to ignore the little tingles from my nether regions.

Lily's Rule #13: When girl parts are reacting overly favorably to the attention of a toxic person of the male persuasion, diffuse the situation with catty gossiping.

"Ashleigh smelling a future ex-husband is she?" I ask, trying to get the dirt from the other house, since Birdie is too sweet to gossip.

Gary doesn't miss a beat. "She has been forcing her collagened lips into a grimace of a smile all morning. Batting her eyelashes, flirting like mad. Poor thing."

"Why poor thing?" Curt asks, still holding my gaze. "Or did you mean Walter?"

"Nope, poor Ashleigh. Bryan recognized Walter as being a gentlemen's gentleman. Apparently he cruises the gay pubs of a weekend, the late wife serving as a sort of long-term beard, since old Walt works for the conservative Republicans as a political analyst." Gary is practically beaming with delight at imparting this information.

"Is that why he came on the show?" I ask. "A public affirmation of his straightness?"

"Seems to be playing out that way. Struck me as odd, a gent of his generation, married so long with no kids. Bryan says he always comes to the bars with a friend of his, plays the innocent straight older guy, just hanging out with a gay friend for a cocktail, uses a pseudonym. Inevitably a pair of younger men will approach the table, conversation will ensue, and some poor bloke will bring him home, thinking that he is initiating Walt the Salt into the illicit world of carnal love between men. Walt slips out before morning, doesn't call, and if the paramour approaches him again in the future, plays dumb, and makes the poor chap think he has mistaken himself."

"That seems to be a lot of detail, Gary. Did you get all that from Bryan?" Curt asks, well, curtly.

"Bryan seems to have participated in a sort of 'homosexual sting' operation. It had happened to a friend of Bryan's and one of Jou's former interns. So they decided to see if third time was the charm and took an opportunity that presented itself to send a third pal into the lion's den. Third verse, same as the first, so they feel pretty confident that it's old Walt's modus operandi. The first shunned boy has been posting warnings all over Craigslist." Bob exits the garage and waves Gary over. Gary kisses my cheek. "Off to play producer, my poppet. Come back inside in about ten minutes to check on darling Mum and Birdie, will you, love?"

"You got it," I say. I will not like him, I will not like him, I will not like him. Yeesh.

"Isn't he just your biggest fan?" Curt says, in a sort of sinister way.

"That was the point, remember? Get him to stop being cold and mean to me? Make him play nice? I'm not trying to win his affection, Curt, I just wanted it to stop being awful." Sounds good, doesn't it?

"As long as you remember that was the plan. It's still none of my business. But there's a difference between friendly and romantic, and I'd just hate to see you get sucked into his fake charm. You can do better."

I lean over and kiss his scruffy cheek. "Thank you, Curt. You're always my champion, and I don't know what I would do without you. Now I must go inside, where my mother is probably discussing her perception of my biological clock on camera with Birdie."

Curt laughs, and turns back to the table at hand, and I square my shoulders for some face time with Renee.

video diary confession:

"Okay, this has been a pretty good day so far. My mom is a trooper, jumping in and helping on all the projects, Curt is rocking and rolling on the carpentry projects, and all in all, I'm feeling pretty good. But I'm not counting my chickens quite yet. It is still Day One, and there are plenty of things that could go wrong. We're pulling up the carpet in the living room, and hoping for decent subflooring or old hardwood. We're taking Walter's bedroom set and giving it a really cool paint finish, at least, I think it will be cool, I've never really done it before. And the weather folks are telling us that we may be in a midwestern typhoon tomorrow, which'll make everything catawampus. But I'm keeping my fingers crossed, and hopefully by tomorrow night, Walter will have a beautiful new space. Now wish me luck, I'm off to get rid of some ugly carpet! Bye!"

"So, ladies, we're going to pull up the carpet and hopefully, what we'll find will either be hardwood floors or subflooring in good shape. I've saved enough money in my budget to put in a laminate floor if we don't get hardwood, but if we do, we'll have enough to refinish the floor and even have some extra money for more accessories." My mom, Birdie, and I are very attractive in our matching *Swap/Meet* shirts, in a tasteful shade of lavender for this episode, bulky work gloves, and plastic safety goggles.

"I'm always so scared when we pull up carpet, y'all!" Birdie says excitedly. "It's like unwrapping a present from a crazy old Aunt Patti, could be an heirloom piece of jewelry, but it could be a half a tomato sandwich. You just never know!"

My mom looks over at me for a "Southern Belle to English" translation. I try to jump in.

"I prefer to think of us as archeologists, Birdie, we could find a treasure under there!" Bob is grinning, we've gotten great letters about the chemistry between me and Birdie lately. *Time Out Chicago* did a full feature article on us, and commented that "strange Southern charm paired with urban Jewish wit" was a "recipe for very watchable television." So Gary and Bob have been trying to have us actually work on more projects together instead of trying to keep the focus on Birdie working alone with the homeowners.

I walk to the corner of the living room and use a crowbar to pry up a small piece of carpet. Gary always makes us leave the pad down and get the carpet out separately, since the padding tends to lift off easily in one piece, making for a cleaner reveal. So I just grab the carpet and start to pull it up. As soon as I have a good section pulled back, I call over for help.

"Okay, guys, how about some assistance over here?"

My mom and Birdie come over and help me pull the carpet up and over. It takes us about fifteen minutes of pulling and folding to get the carpet into a manageable pile. We take a break while the production assistants schlep it out of the room. Bob wants us to get the floor reveal shot before we break for lunch, but since we only need the front half of the room to determine what we'll have, some of the furniture and supplies which had been temporarily moved to the dining room so we could pull out the rug, come back into the room.

"So, shall we see what we have under here?" I ask.

"Oh, yes!" says Birdie.

"Of course, dear," says Mom.

"Here goes!"

I grab the corner of the padding and begin to pull back. Birdie shrieks.

"Oh, sweet Jesus on the cross!"

My mom and I look down to see that what we have revealed

isn't gorgeous original hardwood floor, it is instead a huge nest of carpenter ants, enormous and shiny black, pouring up and out of a three-inch-wide hole in the subflooring that we have uncovered by removing the rug and pad. The three of us run across the room and simultaneously leap up on the wonderful square coffee table I found. It promptly collapses, dumping the three of us into a pile on the floor. My face is buried in Birdie's cleavage, and my substantial tush is up in the air. My mom is making some noises, and as the crew jumps in to help untangle us, Birdie yells out.

"They're coming!"

It's like a horror movie. The swarm of ants is spreading over the subfloor and the dropped padding like an inky layer of icky-ness, and they are indeed headed in our direction. We all jump up, which is when Mom crumples back to the floor. Reg the sound guy (and perfect mensch), puts down his monitor, takes off his headset, and in one motion whisks my mother off of the floor and out the door. I follow behind, with Birdie on my heels. We head for the guest room at the back of the house, where Reg deposits my mom on the bed, and then returns to the front room to see what he can do to help. Mom is rubbing her ankle, a pained look on her face.

"Sprain?" I ask, gently feeling her ankle for broken bones. Since obviously my degree from Harrington makes me practically an MD.

"I just twisted it a bit, I think probably a bruise, dear. Are you both all right?" she asks us.

"I'm okay," I say. "How about you, Bird?"

"I have never seen ANYTHING that HORRIBLE in the WHOLE OF MY LIFE!" she says.

"Poor Walter, living with that sort of thing right under his feet and not knowing it," says my mother.

"I can't believe we broke the fucking coffee table," I lament. "I hope those stupid carpenter ants brought their power tools, 'cause I want them to rebuild me a table!"

"Really, with the complaining, really?" Bob says on his way by the door.

The three of us look at each other. Then the laughing starts.

I wouldn't be a production assistant on this shoot for all the money in the world. It's the morning of Day Two. The PA's were here all night. They had to clear practically half of the first floor for the exterminator, losing nearly two hours of work. Then we all had to vacate the house entirely for four hours after the exterminator left so as not to breathe the fumes. Then the PA's had to come in and clean up the dead and dying ants, finish the painting in both rooms, repair the chewed up subflooring, then lay the laminate. The report from Bob is that they swept up three buckets full of ants. I would have puked for sure.

In the meantime, Curt was also here late trying to repair the coffee table. The top was salvageable, but in need of refinishing since Birdie's heels scratched up the varnish. The legs, however, gorgeous cabriolet legs with ball and claw feet, were totally shattered in the collapse and Curt needed to try and figure out how to create new legs which wouldn't be out of place with the antique top. He did it, of course, genius that he is, but he didn't leave until almost two this morning and was back today first thing so that he could get started on the armoire for the bedroom.

My mom and I spent the rest of yesterday doing as many of the detail projects as we could in the borrowed living room of Walter's neighbor Bruce, who generously lent his space so that we could keep filming while they took care of the insect problem.

Birdie was still pretty shaken, so she spent the rest of the day over at my mom's place helping Ashleigh and Walter. I managed to get out of her that Ashleigh is doing the kitchen and dining room, and that so far it isn't looking too awful.

Renee was a good sport about everything yesterday, bless her heart. She's discreetly limping from the disappointing discomfort of the ankle disfigurement which occurred between the disgorging of ants from the floor and the disentanglement of the three of us atop the coffee table. But she'll heal; it's just slightly discolored. She had a good time at the Peninsula where the show is putting her up for the duration. I sent her a gift certificate for a massage which she enjoyed tremendously after her long day.

Today we're working under the gun, trying to make up for the snafus of yesterday. Mostly everything is reasonably smooth. Mom and I are working on a slipcover for Walter's couch.

"Okay, so now that we've loosely draped the fabric over the couch with the pattern on the inside, we'll start pinning it, and we want this to be pretty tight. Then we'll trim the excess, lift it off gently, and sew along where we've pinned. Then, when we flip it back inside out, we'll have a perfect custom slipcover, and because I've chosen this fairly thick upholstery-weight chenille, no one will ever know that these chintz roses are underneath."

"Well, that's a blessing," my mom quips. Then she looks shocked right into the camera, even though she has been instructed to only do that for the video diary. This makes us both crack up, not to mention Bob and the rest of the crew.

"Okay, let's take a quick break," Bob says. "Jenny, take the slipcover over to May to get sewn. Lily, Renee, we'll pick it up in the bedroom in about fifteen minutes."

Mom and I head over to grab a bottle of water from the cooler.

"Darling, I am starting to wonder how you do this every week.

It's exhausting. Is it always like this?" my mom asks, cracking open her water and taking a deep swig.

"It does tend to be a little wacky. I keep waiting for a 'normal' shoot where nothing goes wrong, and everything flows along like clockwork, and life is simple and beautiful. So far, no go. And according to Curt, I could spend my life in home improvement television and never see a shoot like that."

"He seems like a nice man," my mother says.

"He's become a good friend," I say, trying to nip in the bud whatever strange little matrimonial thought my mother is probably having.

"I was thinking you should introduce him to Hillary."

WHAT?

"Why should I introduce him to Hillary?" My mother has never been remotely interested in my friends' love lives. When I told her that Naomi had come out as a lesbian and was moving in with Toby her response was "That's nice, dear."

"She seems like she could use an older man who wouldn't let her boss him around," my mom says, as if this is the most logical statement in the world. "And he has a handsome face and a very nice body, which I think would be important to her."

"I hadn't really thought about it." I'm dumbfounded. "The only worse idea than fixing up one of my best friends with one of my coworkers would be to date one myself!" Might as well remind myself to behave while Gary is overseeing things at the other house. So much easier to be strong when he isn't in the room with his charm and perfect hair.

"I think a lot of that is just nonsense. Can't people who work together behave like grown-ups and keep their private life activities separate from their professional activities? Where else will one meet people?"

Ah HA! I now get her motive. This is a sly backdoor way of suggesting that I try to snag Gary, sneaky vixen. "It sounds like a good idea, Mom, but let's be honest, it's usually a recipe for disaster. People just don't work and play well together."

"Well, obviously it is your choice. But I think they might be good together." I almost forgot we were ostensibly discussing Curt and Hillary.

"Ladies?" Bob interrupts us. "We're ready for you in the bedroom. Lily, I'm going to want you to take us through the bedding choices, with some specific brand recognition for Tempur-Pedic, since they donated the bed for Walt's bad back."

Saved by the bell.

"C'mon Mom, let's go play with the bedding."

"All right, sweetheart. Whatever you say."

Whatever I say. As if.

My mother is talking to a man, and it is FREAKING ME OUT!

I mean, you know, happy, happy and all that, and it isn't that I want her alone forever, I mean, she's only sixty-one, but this, this is just so fucking WEIRD.

But I have to give Bryan props, she looks fantastic. He took her to Fringe where his friend, the owner, Dawn, gave her an amazing haircut, a very swingy and sophisticated bob, with piecey highlights of ash blond and caramel in her still dark-chestnut hair. Krystiana over at EBella gave her a micro-dermabrasion facial, giving her skin a real glow. And Julie, my favorite Bobbi Brown guru at 900 North Michigan updated her makeup, which hadn't changed much during my lifetime.

Once she had spent the morning being pampered, Bryan took her to Bloomingdale's for new clothes. He dressed her classically in

Ellen Tracy and Tahari, and FINALLY got her to embrace the revolutionary ideas of pleatless pants, lower-rise waistlines, and pointy-toe shoes! Tonight at the wrap party, she is actually radiant, in a gorgeous chocolate brown cashmere sweater, and a kicky tweed skirt with a beaded tulle hem. And she is in deep conversation for the last twenty minutes with Walt's accountant, a distinguished-looking gentleman named Jacob Fein, who is looking at my mother like she's, well, a WOMAN. And she is looking at him like he's, well, DESSERT!

My mother. The hussy.

"She looks fantastic, doesn't she?" Bryan appears at my elbow and hands me a martini glass. It contains a deeply red liquid and is garnished with a piece of chocolate.

"What's this?" I ask, taking it.

"Cherry Pie à La Mode." He says with a wink. "SKYY Vanilla, cherry brandy, and cherry juice, rimmed in vanilla sugar, comes with a chocolate-covered cherry."

I sip, tasting the tartness of the juice with the hit of vanilla and the deep warmth of the brandy; it isn't dissimilar to the sensation of eating a bite of hot cherry pie with vanilla ice cream.

"Thanks," I say. "She really looks fantastic, Bry, thank you so much for taking such good care of her. I don't think I've ever seen her glow like this."

"Well, the number cruncher certainly seems to be noticing," he says, winking at me.

"I know. It's really weird. She and my dad were so sort of asexual in their connection to each other, I guess I never really thought when they broke up that she would want a MAN. I mean, a companion, a friend, sure, but not a MAN in her life in a romantic way, you know?"

"You just don't want to think that your mom might be getting laid tonight and you won't be," he says with a wink.

"Okay, fuck you. I did not need to hear that." Eeew.

"Well, behave yourself, because here she comes." Bryan greets my mom with a hug and a kiss. "You tart! Did you give him your number?" he asks her, all cheek.

"A lady never tells." My mom is being coy and blushing. This is so gross. "How are you, darling?"

"I'm good, Mom, thanks. Did you have a good time doing the show?" Change of subject, change of subject, for the love of all that is holy, please let us CHANGE THE SUBJECT.

"You know, honey, I really did. I mean, I originally said yes for you, since Gary said you wanted me to do it, but going through the experience, well, I feel like a princess and I forgot what that was like. Thank you for letting me horn in on your work for a few days; it was really fun." She kisses me on the cheek.

"You're welcome, Mom. I'm really glad you could do it."

Gary wanders over and throws an arm around my mother's shoulder. "Love, you are ravishing. Are you having a good time?"

She beams at him. "Yes, thank you, Gary. It's been a lovely experience. But I'm afraid I have to go. Jacob is giving me a ride back to Deerfield."

"Saucy wench, leaving us for that old tosser, eh? Well, he'd better be a gentleman, or he'll have me to answer to, all right, darling?" Gary laughs his easy laugh. My stomach turns over. "What about you, my flower? Can I offer you an escort home?" he asks me. Gulp.

"She already has one, Gary." Curt. My savior.

Gary looks at me, then at Curt. "Yeah, Curt and I want to talk about the LA plans, so he's going to get me home. Thanks, though, Gary; I'll take a rain check."

My mother looks at me and raises one newly groomed eyebrow. Then she leans over and kisses my cheek.

"I'll talk to you this week, darling. Thank you again for letting me play with you. I love you, sweetheart." She crosses the bar to the door where Jacob is waiting for her, God help us all.

"Shall we follow them?" Curt asks me.

"Absofuckinglutely," I reply.

"Good night, Gary, see you next week." Curt puts his hand out and shakes Gary's hand. Gary takes it, but doesn't break eye contact with me. Shudder.

"Good night, then," he says, and on his way past, squeezes my arm.

Sure, now that I'm entirely certain I don't want him, the Britiot is making a play for me. And my mom has landed a guy who will probably end up being my stepfather. And my absentee incommunicado dad is the new playboy of Florida, and I'm probably never going to date again.

"Curt, my good man?"

"Yes, my flower?" Such a wise-ass.

"Please take me home."

"You got it."

We walk to his truck, and bless his heart, he doesn't say a word.

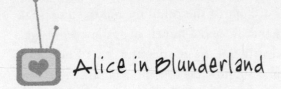 Alice in Blunderland

I pull into HiFi right behind Hillary and Naomi. We park in ad-joining spaces and get out of the cars.

"Tell her she's fucking nuts," Hillary says.

"Tell her she's behaving irrationally," Naomi says.

"Hey, hey, easy ladies, what the hell is going on?" I ask, glad that the irritation is away from me for a change.

"She and Alice are talking about moving in together, already!" says Hillary, holding open the gym door.

"*She's* been turning down invitations from that nice Charlie from Lang's wedding and not telling us!" says Naomi, holding open the locker room door.

"Okay, one at a frigging time, do you mind? Hillary, you first. What's all this about Charlie?" Frankly, my interest is far more piqued by the secret pursuit of Hillary's affections than the prac-tically inevitable cohabitation of my favorite lesbian.

Hillary is hanging up her power suit in the tiny red locker. She sighs. "Fine. If you must know. Ever since the wedding, that dumb ass Charlie Braun has invited me to The Standard Club, ostensibly to encourage me to join; to a Sox Skybox, as if any self-respecting Northsider would accept that invitation when our beloved Cubbies are out of the running; and to some Martini Monday bullshit that he and a bunch of his lawyer friends do every week. He clearly doesn't get the hint, that I'm not interested in dating him. And now the bastard is opposing counsel on a new case. I have half a mind to tell the judge that he has a conflict of interest and should be recused from the case." She looks righteously indignant as she says it, but there is a twinkle in her eye.

"You cunt," I say.

"Really, Lily!" Naomi hates the c-word.

"What?" Hillary smirks a little.

"You're playing hard to get. What a shitty thing to do to a nice man." I know her game all too well; she must really like this guy.

"Am not," she says, weakly.

"Are, TOO! Are, too, are, too, are, too! This is Stuart Hacker all over again." I'm laughing.

Lily's Rule #6: Don't try to pull the wool over the eyes of the people who know you the best, it's a recipe for disaster. Just suck it up and come clean.

"OH MY GOD! You're right! She's right, Hil, it's Stuart. You must REALLY like him, huh?" Naomi is laughing, too.

"Goddammit, I'm not playing hard to get, and I don't like him. And Stuart was sixteen years ago! Can I have some credit for at least a little more maturity?" Hillary's conviction could use a little work here.

We head out to the main gym and jump on three side-by-side

treadmills to warm up and wait for Giorgio to finish with his client.

"Just don't hit this one with your tennis racquet," Naomi says.

Stuart Hacker was the captain of the tennis team in high school with Hillary. She hated not being in charge. He was a senior when we were juniors, cute in a lanky teenage athlete kind of way, terrible acne, but somehow still attractive, and very nice. And very into Hillary, who spent the entire year being mean to him, including "accidentally" knee-capping him with her racket every time they were assigned to play mixed doubles together at practice. In early May he overheard her telling another girl on the team that she couldn't wait for the following year so that they would finally be rid of Stuart, who announced his presence by saying, "I guess this means the prom is out, huh?" To which Hillary said, "Of course not, pick me up at six, and if there is a carnation anywhere in my corsage, you are SO not getting laid." There was, needless to say, no carnation within a five-mile radius of her corsage, and Stuart was rewarded with a lovely prom night and several weeks of pre-college nookie before leaving for Washington University in Saint Louis. It was no surprise that dating Hillary cleared his skin right up.

"You guys are crap. This is not the same thing," Hillary says. "Besides, I'm still sleeping with Chandler. What would I need Charlie for?"

"How about an actual relationship? Like a grown-up? You know, use all that MATURITY you've been developing these past sixteen years," Naomi offers.

"A Shabbas Goy only takes a girl so far, Hillary. I mean, Chandler isn't really dateable. And this guy seems nice, why not cut him a break?" I say, not really thinking that she will listen to either of us.

"I'll think about it. Fair enough, bitches?"

"It's all we ask, dearheart," Naomi says.

"Fine. Can we please focus on the important issue at hand? Naomi, you're goddamned crazy if you think that it isn't too soon for you and Alice to shack up. And I like her. I really like her. I think she could be 'The One.' I'll even give you the frequent flier miles to upgrade to business class when you guys go to China to pick up a kid. But take some time. You haven't even had a vacation together. Or met her folks. Or gotten through the High Holidays. Can't you just take a deep breath and let it move ahead s-l-o-w-l-y?" Hillary is waving her arms over her head.

Giorgio comes over, and the three of us get off the treadmills and follow him down the hall to our little room.

"I tell you what, you who knows so much about relationships, I'll put the moving in with Alice conversation on the back burner for one month. If you have accepted and GONE ON a date with Mr. Charles Braun, Esquire, by that time, we can have another discussion about what is good for me or not. How about them apples?" Naomi says triumphantly.

"Fine," says Hillary, cold as ice, but with a sparkle in her eye. "But I don't have to enjoy it."

"You guys are the weirdest," I say.

"Just wait, missy, you're not off the hook either," Hillary says, laughing.

"Hillary. That's not nice," Naomi says. "It's a good thing, and you're setting her up to be suspicious."

Giorgio starts us on step-ups, pouting because he now knows that Hillary is going to go out with some guy that we must at least superficially approve of.

"Oh Lord, what now?" I shudder to think.

"Alice wants to fix you up," Naomi blurts out.

"What? A blind date? You know I hate that shit. Have you met him? Who is he?" Blind dates never work out for me. Ever. I try to be blithe, but it always feels like a blitzkrieg: this one's a blimp, that one thinks Democrats are a blight, this one blinks too much, that one defines bliss as hours of videogaming. They call them BLIND dates for a reason.

"I haven't met him. He's Alice's brother-in-law's friend. She met him at a barbecue and thought you guys would get along. Please do this. It'll show that you trust her and are welcoming of her, and that will mean a lot to me." I can't resist Naomi when she is like this.

"Fine. Have Alice give him my number. I'm making no promises."

"Ladies, can we please focus for just today on our workout? Hmm?" Poor Giorgio. We are a handful.

"Of course, we can," Naomi says.

"You betcha," I say.

"Fuck you, George. It's our time and our dime. Get over it," Hillary says.

She's a pisser, that one. We settle into our routine and try to actually get some sort of health benefit out of the rest of the hour.

Have I mentioned how much I hate blind dates? Sitting in my lobby, waiting to be picked up by one Dr. Arye Grossman, an orthodontist of indeterminate personality. Wearing my cutest first-date outfit in case he turns out to be great, but buttoned up higher than usual to protect the cleavage in case he turns out to be a troll.

Our one phone conversation lasted exactly seven minutes. He called, introduced himself, asked if he could take me to dinner. I

said yes, expecting that we would continue to chat, and he said great and hung up. But some people aren't good on the phone, so I'm trying to be tentatively optimistic.

A tallish, balding gentleman of certain Jewish heritage comes through the front door.

He is not, as they say, terribly attractive. Nor extraordinarily unattractive. He is sort of nondescript. I rise to greet him.

"Arye. I'm Lily."

"I know, I recognize you from the show." Great. He watches the show. Fan-flipping-tastic.

He extends his arm, indicating that I should go through the door before him. I exit the building and get into the very snazzy BMW parked in the driveway. At least he has a nice ride.

"Can I help you?" says the woman in the driver's seat. I look out the window where Arye is looking puzzled and motioning behind him. I have gotten into the wrong car. Because I am an idiot.

"I'm so sorry, first date, I thought this was his car." I get out of the Beemer, leaving the confused woman behind, and follow Arye to his much-less-exciting Ford Taurus. I'm blushing like mad, and Arye doesn't reference it at all, so clearly we are going to pretend it didn't happen.

Arye drives us downtown. Conversation with him is like trying to get blood from a turnip. I keep asking him questions. His answers are as brief as possible, and he seems completely disinterested in asking me anything. Now, I know I'm not the most scintillating person in the entire world, but I do have a sort of interesting job, you know, I mean even if you don't like interior design, the making of a television show is sort of generically cool. Certainly the kind of thing to be interested in. He talks a little about his work, but not with any particular passion. I ask where we are headed.

"To the Hilton," he says.

"Awfully presumptuous of you," I say, thinking he is joking.

"No, of course not like that. I have a dinner reservation in one of the restaurants."

I still think he is joking, but two seconds later he is pulling into the parking lot. Good grief.

Now, this isn't a hotel like the Park Hyatt or the Peninsula where the restaurants are, in and of themselves, a destination. This is the Hilton. Home of convention travelers and businessmen in need of a burger after a day in meetings.

I indicate that I find this a curious choice, as we enter the hotel and Arye escorts me to The Pavilion, the "bistro" in the hotel.

"I figured this would be a decent place, a little quieter than the usual Saturday night scene."

Yeah, because the last thing a girl wants on a Saturday night date is to be a part of the actual Saturday night dating scene. This is going to be a long evening.

We glance over the menu. I order a glass of pinot noir and Arye does the same.

"So, Alice tells me you like to cook?" he asks.

"Well, I like it, but I don't get to do it that often, since I'm really busy. But yes, I do enjoy it. And you? Do you like to cook?" I sound boring even to me.

"No, I'm all thumbs in the kitchen. I can make my morning cereal and that's about it. I eat the rest of my meals out," he says with a chuckle.

This makes the dinner choice that much stranger, since for a guy who makes a decent living, I assume, and eats out a lot, he must know at least a couple good restaurants. After all, this is Chicago. It's an eating town.

"Where do you usually like to eat?"

"Do you know Chipotle?" His eyes light up.

"The burrito chain?" I ask.

"Yep. I love it. I eat there about six days a week."

You have got to be fucking kidding me.

Okay boys, little tip from your pal Lily . . . if you eat fast food of any kind six nights a week, don't admit to it on a date. And if the fast food you eat six nights a week is of the variety with a reputation for giving any reasonable human being gas and the shits, REALLY DON'T TELL US ABOUT IT.

"Really, that often? You must like it a lot." What else can one say to this?

"I do, it's fresh, quick, and healthy."

Healthy? McMexican?

"They must have a pretty extensive menu if you can eat there that often."

"No, I always get the same thing."

No wonder this guy is forty-one and never been married.

"Really? The exact same thing every night? How long have you been doing this?" Maybe it's a new infatuation.

"About two years."

Sweet Christ.

"You've been eating the same dinner six nights a week for two years?"

"And lunch," he says almost proudly.

"You eat Chipotle for lunch, too?"

"Yep. There's one near my office, too."

Lucky patients. Can't think of anything better than a visit to the orthodontist unless it's an orthodontist with Chipotle breath. "So, Chipotle twice a day?"

"Pretty much. But then again, I don't have a beautiful girl

cooking homemade meals for me . . ." Arye winks. Arye doesn't have a prayer of me ever cooking anything for him. Poor fellow.

"Does your doctor know?" I can't help it.

"Why would I tell my doctor? I mean, it's good for you!" He apparently lives in an alternate universe.

"Well, I mean, I suppose it's a healthier version of fast food, but it is still high in fat, calories, and sodium." I made the mistake of checking the nutritional info when they first opened here. Not a pretty picture. The standard burrito as people get them packs nearly 1400 calories—350 just for the tortilla! I still eat them once in a blue moon, but only if I know there are several salads in my future.

"Well, I get it without the sour cream, so that cuts the fat way down."

"But cheese? Guacamole?"

"Well, yeah. Double rice, double beans, chicken, lettuce, cheese, guac, corn salsa."

Great. Double beans.

"Oh my." I can't help it.

"What?" He seems puzzled.

"It's just, that's like a whole day's worth of calories in one burrito."

"Really?" Duh.

"I'm pretty sure. But whatever, if you like it and it works for you, why not? There are worse vices than Chipotle." Not that any come to mind. All the supposedly worse ones have twelve-step programs. But what kind of intervention can you do for someone who eats at Chipotle twice a day? Flatulence Anonymous?

My wine seems to have evaporated. I motion to the waiter for another. Our salads arrive. Very little discussion ensues.

Arye is possibly the least interesting person I have ever met. The personality that sees nothing wrong with the same meal twice a day for two years also apparently doesn't see anything wrong with having exactly no interests. He doesn't read books. He doesn't follow sports, pop culture, or politics. He belongs to no groups or organizations. He has no subscriptions to anything, neither magazine nor theater. Arye, as far as I can ascertain, gets up, eats his bowl of cereal, goes to work, eats Chipotle for lunch, sees more patients, heads home, eats Chipotle for dinner, watches television, goes to bed. Sometimes he goes over to friends' homes, but they mostly have kids, so he does that less and less. I suspect Arye has an enormous porn collection. Not to mention an irate colon. I order a third glass of wine as our truly mediocre dinner arrives. I decline dessert. It is only 9 PM on a Saturday night. We are at the Hilton. I'm with a man who makes picking one's toenails seem like an exciting prospect for the evening. I'm imagining the slow painful way I would like to kill Alice. It is not my fault.

Enter Madcap Date Girl.

Remember my tough-as-nails, cheeky business alter ego, the one who says all the right things in meetings and interviews? She has a sister. Madcap Date Girl's job is to keep me amused during bad dates so that an entire evening isn't lost. She arrives just in time, when Arye suggests we move from the restaurant to one of the bars in the hotel. I agree. We begin to walk around. I spot a steady stream of people carrying drumsticks coming from somewhere down the hall. Drumsticks as in "stick to beat upon a drum with" and not "the tasty legs formerly owned by a chicken." Madcap Date Girl sees them, too.

"Hey. Let's find out what the drumsticks are about!" I grab Arye's hand and begin leading him like a salmon upstream, through the crowd, to the source of the magical drumsticks. As none of these people look remotely like musicians, I can only deduce that they are a part of some sort of convention or something. We quickly find ourselves in a large meeting room. There are big posters around the room for some bank chain. "Drum up new business!" is clearly the motto for the day. I look around but there are no drumsticks anywhere.

"Oh well, guess we missed them," Arye says, obviously torn between being excited and amused, and totally mortified.

"Not so, my friend. We are just temporarily stymied. Follow me." I grab his hand and pull him back down the hallway. In one of the bars I spot a guy with a name tag and a fistful of sticks. Score. Madcap Date Girl and I mentally high-five.

I walk over and subtly glance down at his tag. Then MDG takes over negotiations.

"Tim, hi!" Big smile, hand extended.

"Um, hi . . ." He's clearly trying to place me.

"Lily. We met earlier, at the breakout session."

"Oh, yes, of course, Lily, how's it going?" Tim, like most mid-level execs, is pretty good at faking remembrance of a client or colleague.

"You remember Arye, from the Carbondale office?"

"Sure, sure, hey man, good to see you!" Tim shakes Arye's hand briskly. Arye looks as if he might throw up.

"Hey Tim, how come you're hoarding the drumsticks when some of us didn't get any?" I'm going with fake petulant here.

"Weren't they under your chair?" He looks confused.

"Do you see me carrying drumsticks, Tim?"

"Well, gosh, here, take a pair of these." He hands over the loot. "Arye, did you need a pair, too?"

"Um, no, thanks, I'm good." Arye is sort of green around the gills, but there's a twinkle in the eye that tells me he's enjoying it at least a little bit.

"Thanks, Tim, we've got to go. See you soon!"

"Sure thing, Lily, catch you at the meeting in Minneapolis!"

"Wouldn't miss it!" I wave good-bye, and Arye and I head off down the hall. I hear music. MDG hears it, too. "C'mon, let's see what's down there . . ." And off we go.

Turns out we are able to crash some sort of Elks Club annual gala, full of women in their most sparkly beaded gowns and men looking uncomfortable in ill-fitting suits. But the cake is good. Arye only eats a couple of bites. I take a flower arrangement.

Finally we head downstairs where I spot a pool table off to the side of a bar. I get a set of balls from the bartender and rack them. Arye is not a good pool shooter. Neither am I. I beat him, but only after what seems like the longest pool game in history. It is nearly eleven. I fake a big yawn, and Arye offers to drive me home.

Standing awkwardly at the front door of the building, drumsticks and flower arrangement in hand, Arye finally lets loose.

"That was the most fun I think I've ever had on a date! Alice said you were awesome. I'll call you and we'll set something up for later in the week." Presumptuous little bugger, isn't he?

"Thanks for dinner, Arye. It was nice to meet you."

He leans in for a kiss. I turn the head to give him my cheek. My doorman comes to the rescue.

"Evening, Ms. Allen."

"Hi, Mike." I head inside.

Upstairs I put the flowers on the table, put my new drumsticks on the mantel, get out of my date clothes, and grab the phone.

"Hello?" Naomi sounds a little less than perky, I hope I didn't wake her.

"Hey. It's me"

"Hi, how'd the date go?"

"Let's see, he is beige, bland, banal, boring, bald, basic, and burrito-crazed. He took me to a lovely little boîte in the lobby of the Hilton. He regaled me with the virtues of Chipotle for the better part of an hour. The evening required an intervention by Madcap Date Girl."

"Really? That's too bad."

"That's too bad? THAT'S TOO BAD? What was Alice thinking? What were you thinking letting Alice think what she was thinking? Who on earth would imagine in their wildest dreams that this man would be the kind of person that I would find remotely interesting in even a platonic, let alone a romantic way? Who, I ask you, who?"

"Well, you know, Lily, there are only so many eligible bachelors in the world." What is that tone in her voice?

"Well, obviously, there are only so many bachelors, but this guy is sort of bottom of the barrel material. Honestly, Naomi, I know we want to make Alice feel a part of the gang, but I can't go through another night like this just to beef up her confidence."

I can hear Alice in the background mumbling something. Naomi clearly has her hand over the mouthpiece. I can't hear what they are talking about. Naomi comes back.

"Sorry. I'll let Alice know that he wasn't your dream date."

"Naomi . . ."

"Yes?"

"What's up?" I know she has something up her sleeve.

"Nothing, I'm just saying that maybe this guy was indicative of the boyfriend market these days. And since you aren't interested in anyone who might challenge you in any way, I guess Alice just thought he might be more your speed." There is a definite

"I told you so" attitude in her voice. This clues me in to the method in her madness.

"Is this still about Ron? Did you let Alice fix me up with a sponge because you think I should be dating Ron?" I don't frigging believe it!

"Would I do such a thing to you?" Naomi giggles. I can hear Alice in the background, clearer this time. "She made me do it!"

"It wasn't Alice, it was YOU?" My mild-mannered little art therapist can be evil when she wants to be.

"Okay. I confess. Alice came home from the barbecue and said her brother-in-law had asked if she knew anyone for Arye, and she told me because she thought he was so dull and I thought you should meet him. Thought it might be a good lesson about taking opportunities, even if they are a little inconvenient. Ron was out with us again after the YLD thing, and he is a really nice guy, and really cute, and I just thought it was sad that you sabotaged a chance to really find out if you guys clicked or not."

"It's like a weird *Brady* version of *Scared Straight*. Naomi, you cow, please let me worry about my dating life or lack thereof, pretty please? Okay? Yes, maybe I totally missed the boat on Ron. But there is a lot of ground to cover between guys like Ron and guys like Arye. Promise me we can not ever do this again?" I'm laughing now, thinking about her little insidious plan, and how proud she must have been to have thought it up.

Naomi giggles, too. "Tough love, baby, tough love."

"Oh my God, it was so awful!" I'm totally cracking up.

"Well, days like this I don't know why anyone would want a relationship to begin with." Naomi is half-whispering.

"Trouble in paradise?" I ask.

"Alice isn't so excited about my asking to not discuss moving in for another month. She's claiming I'm a commitment-phobe."

"Didn't you tell her about Toby?"

"Of course, exes are standard lesbionic first-date fodder. No, she thinks I'm in love with Hillary."

I KNEW IT! I stay calm. "Are you?" I ask casually.

"Of course not. I mean, at one point or another I've been in love with both of you, it's a rite of passage to lust after your straight friends, but trust me, it was total teenage crap, and not at all lasting or current."

"Aw, Naomi, me, too? Really? I'm so flattered!" It's about the best compliment anyone has ever given me.

"Oh, shut up. The fact is, Alice refuses to believe I'm not holding a torch for Hillary and is awfully put out that I won't talk moving in right now. But of course her insistence that I talk about moving in right now as if we are under some sort of deadline makes me a little worried about whether she wants to be with me or just be in a partnership, which makes me even more leery about moving in with her!"

"I can hear you, you know!" Alice calls out in the background.

"Well, of course I know that, no point in pretending I'm not going to be talking about it with her, is there? I mean you know I'm going to talk to her about it. I have nothing to hide from you!" Naomi yells back.

"You are so going to owe me an hour of head for this bullshit, I'm not kidding!" Alice shouts.

Well, there's an image I didn't need at the end of a long day.

"Why don't you guys finish your conversation, I'm going to work on the LA design boards before I go to bed," I say.

"Fine. Sorry about your date," she says, not sounding sorry in the least.

"You're forgiven. But don't ever do that again," I admonish her.

"On one condition."

"What?"

"If another opportunity like Ron comes along, don't be a fucking idiot. Deal?"

"Fine. Deal."

"Good night, sweetie."

"Good night, Naomi. And good lick. I mean luck."

"Very funny."

"Bye."

Wait till Hillary hears about this!

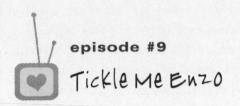

episode #9

Tickle Me Enzo

Bravo *Wednesday August 2* 8PM–9PM

SWAP/MEET Enzo and Isadora: The Hollywood Edition

The two hot, hot, hot stars of *Hit List*, Enzo Mangiafiore and Isadora Gregg, step up for the sake of charity and publicity. They submit to the usual home improvement and personal styling as the regular Joes, but access to the wrap party carries a $500-a-head price tag, matched dollar for dollar by BBC Productions, with the proceeds going to the Susan G. Komen Breast Cancer Research Foundation. A $50 per ticket raffle will give guests a shot at travel prizes, food and wine packages, and, for two lucky singles, dates with Enzo and Isadora.

I never want to move off this bed. We are happily ensconced in the Sheraton Delfina in Santa Monica after a truly tedious flight from Chicago. Since we are still far from major players, we were booked in coach, and since we needed nearly forty seats on one plane, we had to take the very undesirable three o'clock flight, getting us into LA at five in the evening, just in time for rush hour. I was squished into an exit row, a twelve-year-old seat-kicker behind me, a push-the-seat-all-the-way-back businessman in front of me, and no less than three shrieking infants of varying dissonance and decibel level within five rows fore and aft. The coach Gary hired to schlep us all from LAX was unair-conditioned and miserable. Jake insisted on sitting with me, trying to slither his way into my good graces, much to the amusement of Curt, who was sitting behind me eaves-dropping, and much to the chagrin of Ashleigh, who was in the seat opposite glaring as best as she could without benefit of mobile eyebrows. It took over an hour and a half to get to Santa Monica from the airport.

I was never so happy to see a hotel room in all my life. Nor so distressed to see a well-stocked stash of snacks atop the desk. Pringles shall be the death of me. Especially Sour Cream & Onion. And gummy bears. Damn you, Sheraton.

Tomorrow we meet our illustrious homeowners, and I'm just going to admit it, I'm excited and nervous as hell. If Enzo Man-giafiore is even half as handsome and charming in person as he was in *Hit List*, I may turn into a complete idiot. I've never been so grateful in all my life to anyone as I am to Samuel Diaz-Perez right now. Birdie is so over the moon in love with him that she wouldn't notice Enzo if he were the second coming of Cary Grant himself. Not that I have any intention of being anything but very professional with Mr. Mangiafiore. Unless he offers.

"Knock knock . . ." Who the hell is that?

I open the door to find Gary, a most unwelcome sight.

"Hello, love, just checking in on my star. Everything all right in here? Have everything you need?"

Oh, good Lord.

"I'm fine, Gary, thanks."

"Fancy some dinner? I'm just headed down to the lobby to grab a bite, come with me?"

Nope. Shouldn't do that, that would be a bad idea. I'm tired, my defenses are down, there will be wine involved, and I'm in a hotel. Hotels are bad news. Show me a king size bed with decent sheets and I'm immediately horny. I remember dimly that I have my usual stash of travel condoms in my toiletry bag. And I can't help but be reminded that the last time I had sex was at another hotel with the very gentleman who is currently offering to take me to dinner. This is a time for Morning Girl to be in charge. It's one thing to do the walk of shame from the Wyndham in downtown Chicago where the inappropriate guy you have just slept with is the only person you know in the vicinity. It's quite another to do it in a hotel in LA where everyone you work with is also staying. Yep, dinner is a no go.

"Okay, but I need to shower, get the flight off me. I'll meet you downstairs in a half an hour, okay?"

That fucking Night Girl is bound and determined to get me into trouble.

"Want me to do your back?" He winks at me.

"Gary . . ."

"I know, darling, just kidding. I'll meet you downstairs like a good boy, I promise." Gary kisses my cheek and disappears.

In the shower, Morning Girl goes over the plan with Night Girl. No wine, just water to rehydrate after the flight. Just a light supper, nothing heavy that might make me stuporous. And for sure, no going back to his room or letting him into mine. That would be deadly. Lord knows the combination of cocktails and convivial conversation with this colleague could have me consenting to coitus.

I run some styling lotion through my damp curls, and go with no makeup, a simple black T-shirt, and jeans. I meet Gary in the bar, and we decide to eat outside by the pool. The waiter comes over.

"Miss, a cocktail before dinner?"

"Pinot grigio please." Doh! Bad Night Girl. Okay. Now we have to rethink food. I haven't eaten for hours. Oh, the fucking Pringles don't count! I need something to soak up the booze and keep my wits. Some protein, but nothing too heavy. Maybe the salmon.

The waiter brings my wine and Gary's whiskey.

"And for dinner, Miss?"

"I'll have the New York strip, rare, please." Jesus that Night Girl is unruly.

Gary orders the same and we chat. We chat with the same sickening ease as we did that first magical day in Paul's office. Damn his eyes. The food is good, the wine goes down so easy it needs another glass to keep it company. Gary is charming and funny. He talks about some of the other shows he has worked on, he talks about his ex-wife, he talks about his vision for the show, and then he slams me with the coup de grace. He talks about his desire to bring me to London to redecorate his house. Evil, evil man. Then he does something I never would have expected.

"Lily, I wanted, well, I wanted to apologize."

Huh?

"For what?"

"For how we began and how I behaved after. That night was really wonderful, and then I just, well, I just had a right old freak-out. I'm trying to move up from series producer to exec for the company and sleeping with the talent is no way to get promoted. I know I was a shit, but frankly, I was pretty well gobsmacked by the whole thing. I was sort of bluffing when I invited you over, and when you called that bluff . . . well, obviously I handled the whole thing badly. And then when you upbraided me in front of the whole crew at the wrap party, my ego was bruised. I behaved like a child, and an ass, and I want to know if you forgive me."

Check out who's looking for absolution.

"Gary, let's call the whole thing water under the bridge. That night was very unlike me. I'm never the girl who gets the indecent proposal from someone desirable. Usually the 'come up and see my etchings' offer comes from some toothless alcoholic in the range of seventy-four. I think I called my own bluff when I accepted your offer. And yes, I was somewhat put out that you totally ignored me after, and that probably made me harsher than I might have been, even in my anger, at that party. But I like this gig, and I hope it can continue, and I want us to be able to work together the way we have these past couple of weeks. So I accept your apology, and think we should just start over."

"I'm so glad to hear it, poppet. I have good news, but it's a secret; you can't tell the rest of the crew, I'm announcing it to them tomorrow. Promise?"

"Of course." I love a secret more than just about anything, how sick is that?

"We're getting picked up for next season. Thirty shows. And I'm replacing Paul permanently."

"Gary! That's fantastic! Congratulations."

We toast our future success, we toast our newfound parity, we toast tomorrow's shoot. And in spite of letting me down consistently all evening, Night Girl finally relents, and when Gary offers to escort me back to my room, I'm able to decline.

"I'm good, Gary, thanks for the offer. What time is wheels up?"

"Eight-thirty."

"I'll see you then."

"Sleep well, love. And try to act surprised tomorrow when I make the announcement, there's a darling."

"I will, I promise. Good night, Gary."

I head back to my room, full of wine and steak and self-love. I'm so strong. I'm a rock star.

video diary confession:

"Okay, this may be my favorite episode so far. And I know all of you out there in TV Land are thinking, 'Of course this is her favorite, she is hanging out with Enzo Mangiafiore for two days, how bad could that be?' but the truth is, really and honestly, I'm just so excited about this design. First off, I haven't done an outdoor space before, which is really cool, and I think Isadora is going to be amazed at the transformation of the storage shed into a luxurious poolside cabana to complement the work we are doing outside. It is all flowing together, and yes, Enzo has been charming and handy. And handsome, okay, you got me, the man is very attractive. Whoever wins that date at the raffle is one lucky girl! Back to the trenches . . ."

Oh. My. God.

Can we just talk about Enzo for a very minutely brief moment, hmmm? This man may in fact be the single most attractive person I have ever met in my entire life. Unlike most movie stars, he is tall. Like six foot two or something. And of course, as we all saw in the infamous shower scene from *Hit List*, the body is slammin'. The chiseled features, the olive skin, the liquid brown eyes, the white smile . . . no living human being can deny this man's physical beauty.

But it isn't his beauty that makes him so irresistible, no, not at all. This man is so silly funny that so far today I have almost peed my pants three times. He could have been a stand-up comic, he's so funny. And really sweet. He requested that Ashleigh do his basement as a playroom for his seven nieces and nephews, and redo his guest room with his mother in mind so that she will have a little retreat when she comes to visit. I mean, really, a solid ten on the adorable scale.

And it turns out that before his big break, he was in construction, so he and Curt are getting along like gangbusters. He has two adopted dogs from the pound, his best friend is gay, the *Hit List* paycheck paid off his four sisters' student loans and mortgages and bought a retirement condo for Mom in Florida. He drives a beat-up 1997 Chevy pickup truck because, and I quote, "Actors driving flashy cars is just too stupid and cliché, and most of the fancy ones are gas guzzlers anyway. This gets me around fine for now, and when it dies, I'll probably get an electric car or something."

Sigh. I just want to lick him.

Isadora's house was clearly decorated by a local pro, and not much in need of my services, so she has turned us loose in her backyard, where the retro kidney-shaped pool was surrounded by cracking concrete slab, aging pool furniture, and a storage shed. We demoed the concrete and brought in a local team to put in this fab new pool decking that doesn't heat up, so no more burned feet on those hot LA summer days. Curt and Enzo extended the roof off the back of the house to create a shaded deck area, which I'll be pulling together with teak furniture, and a million twinkling fairy lights. I got her new Tropitone chairs and loungers for around the pool, and I'm converting the storage shed into a cabana, complete with changing room, minifridge and microwave, and a massage table.

Now that my Day One video diary is done, I head out to see

what craft service is tempting us with for lunch. I'm sort of hoping Enzo is on the menu.

"All right, kids, it's going to take the guys about an hour to get the coating on the new pool deck, and apparently this stuff is sort of toxic, so hang out in the house until we call for you," Bob yells out.

"Well, a break isn't unwelcome, I have to admit," Enzo says to me in that honeyed voice. "Do you guys always work this hard on this show? I'm pooped."

He flops his perfect frame down on Isadora's couch and runs his hands through his dark hair. Our kids would have the best hair ever. I'm not saying, I'm just saying.

"Well, yeah, actually, we do. I'm always cashed by the time we finish the two days." I flop across from him, and tilt my head side to side in an effort to loosen up my neck muscles.

"C'mere. Let me work that for you." He pats the seat next to him on the couch. I obey like any good puppy. Before I know it, Enzo Mangiafiore is kneading my sore neck with his strong hands, and I am all-atwitter. This may be my favorite day in my whole life. And we still have another day of shooting and the party! I love my job. Curt wanders in from the backyard and sits on the ottoman.

"That crap out there stinks to high heaven, even with all the blowers going. You just had to be that concerned about her poor wittle fweet getting hot, didn't you?" He whips a small throw pillow at my head, which Enzo, my hero, catches before it can do me any bodily harm.

"Hey, not me, the company donated the product and installation, talk to Gary about it."

"Children, no fighting," Enzo says. "Especially when it means we get to sit on this lovely couch for an hour and not build or hot glue or faux or slipcover or make a window treatment for anything or . . ." Enzo is ticking off our offenses on his fingers, and Curt and I make eye contact. Then we pounce.

"Ungrateful bastard," Curt says, walloping Enzo with a pillow.

"After all our efforts to make you look good on camera!" I say, throwing the lap blanket over his head.

"Not the face, NOT THE FACE!" he yells in mock horror.

"Really, with the wrestling, really?" Bob says on his way past the living room to try and set up the next shot.

The three of us collapse back on the couch.

"Hey, wait," Enzo says, leaning toward me. "You have some snibblechiz there." He starts picking some fuzz off my sleeve.

"What the fuck did you just say?" Curt asks.

"What?" Enzo looks puzzled.

"Snorkelcheese?" I ask. "What on God's green earth is snorklecheese?"

Enzo laughs. "Not *snorkelcheese*, silly girl, snibblechiz. You know, *snibblechiz*." Because that is so different. But, not wanting him to think I'm an idiot, I figure I'd better play along.

"Oh, I'm sorry, I misheard. I thought you said *snorkelcheese*. My bad."

"Lily, princess?" Curt turns to me.

"Yes?"

"Do you know what *snibblechiz* is?"

"Um, well, it's like . . ." Uh. Oh.

Enzo interrupts. "You know, like you have some *snibblechiz* on your shirt, like lint. Haven't you ever heard of *snibblechiz*?"

"Can't say as I have," Curt says.

"My mom used to say it all the time," Enzo says. Then he pauses. "Maybe it isn't a real word?"

"No, I wouldn't imagine that it would be a real word." Curt starts to laugh. "*Snibblechiz?*"

Enzo starts to laugh. "I guess it does sound pretty silly when you think about it."

"It's ridiculous," Curt says. "But at least Lily knew what you meant," he adds snidely.

"Not fair, I just didn't want to make Enzo feel bad!" Because I do so want to make him feel good.

"See how sweet she is?" Enzo says. Curt nods.

"She's very sweet."

Then he and Curt start pummeling me with the pillows.

"Don't get me all covered in snorkelcheese!" I yelp between laughing.

"SNIBBLECHIZ!!!" yell Enzo and Curt in unison.

"Really, with the pillow fighting and screaming, really?" remarks Bob on his way back through the living room toward the bathroom.

The three of us fall back on the couch, tears streaming from our eyes, out of breath from laughing so hard.

And we all have snibblechiz on our shirts.

The Sheraton sneaks us in the back door. Enzo is wearing a *Swap/Meet* shirt, Curt's worn Cubs hat, and a pair of sunglasses. He keeps his head down, and we get into the small building next to the pool without the paparazzi spotting us. As it turns out, Enzo is in the same section of the hotel as I am. In the room next door. We are sharing a wall. I may end up humping said wall at some point later this evening.

"Hey, you up for some room service?" he says, taking off the sunglasses. "I'm starved, but I don't feel like dealing with the tourists in the lobby. Keep me company?"

Would I like room service? Would I like to service him in his room? Be cool, Lily. "Sure, that would be great. Your place or mine?" Suave. Very suave.

"How about yours? Mine seems to smell the tiniest bit like feet. Which doesn't bother me a whole lot, but isn't really that appetizing as a fine dining location. That okay?"

Said the fly to the spider.

"Sure that's fine. I'm going to jump in the shower, come back in, like, twenty minutes," I say, my heart racing.

"Me, too. I'll knock thrice." He winks and heads into his room.

Thank God I'm far neater in hotel rooms than I am at home. Something about the cleaning crew knowing I'm a slob keeps me on the straight and narrow. At home I have to stay up and clean the night before my cleaning lady comes so that she doesn't know what a pig I can be. But the room looks pretty good, so I strip down and get in the shower. I scrub the day's grime off me, shave my legs and pits and my bikini line. I wash and condition my hair (curtains and carpets, if you know what I mean), and all with cold water to tighten the pores and freshen the skin. A little light oiling to moisturize. Some quick product in the hair, a little mascara and lip gloss, and into my most favorite casual hanging-out duds, a pair of black cashmere lounging pants that I bought on sale at Bloomies, and a light blue long-sleeved T-shirt with just the right amount of fraying around the edges. The littlest bit of spritz of my Fresh Cucumber Boie perfume, a crisp vegetal scent that I adore.

Knock, knock, knock. Comes the knocking at my door. Rap,

tap, tap, a handsome fellow, rapping at my chamber door. It is well that I'm not napping, as the man comes gently rapping, perhaps my ass he'll later be tapping, quoth my nether parts, nevermore. With my mental apologies to Edgar Allan Poe, and a deep breath, I open the door.

He is wearing a very old and worn pair of cargo pants, a vintage Aerosmith softball-style T-shirt, and his hair is damp, his skin glowing. He is barefoot. He has perfect feet. Not in that metrosexual "I'm man enough to get pedicures" way, but in that "I own a toenail clipper and a pumice stone and remember to wear flip flops in the gym shower" kind of way.

"Hey!" he says walking inside. "God that shower felt good."

"I know. I always feel like I need to take a layer of skin off at the end of a shoot day!"

He grabs the room service menu off the desk and drops onto the love seat in front of the television. "I could eat everything on this menu!"

I could eat everything on this love seat.

"Well, I can recommend the steak."

"I love it, a girl who knows that life isn't lived on salad alone. I can't tell you what a treat it is to meet a girl who actually eats. All the women out here eat one carrot and then throw it up, making more room for vodka with Red Bull Light." He sounds genuinely disdainful. Suddenly I'm not so terribly ashamed of my Russian Peasant tush or the enormous plate of lasagna I put away at lunch.

"Well, I'm a Chicago girl, we like our steak."

"How do you take it?" he asks like it's a dare.

"Just walk it through a warm room. I like it mooing."

He claps his hands together. "NOW we're talking!" He jumps off the couch and grabs the phone. "Yeah, hi, room two eight-seven. Sure, I'd like two New York Strips, rare. Two salads with

prosciutto and goat cheese . . ." He shrugs at me and I nod appre-
ciatively. "And a bottle of the rioja." I love his choice of a spicy
Spanish red with the steak.

He hangs up and returns to the sitting area. "Did I do okay?"
he asks me.

"You did perfect." I just don't know how I'm going to eat a
steak with these butterflies taking up all the room in my stomach.

"So tell me your life, Lily Allen. How do you get to be the reluctant it-girl of home improvement television?"

"I like that, the 'reluctant it-girl.' Makes me sound popular,
but still humble." Uh oh, looks like Night Girl is awake. And she's
flirting.

"Well, I think you're the best reason to watch the show. You
explain everything simply, but without making it sound like
someone would be an idiot for not knowing it already. And when
you have problems, you seem really genuinely remorseful. Ashleigh, when she talks about whatever she's doing, she's got that patronizing air about her. And when that Jake guy messes something
up, he acts like he doesn't really give a shit, and sort of thinks it's
funny. I mean, Birdie's cute, and the banter with you and Curt is
good, but you're the one I really watch."

I can feel my face flushing red as anything. "See, and mostly
what I like about watching you is the way your butt fills out your
pants." Boy that Night Girl is sassy. Makes me think that her back-
ing down last night with Gary was just saving energy for bigger
fish. And apparently even Morning Girl likes this guy, because she
is sitting back and letting Night Girl make all the decisions.

Enzo laughs. "I do most of my best acting with my butt."

"And the winner, for best performance by a fabulous read end
is . . . Enzo Mangiafiore," I say in my best award-show-announcer
voice.

"Hey, couldn't my ass at least tie with my abs? I mean, some credit for the endless crunches?"

He makes me laugh. "Absolutely."

We talk about our different career paths. He started acting in high school in Pasadena, where memorizing lines and taking on different characters helped with a stutter. He was a double major in theater and special ed, teaching during the summer at a drama camp for disabled children. He lived with one of his sisters while auditioning and doing construction until he got a small guest spot on some Fox show and they got a lot of letters, so they made his character recurring for a couple of episodes. He got cast in *Hit List*, which was a major sleeper this past winter. Now he's everywhere, just finished wrapping a movie where he plays Colin Farrell's brother, and another where he plays a closeted gay haplessly wooing a clueless Kate Winslet, not to mention getting an invitation to be on *Celebrity Poker Showdown*.

"You get to meet Phil Gordon!" I'm so jealous.

"Yes, I do. You a Phil fan?"

"I love him. He's the second most attractive man I think I've ever seen."

"After me?" He winks.

"After Cary Grant. You're somewhere after Cary, Phil, Harrison Ford, Matthew Modine, Jon Stewart, and Clive Owen."

"That's a pretty good group, I suppose I can hang back around seventh place for the time being. I'm a little hurt about the dead guy, but I understand the impulse."

There is a loud knocking, interrupting the really good banter we had going. Enzo jumps up and answers the door. He signs the bill, and a sheet of paper off the desk for the awestruck waiter to give to his girlfriend, and wheels the table over to the love seat.

The steak is just as good as it was last night. The wine warms the blood, the fingerling potatoes are creamy and earthy, the salty prosciutto and creamy goat cheese in perfect contrast to lightly lemony greens and sweet figs. This couldn't be more perfect.

Until it is.

The room service cart safely moved out to the hallway, Enzo and I are sitting facing each other on the love seat finishing the bottle of wine.

"How are you single?" he asks me.

"What do you mean?" I think the answer must be obvious.

"Well, you're smart, funny, talented, sweet, and totally gorgeous. What's up with those Chicago boys?"

I snort a tiny bit of wine through my nose. This makes me cough. Enzo laughs at me and hands me his napkin.

"Easy, killer. Just a question."

"I'm sorry, did you just call me gorgeous?" I'm stumped. Even Night Girl can't get out of this one gracefully.

"Lily, have you seen you? The gray-blue eyes? The curly hair? The porcelain skin, the perfect smile, those little freckles on the bridge of your nose . . ." He is tracing those freckles on my nose with the tip of his finger. "You're beautiful, Lily. You should know that about yourself."

I swallow loudly. "Do you really and truly think that?" I ask him.

"Yes. I do," he says.

"I'm going to need some proof of that, Tiger."

Enzo leans forward and kisses me. A total Jake Ryan end of *Sixteen Candles* over the birthday cake kiss. Small and sweet and gentle. I kiss him back, leaning forward and feeling his arms move around my shoulders.

"More," I whisper when he pulls back, and he kisses me again, more firmly, and I can feel my body melting against his, my arms snaking around his waist, holding him close.

When we part, he is smiling at me. I touch his cheek lightly, and taking his hand, I lead him to the bed, and we sink together on the soft surface. We lay side by side, kissing deeply, caressing, talking, laughing, and slowly kissing deeper, longer, items of clothing unbuttoned, unzipped, pushed aside, time disappearing like cotton candy on our intertwined tongues until after nearly an hour we are naked together under the comforter.

"I can't believe we are here." I have to say it.

"Me, either. I've had a crush on you since the first time I saw the show."

"You've had a crush on me?"

"Yes, Miss Lily. Why do you think I agreed to this whole thing?"

"I can't believe it."

"Well, I can't believe how soft your skin is."

He kisses my neck and shoulders. It takes both of his hands to properly bring my breasts to his mouth, my nipples fairly jumping on his tongue, my hands massaging his neck and shoulders, my fingers in his hair. There is voodoo in his kisses, he is bewitching.

"Do you know what Mangiafiore means in Italian?" he asks.

"I thought it meant eat fire." Seems like a reasonable guess to me.

"Nope, but close." He smiles.

"Well, what does it mean?"

"Eat flowers, my Lily." The grin gets sillier. I blush, but Night Girl finds her tongue.

"Well, you'd better not disappoint the ancestry!"

He explores my body slowly with his hands, his mouth, finally coming to rest between my legs, tasting the warmth of me. I can feel my hips bucking slightly with every caress of his tongue. He raises his hand, letting his fingers slip inside me, feeling the wetness of my excitement. I try to muffle my moans in a pillow, calling his name in a hoarse whisper. It feels so good to have him really paying attention to me, not just lip service, for lack of a less tacky pun.

He sucks gently while moving his fingers rhythmically inside me, until he seems to guess that I'm close to coming, then he slowly moves away, kissing back up my squishy belly as if he is thrilled to find no six pack, nuzzling between my breasts, nibbling my shoulders and earlobes.

Two can play at that game. I push him down beside me and begin my own exploration, tweaking his nipples, running my hands through the soft, downy hair on his chest, slipping my tongue for a brief moment into his belly button. I lean down, caressing his chest and stomach with my hair, and he giggles.

I let my hair run over his perfect abs and get my first up close look at the equipment. Not nearly as impressive as the rest of him. I suppose it would be fair to refer to him as being on the larger end of the average scale, and not quite as thick as I might prefer, but still, considering who it is attached to, and what he can obviously do with his tongue, I'm not going to be complaining. I run my hair over his cock and balls, one hand stroking him with the still slightly damp tresses. He lets out a guttural moan.

I move lower on the bed and plant myself between his legs and attend to him with my mouth and hand, until I can tell that now it's him on the edge.

"Stay where you are for a minute," I say, getting up and heading for the bathroom. Please don't let him be horrified by the ass. I grab the condoms out of my toiletry bag and head back to the bed.

I help him put one on and then straddle him. We move together for a few strokes and then he reaches up and grasps my hips, rolling me off to the side, and, kissing me deeply, repositions himself on top of me, and with one perfect thrust, reenters me. It feels amazing to have his weight on me.

It doesn't take long for him to come, biting my shoulder and grunting. He reaches down and I help him finish me with his hand, feeling the exquisite release of a truly deep and powerful orgasm. Spent and sweaty, we lay entwined, talking about nothing, giggling, taking sips of the water bottle I have on the bed stand.

Eventually, the trials of the day win out. We both crash hard, with the lights on, all tangled. I dimly recognize when he gets up out of the bed, hear the sound of running water, the flush of the toilet, the darkness when the lights go out, the weight of him settling back in the bed, the warmth of him spooning me. And then delicious sleep.

At the wrap party, Isadora comes over to the booth where Enzo, Curt, Bryan and Jou, and I are hanging out. It's been an amazing few days, but we're all glad to be heading home tomorrow. Ashleigh is trailing Isadora, obviously sensing an opportunity to get some face time with Enzo. I'm just waiting for the party to be over, since based on the fondling that is happening under the table, there will be a fourth night in a row of "sucking face" time with the everdelicious Enzo. I feel like such a vixen, I can't even describe it.

"Room for a couple more?" Isadora asks, sliding in beside Jou, who continues to squish over so that Ashleigh can fit as well. "I'm so glad this whole thing is over, I'm exhausted!" she says. She doesn't look exhausted. She looks radiant. She looks as if she has her own personal lighting designer following her around. Debbie

Messing is like that. She and I overlapped at Brandeis by just a year, and I used to see her sometimes of a Saturday or Sunday morning in Sherman cafeteria for brunch. Hair mussed, no makeup, in sweats, she always looked luminously beautiful. And from the few brief conversations we had in line waiting for pancakes, smart as a whip and sweet as could be. Bitch.

"Well, you guys were great, and we raised a lot of money for a good cause." Bryan, who lost his mom and grandmother to breast cancer, raises his glass. We took in just over $50,000 from the entrance fees and raffle tickets, which BBC Productions matched dollar for dollar, so the show got to present a check for $104,500 to the foundation. Not bad for a week's work.

"It was an honor to be a part of it and totally fun," Isadora says. "Now, here's the more important thing . . . Ashleigh? When might you have some time to come back?"

"Pardon?" Ashleigh seems surprised.

"Back to LA, when can you come?" Why is Isadora asking her this, and Enzo, with whom I have spent three (about to be four) extraordinarily passionate nights, has not asked me?

"I would think probably during our sabbatical in a few weeks. Why do you ask?" Ashleigh says.

"My production company just bought a building to use as office space, and it's totally raw. After seeing what you did for Enzo and working with you, I want to hire you to design it for me."

"Wow, Isadora, I'm so flattered, of course we'll make it work. Thank you." Ashleigh beams.

"No, thank you, I know it'll be perfect. I'll call you in the next week or so to figure it out. And now, I'm going to go schmooze the guy that won the raffle, he's actually kind of cute!" Ashleigh gets up to let her out, grins at me with thinly disguised gloating pride, and wanders across the room toward Gary.

Wow. That is amazing. Ashleigh is the one who thought that white carpet would be a good idea in a kid's playroom, and she did the guest room for Enzo's mom in shades of black and gray, with flea market melamine furniture that she spray-painted silver "to look like brushed chrome on a budget." Not.

I can't believe that even after she loved what I did for her house, Isadora wouldn't even consider asking me to do this project. It is a slap in the face. And Enzo said that he'll be changing both rooms ASAP. Can't Isadora see how awful Ashleigh is? I mean, some of her stuff turns out all right, and while it is rarely my taste, a bunch of the homeowners have liked their rooms. But Enzo couldn't have been more disappointed in her work. Then again, he didn't ask me to come visit and fix them either.

The past three days have been like a dream. Enzo and I have holed up in my hotel room every night, ordering room service, watching in-room movies, talking, and making love. It's been totally incredible, and as far as I can tell, no one knows. Everyone else is housed in the other building, so no one has seen us tiptoeing around in the morning. We haven't talked about what happens when I leave tomorrow, but I assume we'll be keeping in touch. Obviously, much as the fantasy would be for us to try and do the long-distance thing, I'm a grown-up. I know how difficult and ultimately unsuccessful that would probably be. But still, I think we'll be friends, maybe with benefits if we are ever in the same place at the same time. I mean, you can't just get this close to someone and then never speak to them again, right?

"So then he said he didn't think we should communicate at all, it would just be too difficult!"

"Get out!" Hillary says. "What a tool!"

"Well, I mean, it's awful to be sure, Lily, but did you expect that you would be his girlfriend or something?" Alice asks.

"Now, Alice, I'm sure Lily just thought that they would at least stay friends, maybe try a visit or two, after all, they were so compatible!" Naomi steps up for me.

We're at my welcome-home dinner at the Athenian Room on Webster. Naomi, Alice, and Hillary picked me up at the airport, and while we were stuck in evil Kennedy Expressway traffic, I filled them in on the details of my LA fling. It was Hillary's idea to hit the A-Room, as we call it, and to indulge my Hollywood-bruised heart, I am now chin deep in a king-size gyros dinner with Greek salad and extra *tzatziki* sauce for dipping the vinaigrette-marinated steak fries. I'll probably have heartburn later, but at the moment the spiced lamb and tender pita are soothing my mood tremendously.

"I don't know what I thought, but I didn't think he would say that it was lovely to meet me and wish me luck in all my endeavors. I mean, he knows Ashleigh's coming back during the sabbatical to meet with Isadora about her space, so he knows I'm available then, too. He could have suggested that I come fix his house back up. He doesn't start filming his next project for three months. And press stuff is going to bring him to Chicago periodically. I feel so used!" But I'm grinning like an idiot.

"Yeah, look how awful it is for you. You spent four nights in a row shagging your brains out with the hottest ass in Hollywood. And all you have left is your memories . . ." Hillary shakes her head at me. "Get over yourself. I don't mean to continue to point out a pattern, but . . ."

"Yet another safely impossible man!" Alice chimes in, excited to know enough of the inside scoop to jump in. The three of us turn to look at her, and Naomi blushes beet red.

"Everyone's a critic," I say. What can I do? I don't want to fight with them about my relationship crap tonight.

"At least Lily stays awake on the job, even if it is to seduce the guest talent!" Naomi jibes.

"Uh, oh, what'd you do?" I ask Hillary, who is glaring at Naomi.

"Nothing important," she barks.

"Fess up, Miss Hillary, it's pretty funny," Naomi says.

"Fine, you want a chuckle at my expense, here you go. The day before we're set to go to trial, I get a call from my boss, who tells me that a different judge is taking over, and he has much more leaning him in favor of Charlie's petition. So I stay up all night making sure that my ducks are in a row, because now I do mean to crush him."

Alice snickers. Hillary shoots her a look. "Sorry," she says.

"Anyway, when I say I stay up all night, I mean ALL NIGHT. Like, get off the couch, take a shower, go to the Daley center. So we start the trial, we give our respective opening arguments, then Charlie starts direct examination of his client. It's a little boring. It's mostly exposition of crap I already know. So . . ."

"She falls asleep!" Naomi can't help but jump in.

"You didn't!" Hillary is the most professional person I know. I can't imagine her actually falling asleep in trial.

"I just sort of dozed off a little bit." Naomi looks at her. "Maybe more than a little bit."

"What happened?" I can imagine at least seven television courtroom drama scenarios.

"My co-counsel noticed and kicked me under the table. Which woke me up and made me shout out."

"Tell her what you shouted!" Alice says.

"You shouted something specific?" I ask, thinking she had probably just yelped in surprise.

"Yep." She smiles wickedly.

"What did you shout?" I can't stand it.

"OBJECTION!" Naomi and Alice yell.

"No way!" Figures she would be professional even when she was being unprofessional.

"Way," she says. "And guess what?"

"What?"

"It was sustained!" she says proudly.

"Oh. My. GOD! That's priceless." The four of us are laughing loudly, probably disrupting the rest of the diners around us.

"Yeah, I thought I totally got away with it, but when I got back to the office there was a package waiting for me from Charlie . . . Hot Cocoa Mix, Sleepytime Tea, natural melatonin sleep-aid pills, a special buckwheat husk pillow, a lavender-infused sleep mask, that Badger Sleep Balm stuff you love so much, Lily, and a set of pajamas with gavels and law books all over them. A card that just says, 'Get a good night's rest. CB'

"Then, in the morning at like six-thirty, my doorman calls up and says I have a package. I schlep down to get it, and it's from Charlie again. A French coffee-press, Kenyan coffee beans, a coffee grinder, a thermos, a four-pack of Red Bull, a six-pack of Jolt Cola, a box of No-Doz, and a pound of chocolate-covered espresso beans. And a card that says, 'I'm trying to impress you with my legal skills, please try to stay awake to appreciate me. CB'!"

"That is so cute! Aren't you warming to him at all?" If some guy as nice and handsome as Charlie did that for me I'd have shown up on his doorstep that night wearing the pajamas.

"Frankly, I think he's bonkers. And I'm still tempted to try and get him thrown off the case."

"You wouldn't." I can't imagine her being that mean.

"No, I wouldn't. But it is a little sweet to think of. Just a little." She grins. We do like to paint her as the wicked bitch of the west, but deep down she's really a good person.

Naomi is shaking her head. "What am I going to do with the two of you? You guys suck at relationships."

"At least I get my wish: we're looking at apartments this weekend, just to see what might be out there," Alice says.

"Hey, we had an agreement," Hillary says to Naomi.

"I said you had to go out with him."

"I still have two weeks!" Hillary says.

"I'd be amazed," Naomi says.

"Watch me work. Two weeks." Hillary sticks her pinky out for Naomi to shake with her own.

Alice pouts subtly, but she clearly thinks that there is no way in hell that Hillary can pull this off.

"Now, who wants Tom and Wendee Italian Ice?"

We all raise our hands, and Hillary waves at the waitress to bring a check. As weird and wonderful as LA was, it's sure as hell good to be home.

♥ Death Be Not Loud

"Okay Lily, love, this is the last promo shoot, I promise," Gary says, as we get set up outside Buckingham Fountain. It's been a very, VERY long day. Who knew those little commercial spots were so hard to do? We started the day at Pillow-A-Go-Go, this really cool store where you can design and make your own throw pillows, including reproducing photos on them. We shot me making a throw pillow with the *Swap/Meet* logo, which will eventually be filmed with the whole on-air crew tossing it around to each other, when we shoot the new intro.

Then we did a segment at American Mattress on Clybourn, where I pretended to come in to buy a bed for a homeowner, and when I leave, all the formerly bare mattresses are completely made up with all different kinds of comforters and pillows and things . . . with the bed by the door done in the *Swap/Meet* logo colors, with the pillow I made center stage. It was a nightmare, making and unmaking all of those beds; luckily the two guys working there were really entertaining, kind of like the Oscar and

Felix of the mattress-selling world. American Mattress just signed on as a sponsor of the show, so from now on they will be donating the mattresses anytime we need a new bed, hence their prominent placement in the promo.

That Gary is a genius for product placement. Pottery Barn, Restoration Hardware, Pier One Imports, Crate & Barrel, Room & Board, The Container Store . . . all of my favorite places to shop have sponsored at least one show, and now I get personal phone calls from the sales associates when something they think I might like comes in or goes on sale. Aren't I a rock star?

We did a quick fly-by at the Home Depot, our major sponsor, and now we are doing the final shot, the one that reminds everyone we are based in beautiful Chicago. Buckingham Fountain, with the amazing skyline behind me. All I have to say is "Have you seen what we've been up to at *Swap/Meet*? Well, wait till you see what's coming next!" in front of the fountain. My hair and makeup have been touched up, and now we are getting the lights set up. Gary is massaging my shoulders.

"You've been a trooper, darling. I think this is going to be terrific. You ready to do the last shot?"

"I'm ready for a hot bath and a glass of wine, so if I have to do this last shot in order to get there, let's do it!" Luckily I'm close to home, and I can taste the Prosecco already.

"We're ready to go, Lily," Bob says, coming over.

"Let's get 'er done," I say.

I walk over to the fountain. I stand slightly off-center in relation to the camera and wait for my cue.

"Lily, we're speeding. And, action!"

And, action.

And, action.

And, action.

And, action.

And, action.

And, action.

And, action.

And, action.

And, action.

And, action.

And, action.

And, action.

And, action.

And, action.

And, action.

And, action.

And, action.

And, action.

And, action.

"Okay, Lily, that one was pretty good, but Gary wants to try something else."

Twenty-two fucking takes, and I'm about ready to kill Gary. I can't say it any other way unless I translate it into fucking Swahili.

"Poppet, I know you're tired, let's just try this one last thing, and if it doesn't work, we'll go with one of the other takes, alright, darling?"

"Fine. What do you want me to do?"

"Can you do it walking along the rim of the fountain?"

"In these heels?" I point to my shoes, which are killing me after such a long day on my feet. But Bryan said they make my legs a mile long, which is a compliment no girl five-feet-five-inches can resist.

"I'm thinking barefoot."

Reg walks over and whispers something to Gary, who seems to shake him off.

"Fine, I just want to go home." I hand Gary my shoes. I'm cranky, and at the moment, I don't particularly care if it is making me a little petulant.

"Just this last take, let's just try it!"

I walk back over to the fountain, where Bob helps me get perched on the rim. Gary smiles widely at me. Bob wanders back over near the camera guy and yells out, "Lily, we're speeding. And, action."

"Have you seen what we've been up to at *Swap/Meet*? Well, wait till you see what's coming up next!" Suddenly a big gust of wind from off the lake blows right at me. I can feel my skirt beginning to whip around my knees in a way that makes me know that I'm about one second away from a *Seven Year Itch* moment, except I'm no Marilyn. I reach down, trying to keep my skirt in place, and I can feel my footing slipping. I hear Bob yelling something at Reg, and then I'm falling.

My head hurts. I can hear a lot of muffled noises around me. I open one eye. It's bright out there. I open the other eye. Gary's head is enormously large in front of me.

"Lily, darling, are you okay? How do you feel?"

"My head hurts. And I feel all weird and tingly."

"You've had a little accident, the paramedics will be here any second." I can hear sirens in the background. Paramedics?

"Really, with the electrocution, really?" Bob says from my left elbow.

Electrocution? "Am I electrocuted?" I ask.

"Just a little. Reg managed to turn your mike pack off pretty quick, so you just got a shock as you hit the water."

I turn to Gary, who looks ashen. "Lily, I'm so sorry. If I had known you were in the least bit of danger, I never would have let you get up there. I feel awful."

"Yeah, well, I feel like hammered shit myself, so we're even." The sirens are really close, and I can hear new voices. I'm also cold, and wet, and suddenly feeling a breeze in the general arena of my cooter, so I'm pretty sure that my skirt is up around my waist. Great. I'm lying on the gravel in front of Buckingham Fountain with my ass hanging out all wet and electrocuted.

I'm so glad I wanted to do this promo. It's really working out well for me.

"Can I get you anything else before I leave?" Gary asks.

I'm home on the couch, wearing my robe and my pajamas, with a throw blanket tucked around my knees. Gary went with me to the emergency room, where they did a bunch of tests to assure that the shock hadn't damaged my heart or brain or anything, and then they sent me home with some Tylenol for my headache, and an order to drink a lot of Gatorade for a week or so, since apparently even mild electrocution sort of makes all the electrolytes in your body disappear. Which is also why I'm so hungry. Which sort of sucks, since the only good thing about any sort of illness is the accompanying couple of pounds of weight loss.

But nope, I'm ravenous. I made Gary stop by Al's Beef on the way home to get me two, dipped, with no peppers and a large fries. And yes, I ate both of them. In the car. I'm such a delicate flower. And Gary had better make haste, because within the next thirty

minutes I am going to begin to create a toxic miasma around me.
The sandwiches might be flavorful, but the resulting flair for the
flamboyant flare of flatulence is a definite flaw, and he'd probably
be flabbergasted and give me flak about it.

I'm nursing a huge bottle of lemonade-flavored Gatorade out
of a straw, and I just want him to leave. I feel shitty and for whatever reason, embarrassed.

"I'm fine, Gary, thanks for helping me." Now get out.

"Are you sure you don't want me to stay and keep an eye on
you, love?" He does look really concerned, bless his heart.

"You heard the doctors, I'm fine. A mild shock. I'll be right as
rain tomorrow."

"All right, then. I'll go. Promise you'll call if you need anything, at any hour, do I have your word?"

"You have my word."

Gary kisses me on the head and finally leaves.

I wait until I can hear the elevator dig outside my door. Then
I let rip.

BBBBRRRRRRRRRRRRRRAAAAAAAAAAAAAAAAAPPPP
PP! I wait a moment. *BBRRAAAP BBRRAP BRRRRAP BRP.* Ah-
hhh. The relief is short-lived, since within seconds the scent of
two hastily digested Italian Beef sandwiches wafts up from under
the blanket.

Yikes, what a stench. I'm killing myself.

I get up to go find the room spray. It takes the better part of
an hour to subside. Fart. Spritz. Fart. Spritz. Fart. Spritz. My
apartment smells like fart mixed with orange blossom. When I
think the barrage is over, I grab the phone. I've called everyone
and left messages, but so far no one has called me back. I know
Hillary is at Chandler's, releasing the tension of the trial which
ended yesterday in victory, poor Charlie. Naomi and Alice are

spending the weekend with friends in New Buffalo. Bryan and Jou are in New York for some fashion charity thing with the *Queer Eye* guys. Curt is at a party with his friends who just had the baby. My mom is out with Jacob, their second date since the wrap party. She seems to be having a good time. It's still weird. I called my dad, but some woman answered his phone, so I hung up. He keeps leaving me messages that he has seen the show and that he's proud of me, but he always calls me at home midday, I assume because he suspects I'm not there.

I hate this feeling.

I want to be alone with my spastic colon, but I don't want to be lonely. I want to be able to talk about my trauma with someone. But the only person I know I can call is Gary, and that is stupid, since I just kicked him out. I'm mopey. I still have a little headache. Luckily the hair on my arms is finally lying flat again, so that is something.

The phone rings. FINALLY!

"Hello?"

"Dollface, what the hell happened today?"

Great. Jake. I hate how fast the *Swap/Meet* grapevine works.

"Hey, Jake."

"Are you okay? I heard you almost died!"

"I didn't almost die, I had a little bump on the head and a minor shock from my mike pack. Nothing serious at all. How'd you find out?"

"Reg called Billy to vent. Sounds like he was really pissed." Billy is the other team's sound guy, and he and Reg are pretty tight.

"Why pissed?"

"Because he told Gary that if you were going to be working that precariously on the fountain that he should switch out your mike pack for a waterproof one, but Gary didn't want to take the time. It's why he had his finger on the kill switch when you went in."

That fucking Gary. Never changes. I'm frankly not surprised. But I'm sending Reg a case of beer tomorrow.

"Well, everything turned out okay."

"That's a girl. Don't let the bastards get you down!"

What an idiot.

"I'll try, Jake. I'll really try."

"So, what can I do, what do you need, what can I bring you?" As if I'd let him come here!

"Actually, Jake, I'm really fine. It's sweet of you to offer, but I don't need anything."

"How about company? Should you be alone after all you've been through?" He's practically purring at me.

"Really, Jake, I appreciate the offer, but I think I'm probably going to go to bed pretty soon."

"If you say so, gorgeous. But you can call on old Jake if you change your mind, okay?" Boy, I've got nothing but great offers tonight, huh?

"Okay, Jake, thanks again. I'll see you next week at the production meeting for the last three shows."

" 'Night, kiddo."

"Good night."

I give up. Bed turns out to be the best option, so I grab the latest Ann Patchett novel, and crawl between the sheets. But I can't seem to stay focused, and after reading the same page four times, I just turn the lights out.

But I can't seem to get out of my head. I wish there was someone really taking care of me. Not offering for their own insidious purposes like Gary and Jake. But wanting to really be there for me. I wish there was someone here, holding me, not for some sort of sexual gratification, but just because he thinks I'm nice to hold on to.

I hate crying over stupid shit. I mean, I know my life is awesome. I have a job I have always loved, which has recently become something even more fabulously unexpected and wonderful. I have great friends who love me and keep me on the straight and narrow. And I have reasonably good luck in the sex department, which if one is going to be relationship-phobic, at least keeps a girl perky. So what if my parents are each a little difficult in their own ways, whose aren't? I know they love me.

But that doesn't seem to matter to my tear ducts. Deep down, understanding intellectually that one is blessed and usually happy, well, it doesn't mean a fig when the spirit is blue.

> *Lily's Rule #20: When the soul wants a good cry, give it what it wants. (See also Rules #7, 39, and 61 regarding chocolate, ice cream, and French onion dip.)*

Fine, if I'm going to be blubbering, let me blubber. I get out of bed and pull my robe back on. I head out to the living room and turn on the TV, pulling up the TiVo list. TiVo never lets me down. I am a TiVangelist. Everyone should have TiVo, it is the best thing EVER. I scroll the available shows. There it is. Extreme Home Makeover. A two-hour episode. Guaranfuckingteed to inspire a sobfest. But at least I'll be crying for some other people who are down on their luck getting something wonderful and not with self-pity. I grab the box of Kleenex and my now warmish Gatorade and settle my electrocuted lonely self in for a bacchanal of tears.

♥ Bye, Bye Birdie

Gary calls us to order. "All right, I know everyone is excited about getting picked up for next season. I know I'm certainly thrilled for us all. And I wish Paul all the luck in the world in his new endeavor." A newly forty-five-days-sober Paul is going to be series producing for TLC, a new show where he helps people stage interventions, and then follows them through their rehab. "But I'm especially glad that the powers that be have decided to let me continue with you all, and that most of you have signed back on."

A few of the crew have bailed. But all of the principals said yes to the new contract. It's nearly a forty percent increase over the previous contract with a bonus structure based on things like awards and ratings. It includes a lot more requirements for public appearances and such, and will mean another decrease in my private design work, but my little nest egg is growing, and after next season wraps I'll finally be able to afford my dream of moving into a house.

Well, to be perfectly frank, the dream always included a guy, usually a handsome one, who would get into a sexy paint fight with me, bring in a Chinese takeout picnic to eat on packing boxes, make love to me on a mattress on the floor . . . you know, the standard television movie idea of a couple's first home move-in sort of fantasy.

Gary says something that breaks me from my reverie.

"Birdie, do you want to make your announcement now?"

"Thanks, Gary darlin'. Oh, you guys. This is so HARD!" She seems really flustered. Then I notice the flash on her left hand. "See the thing is, Sam and I got engaged!" We all begin to applaud and cheer, but she shushes us. "Thanks for that, we're excited, too, and we expect y' all to be at the wedding for sure, now! But the other news is that the press conference is today, Sam has been traded to the Angels, and these good people have allowed the Angels to buy out my contract so that I can move with Sam and not break his streak, so I'm afraid I'm leaving the show." He blue eyes sparkle with tears. Her little chin quivers appealingly.

I can't believe the Sox traded their power-hitter. I can't believe the Angels think that Birdie is so essential to Samuel's success as to actually buy her contract from the show. I can't believe a network filming a show almost entirely in Chicago is supporting a rival city's team by glibly taking money for the continued success of a former White Sox. Or White Sock. Or whatever the singular of Sox is. I can't believe we have to figure out how to work with a new host with only three shows left in the season.

Everyone is talking at once, looking at Birdie's spectacular rock, wondering aloud about who will be replacing her.

"Alright, poppets, let's settle down. We are going to miss our lovely Birdie, but we wish her all the luck in the world. And while we looked high and low for a young lady who could fill

Miss Birdie's shoes, we couldn't, so we decided to go in another direction. Next week I'll expect you to make Richard Merriam welcome as our new host."

Curt elbows me and grins.

Richard was the host of a series that didn't get picked up, an organization show where he served as combination carpenter and cohost. The show was badly executed, but Richard was very winning, and the exact type of host that Curt was suggesting they should have gone with when we first started. Tall, boyish good-looks, more carpenter body than gym body, dark hair, fantastic smile. Really attractive, but not in that "make the girls stupid or make the guys disdainful of the pretty boy" way. A quick wit and goofy sense of humor, with a tinge of suspected ADD, but some serious design chops and carpentry skills, and the camera just loves him. If he turns out to be a nice guy to work with, we might be onto a really special combination.

"Please don't sleep with this guy," Curt whispers in my ear. I confessed the Enzo fling when he brought me breakfast the day after my electrocution.

"Fuck you," I whisper back.

"Well, I appear to be the only one who hasn't gotten that offer yet!"

We snicker, then shush when Gary looks over. We've irritated teacher.

"Okay, let's look at the brief on the last three shows, so that we can go out with a bang. Episode number ten will be Randy and April. Ashleigh, you'll be working with Randy on April's place. Her personal style and house are both stuck in the 80's. Lily, you and April will tackle Randy's place, which is a shrine to sports. Episode number eleven we have Zoë and Ron. Zoë just got transferred here from Houston and has moved into a totally bare loft space. Ron owns a successful packaging company, but his place is an organizational mess and his personal style doesn't show him off to his best advantage. Ashleigh, you and Zoë will take on the bachelor pad and Lily, you and Ron will give Zoë a place she can call home. Finally, the season finale, we've found two design students from Harrington, and we're going to let Ashleigh and Lily guide them through the execution of their own design plans for the spaces. Ashleigh, you and Liza will work on her plan for Webster's place, and Lily, you'll help Webster figure out a good scheme for Liza."

What was that second one again?

I look down at the typed brief for episode #11. Ron. Ron Schwartz. Owns a packaging company. As if springing my mother on me wasn't bad enough. Then I see the note at the bottom. Application was from "best buddy Dave" on Ron's behalf. Fucking Dave. Probably thought it would be funny. But why the hell would Ron agree to it? I wonder if Hillary knows. I'm going to kill her at the gym today if she had anything to do with it.

"He OWNS the company?" Hillary asks. "He never mentioned that, he just said he worked for a packaging company. Interesting. He must be worth a fortune."

"Money isn't the issue, Hil, the issue is that he is a really nice guy!" Naomi says.

"The ISSUE is that fuckhead Dave thought it would be funny to sign him up for the show, and for whatever reason, probably to get back at me, Ron has agreed to do it." They are missing the point completely.

"The ISSUE is that you three are gabbing and not EXERCISING, and if you don't start SWEATING I may have to kill all of you!" Giorgio is frustrated as hell. Can't say as I blame him. We haven't exactly been diligent either about our time together or working out on our own.

"Cork it, George. This is a serious problem, so you are just going to have to deal with these step-ups at a pace that leaves us breath enough to discuss Lily's current dilemma."

"What Hillary means, Giorgio, is that maybe we should do a slower-heart-rate-fat-burning pace today instead of faster-cardio-building pace," Naomi says.

"I give up," Giorgio says. "Fine, keep the pace, I'm just the trainer, what do I know? You girls are really trying my patience!"

The three of us step up and down in unison.

"What am I going to do about Ron?" I ask.

"I think you should call him," Naomi says. "Tell him you want to clear the air before the show."

"Bad idea," Hillary says. "Never let a guy think YOU think you are in the wrong, or that you have anything to apologize for. Better to just let him show up and pretend that there is nothing at all amiss. By the end of the first day, he'll be wondering if HE isn't the one who owes YOU an apology."

Lily's Rule #53: The best advice usually lies somewhere in between the advice you are getting from your two best friends, and almost always at the opposite end of the spectrum from what you yourself would prefer to do.

"I just have to think about it for a while, that's all. Luckily the shoot isn't for a couple of weeks. I've got some time to figure out the best course of action."

"Well, one thing is for sure," Naomi says. "You're having a helluva first season!"

"It's certainly been an adventure." I have to admit.

"Adventure?" Hillary snorts. "Let's recap, shall we? So far this 'adventure' has included some bonding with Mom, a guest appearance on a prank show, a fling with a movie star, a one-night stand with your producer, and now you'll be doing work with a former drunken booty-call boy! I'd say that was the kind of adventure usually reserved for the anorexic party children of the ancestrally wealthy."

She sort of has a point, huh?

"Well, some adventures are more interesting than others!" I say.

"And some workouts are more beneficial than others." Giorgio pouts. There is a knock on the door. Marc enters.

"Ahhh, I was wondering where we were keeping all the beautiful women!" His typical greeting. "G, you have a phone call, I'll watch the dream team for you if you want to take it."

"See if you can get them to do something, Lord knows I can't do anything with them!" Giorgio leaves.

Marc rubs his hands together like a mad genius. "I've been waiting forever to get the three of you all to myself!" Then he notices our leisurely pace. "Oh, no, no, no, my lovelies, not so slow. C'mon!" He starts stepping with us, setting our pace faster. "Yeah, that's more like it!" He runs to grab three sets of dumbbells, which he hands to each of us one at a time.

What is it about the really pretty boys? They can make you do stuff you don't want to do even a little bit. The three of us were talking about it over dinner once, and I admitted that while in general, nothing in the world could make me do something scary like skydiving, the only exception would be if a really hot guy presented me with the opportunity in such a way that made me believe he would think me cool and sexy if I went. How lame does that make me?

Then again, lovely Marc has Naomi just as pumped up as the rest of us, and she doesn't even like men!

The door opens, and Giorgio pokes his head back in. He sees us hustling and sweating, and Marc motivating us with a constant barrage of "C'mon, you can do it!" and "Damn, you all are so gorgeous when you sweat for me. Bring it!"

"I GIVE UP!" he yells, and shuts the door again.

Oops. We may have been overenthusiastic with the overzealous Marc, of whom we are overfond, and accidentally insulted Giorgio, who can be oversensitive, and now he has caught us overexterting ourselves, and is likely to overwork us next time.

Oh well. All's fair in love and fitness.

I'm working on the design boards for the next episode, when my phone rings.

"I did it," Hillary says.

"What did you did?" I ask, gluing a paint chip to the corner of the board.

"I called Charlie."

"Get out! What did you say?"

"I got his machine. But I left a message apologizing for having been so rude to him, and asking if I could take him to dinner to start over. What if he doesn't call back?" She actually sounds, well, *vulnerable*?

"You really like this guy, huh?" I'm trying to be as delicate as possible.

"I dunno. I mean, I thought I hated him. I thought he was obsequious and disingenuous. I thought he was arrogant and was just playing around for the sake of the game. But then Naomi gave me her whole 'The things you hate most in someone else are often the qualities that you hate most about yourself' speech, and I keep thinking about his attitude, which seems more and more confident and not arrogant. And he is attractive. And he has put himself out there in unique and creative and fun ways. Maybe I just need to be open to a guy who wants to get to know me."

Oh. My. GOD!

"Miss Hillary, is that an open mind in the relationship sector I'm hearing?"

"All right, now, don't get all Renee on me. I just think that even though I still don't know about marriage and kids, I know that the whole Shabbas Goy thing isn't really enough for me. So if a reasonably smart, nice, attractive man wants to actually date me, well, maybe it's time I started seeing how that feels."

"I'm very proud." Which I totally am.

"What if he doesn't call?"

"He'll call."

"What if he tells me to fuck off? He could, you know, he'd be well within his rights."

"He won't tell you to fuck off." Good Lord. From tough broad to insecure schoolgirl in one fell revelation. Goddamn Naomi and her therapy platitudes. She will have created a monster. "You'll apologize sincerely and he'll accept your apology, and you'll start over."

"You think that will work?"

"Yeesh. Yes! I think that will work. You'll either end up lovers or friends but at least you won't have to try and destroy his career anymore."

"Sounds like excellent, mature, sensible advice. Now, what do you say you follow that same sage wisdom you've just handed down to me, hmmm?"

"What on earth are you talking about?"

"I'm talking about Ron. Call him. Apologize. Tell him about

your particular brand of crazy. Tell him that you want the shoot to go well for you both, and that starting over might be a good way to guarantee that."

"You're joking." Sneaky minx. "You aren't worried about Charlie at all are you, you just wanted to be able to throw my own advice back in my face!"

"C'mon, how long have you known me? Of course I'm not worried about Charlie. Charlie is taking me to dinner on Saturday. But you have only two weeks before you have to spend some time in close quarters with Package Boy, and I know you'd love to pretend it isn't going to happen, but it is, and you'll be miserable if you don't take care of it like a grown-up."

"Hold on, Charlie is taking you to dinner on Saturday?"

"Yup. To celebrate my win."

"You are amazing."

"And you are a coward. Call Ron. I mean it. You'll feel better."

Sigh. "Fine, I'll think about it." Which I suppose I'll have to actually do.

"Fine. Call me and let me know how it goes."

"You, too."

"All right. Go call Naomi, I know you're going to. Tell her I'll talk to her tomorrow."

She could always read my mind. "Fine, I'll send her your love."

" 'Kay. Bye."

"Bye."

Crap. Now I have to call Naomi, who will tell me to call Ron, and then I have to call Ron and that is just going to suck out loud.

Fucking good advice.

I should learn to keep my wisdom to myself. Always comes back to bite me in the ass.

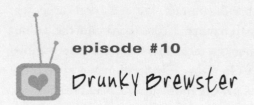

episode #10

Drunky Brewster

Bravo *Wednesday August 9* 8PM–9PM

SWAP/MEET Randy and April

The team faces a challenge with one homeowner stuck in the 80's, and another who has their own idea of what their personal style says about them, making things difficult for stylist Jou DuFresne. Can new host Richard Merriam fill Birdie Truesdell's stilettos? Highlights include a table-building contest between newbie Richard and veteran carpenter Curt Hinman, and an unusual use of industrial chain by designer Ashleigh Benning.

Okay, the universe is officially forgiven for its usual ironic sense of humor, because sending us Richard Merriam has, in just one week, taken this show to the next level. It's as if we were on a boat, everyone rowing, heading in one direction, but slowly, and then this guy shows up and says, "Hey, wanna use my motor?"

Yes, he's just that awesome. He and Curt bonded after the first production meeting, heading off to Home Depot together to do the shopping. Not in Richard's contract, but as a good carpenter himself, he was just happy to have an excuse to go sniff the wood, and I think Curt was glad of the company. Gary hosted a combination Welcome Richard/Good-bye Birdie dinner a couple of nights ago, taking over the private room at *Scoozi!* and feasting us on the Italian delicacies. Richard showed in his general conversation that he has seen all of the episodes, complimented Ashleigh on her willingness to think outside the design box and commiserating with me about the Zen garden. He said on his second episode he built a huge bed, very tall off the floor, only to find out that the person he was building the bed for was only four-feet-eleven-inches and had an elderly basset hound that slept on the bed with her. Neither of them could apparently get onto the bed without a boost.

Yesterday, after a pretty uneventful Day One, we all went to Howl at the Moon, where Richard got up and sang with the band. And unlike my last endeavor in that direction, he was not only made welcome, but allowed to do three songs, one of which was totally improvised new lyrics to the tune of Wild Thing. "*Swap/Meet!*" he sang loudly "You guys are so sweet! You make everything improovy! Oh, *Swap/Meet . . .*"

I did not look so attractive with Budweiser Select coming out of my nose.

This morning, he went out to do a brief segment in the land of carpentry where Curt was building one of a pair of end tables I had designed for Randy's living room. Suddenly, the whole crew was running outside, where a spontaneous table-making contest had erupted. Within thirty minutes I had both my tables ready for staining, and Bob had some great footage for the episode.

And thank goodness Richard has been so terrific, because things have been a little wonky today. April, who was bland and boring yesterday, began the day in a very good mood. Perky and chatty, almost a little frenetic, it was like invasion of the homeowner snatchers. But she's been disappearing every twenty minutes or so to the bathroom or something, and never seems to be where she is supposed to be.

Gary is over at April's house, addressing some complaint of Ashleigh's. My guess is the complaint is that Gary spends more time on site with my team than hers. Which I flatter myself believing it has to do with still carrying a torch for me, but probably has more to do with the fact that Jake and Ashleigh as a team are a little much to take, and Afton, the director, is a grumpy older gentleman who isn't very interested in the input of an upstart producer type. He keeps telling stories about the good old days when series producers never showed up unless there was a problem of some sort.

When Gary said that Randy's apartment was a shrine to sports, he wasn't kidding. Every room has a different theme, football living room, basketball dining room, baseball bedroom . . . the memorabilia is everywhere. Both living room and bedroom even have Astro Turf–green carpet! No wonder Randy is single.

Lily's Rule #51: Theme rooms are hard to do well. The key is to go for "generally inspired" and not "specifically connected to the theme to the nth degree." And when in doubt, buy everything you think will be cool, and then return two of every three items.

Randy's job as a Chicago-based sports writer for *Sports Illustrated* does nothing to curtail the instinct to feed the sports monster that has consumed his design scheme. I wish I could redo the entire apartment, but as I am limited to two days and two rooms, I've chosen the living room and bedroom. I figure those are the two rooms most inhabited by female company. I'm relegating the actually interesting and valuable collectibles to a new wall unit, which will have display shelves, but the cheap giveaways and posters are all being stored in Rubbermaid bins in Randy's storage room.

I'm also getting rid of the football-shaped coffee table (no I'm not kidding) and the football helmet phone (God help me). I'm bringing in a new leather couch in deep green, with a secret recliner actually embedded in one seat. Curt and Richard are teaming up on the entertainment center wall unit, a (hopefully) gorgeous full wall of shelving and space for the television and stereo equipment done in a light wood which will complement the laminate flooring I'm installing. A great rug, two simple wood end tables (thanks to Curt and Richard), and a pair of comfy chairs, and the room is ready for lighting and accessories. Hopefully Randy won't mind too much.

The bedroom is even worse. A bed actually constructed of baseball bats. Bedside tables with painted baseball diamonds on the top. A catcher's mask lamp. A dresser with minibaseballs as drawer pulls. It couldn't be more nine-year-old-little-leaguer. It couldn't be less thirty-two-year-old-writer. It sure as shit isn't a room that would get Randy laid. It's the equivalent of a grown woman's bedroom filled with Barbie dolls.

I'm going clean and masculine in the bedroom. I've designed a really cool platform bed that I'll be upholstering with good quality faux leather (read: vinyl) with a slight texture in a chocolate brown. "The key to fooling people with vinyl," I got to explain earlier, "is to use the textured versions, since the smooth ones are always just a little too shiny to be mistaken for real leather. But the embossed versions look fantastic, and are very easy to work with." Aren't I full of excellent advice? The linens are shades of taupe and cream with slate blue accents. I found a pair of heavy woven cane trunks, perfectly flat, which I'll be putting on two suitcase racks to create bedstands. The carpet will be replaced with my favorite, the ever popular carpet tiles, in a subtle tone-on-tone stripe in the blue.

video diary confession:

"Okay, so far things are looking pretty good here. We're going to be a able to tone down a little of the sports theme that Randy has going on, but still acknowledging his interests. I'm a little worried about my art project, to be honest. I tried a small version at home last week, and that worked, but you know how things tend to go when we get in front of the camera with a deadline looming! But I just want to take a small moment to acknowledge the change in personnel that has happened. Birdie, we all love you and miss you, but we know how happy you and Samuel are, and we wish you the best. But as you will be able to see when you watch this show, Richard is a trooper, and he's just jumping right in and making himself a part of the team, so we seem to be in good hands! I've got to go, because they are about to pull up the carpet in the living room, and as you can imagine after the last time, I'm going to be as far away from that as possible!"

That's right. I'm letting the crew take care of pulling up the carpet without me. After the ant incident at Walter's, Gary promised me I could take a brief sabbatical from the "carpet reveal." April has disappeared for the umpteenth time, and I'm off to find her so that we can do an art project for over the bed. I've gotten a huge stack of baseball cards which we are going to tear up and use to collage over a large poster, following the color scheme of the original and making a textured impressionistic version.

And find her I do. In the laundry room. Sitting on the dryer. Asleep. This girl is really strange.

"Hey, April, wake up," I say. She starts. I get a distinctive scent of the combination of new booze on the breath and old booze seeping out of her pores. I'm beginning to have an understanding of why she's been going missing so often, and why her behavior was so different today.

"Mmmm." She sits up and rubs her eyes. "Sorry, Lily, I didn't sleep that well last night. Must have caught up with me a little. Now, why did I come in here?"

Oh Lordy. This girl is a disaster. And alas, although alleged alcoholism doesn't always allude to an inability to function, I'm still alarmed that April's alacrity is altogether temporary, and the alternative could be an altercation, and I want to be an ally right now.

"I don't know, April. Maybe we should get a Coke or something, what do you say?" I'd better get some caffeine in her or the rest of the day is going to be a disaster.

"Yeah, that'll probably help." April stands, sways a little, then finds her balance. I follow her out of the laundry room and down the hall to the kitchen where craft service is set up. She is weaving only the slightest bit.

I grab two Cokes, figuring it will be better to not make it appear that I'm attempting to sober her up, but rather that the two of us are just taking a quick refreshment break. We sit at the kitchen table and drink. I reach forward and grab a bagel, which I'm not terribly hungry for, but I hope April will follow my lead, since some food in her stomach probably isn't a bad idea either. Thankfully, she does grab a bagel as well and begins to pick at it listlessly.

Richard comes in from the land of carpentry.

"Hello, ladies!" He grabs a bottle of water and chugs half of it before continuing his banter. "I'm heading over to spend the rest of the afternoon at your place, April. Anything you need done while I'm there? A little laundry? A little straightening up?" He puts his arm around her in a friendly gesture, does a tiny, almost imperceptible double take, and then looks at me pointedly and raises one eyebrow. I nod one quick movement to indicate that his nose hasn't led him wrong. He smiles at me over her head, and shrugs his shoulders.

"Well, lovelies, I'm off like a prom dress. You play nice, and I promise I'll do something great over at your house, April." He walks around the table and leans over as if to kiss my cheek. "If she's tanked, keep her away from the carpentry tent," he whispers in my ear. Then he squeezes my shoulder and heads off in the direction of the door.

"He's really sweet, that guy," April says. "I could fall in love with him in, like, ten seconds."

"He's a good guy, and extremely talented. We're really lucky to have him." I spot Bob coming our way. With Gary over at April's today, Bob is Papa Bear. I'd better fill him in on the situation. "April, I just have to check in with Bob about the next segment, I'll be right back."

"No problem. I have to go to the bathroom anyway."

Great. Just what I need, for her to sneak another swig.

"Bob, we have a problem."

"You mean Tipsy McSchickered?" Bob will never cease to amaze me. He seems to know everything, even though he always appears to be totally focused on the moment-to-moment shooting. It makes me wonder if he guessed about Gary and me. God I hope not.

"Yeah. She's totally out of it. I went to get her to set up the art project and I found her asleep in the laundry room. I'm afraid to let her use the hot glue gun. What are we going to do?"

"Well, if Gary were here he'd probably want to try and film her sneaking off to drink or screwing something up, but I think this poor girl has a problem, and I'd rather let her keep as much dignity as possible. So I think we're going to show you explaining the project, but not her actually doing the project. I'll have you and Curt do one of your little banter moments out in the tent, and that along with the usual room-dressing footage should be enough. I just hope for her sake that she keeps it together tomorrow, or Bryan is going to have a heck of a time of it." He runs his hand through his hair. Then he chuckles. "Ironic, though, isn't it?"

"Ironic? Why?"

"Paul's supposed to stop by later today. Wants to say hi, show off his sober self. Wait till he gets ahold of our little tippler over there."

"Oy. Won't that be fun?"

"Yep. Why don't you go see if the PA's got your project set up properly in the dining room, and I'll go talk to her." Bob heads off to find our wandering lush, and from the other room I can hear him say "Really, with the no taping, really?" meaning that once again one of the PA's has decided to skip the laborious process of taping out the edges of a room before painting, assuming a steady hand, and has probably gotten paint somewhere that will need fixing. I go to check on the art project. I should have known something was brewing. Because this shoot was going far too smoothly.

"So, Paul comes by the shoot, looking trim and healthy, wandering around catching up with everyone." I'm telling Hillary about the shoot over a quiet dinner at MK, just the two of us. Naomi and Alice are at some therapist conference in Toronto.

"Did he meet the drunk girl?" she asks.

"Oh, yeah. Spotted her in a heartbeat. And which is worse, gets the bright idea to do an intervention for her as part of his new series. So he makes all these phone calls, gets a crew ready, and brings them to the wrap party."

"Isn't the premise of his show that people apply to have an intervention done for one of their friends or family members?"

"Yeah, that's the premise. But Paul had this bee in his bonnet. Now he isn't trying to pull another thing like the *Spanked!* business, they stay out of the way while we are doing our stuff. But after our crew is totally finished filming, Paul grabs all her girlfriends and April and gets them to gather in one section of the bar and begins to just "intervene" away. Before we know it, sixteen twenty-five-year-olds are screaming at him. Turns out, there was a bachelorette party the night of Day One, with many, many shots consumed, and poor April woke up still drunk and totally panicked about the hangover hitting her in the middle of shooting on Day Two. Her friend Georgia suggested she take two sips of booze every half an hour to prevent this. She isn't any bigger a drinker than the rest of us!"

"Poor Paul! Was he just so embarrassed?"

"Oh, yeah. And his team was pissed, because they were all called in last minute and lost a night off for nothing!" I take a sip of my port, and one more bite of the luscious chocolatey goodness of the dessert we are splitting.

"Poor Paul." Hillary waves for a check.

"Yep. So what are you doing tonight?"

"I'm supposed to meet Charlie." Hillary has been very mum

about the whole Charlie thing, but she has admitted that she and Chandler are no longer sleeping together.

"How's that going?" Naomi and I are trying not to pry too much, we're afraid if we're too excited, Hilary will spook.

"It's weird. He's weird."

"What do you mean, weird?" Uh oh. Sounds like she's psyching herself out already.

"He hasn't fucking touched me. I mean, first, we go to dinner after the whole trial debacle. He takes me to Kiki's Bistro, orders good wine, decent conversation, and about halfway through dinner I'm thinking 'Okay, this guy is pretty cute.' Which you know, for me, means I'm totally going to sleep with him." Sounds like Hillary.

"Okay, so what happened?"

"He drove me home, walked me to the door, said he had a great time and that he'd like to do it again. We set another date. He gives me a hug and leaves. Doesn't even try to kiss me. Okay, fine. So then second date, dinner and a movie, doesn't try to hold my hand or put his arm around me in the movie, and end of the date same thing, walks me to the door, sets the next date, and then nothing! What the fuck is wrong with this guy? I don't think he's gay, and he's pursued me like mad since Cliff and Lang's wedding, what is his DEAL?"

Poor Hillary. I don't know that she's ever actually dated in the way that people date. She's always fucked first and gotten to know them later. Sleep with a friend, sleep with a stranger, wake up in a non-relationship where she holds all the cards.

"Hil . . ."

"What?"

"It's only been two dates. If this guy really likes you, which he seems to, he's probably taking it slow, getting to really know you. Just give things a chance to develop organically."

"Fuck. Maybe I retired Chandler too soon?"

"Jesus, Hillary, get a grip would you? Give your cooter a vacation for a couple weeks. Did you ever think that the sex is hotter if you go slow for a change?" This girl is insane.

"If a guy doesn't at least try to get some action, doesn't that mean he isn't that interested in me?"

"Or maybe it means that he's really extra-special interested!"

"You don't think that all this spending time with me and not making a pass means that the more he knows me the less attractive I'm becoming?"

Holy shit, Hillary's actually a little out of her element here! "Poor baby, sucks to be out in the world not in control of other people's actions and intentions, huh?" I have to give her a little shit.

"Fuck you."

"I'm sure you're not that desperate yet, but Naomi is probably a better place for that offer."

"So you're saying I'm a crazy sex-starved ho, and that a guy who doesn't try to grope me under the table at our first dinner isn't necessarily immune to my charms, but might actually want to know me as a person before jumping into bed with me?"

"Pretty much."

"Fine. I'll give him one more date. But if this idiot doesn't kiss me tonight, I may fucking kill him."

"Fair enough."

Hillary pays. "What are you doing tonight?"

I pause. "I'm supposed to hook up with Gary for a drink."

"Lily . . ."

"Not like that. We've been working really hard to have a friendship and good working relationship, and he just had his review and was essentially told that while they love the way he works as a series producer, at the moment they don't really see him as executive producer material. He's blue and I'm just going to have a drink and try and get his mind off of it."

"Just be careful, Lily. I still don't trust that guy."

"I know, neither does Curt. I promise I'm not going to sleep with him."

"Well, I promise that if I get the opportunity, I am going to sleep with Charlie!"

I laugh. "Sounds like we both have a solid plan for the evening."

We wait for our cars at the valet station. Hillary's arrives first. "Be good," she says.

"I will. Be bad!" I say.

"I'll try!" She gets in the car and heads off toward an uncertain future. And when my car arrives, I do the same.

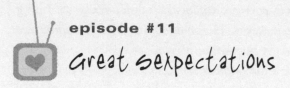

episode #11

Great Sexpectations

Bravo *Wednesday August 16* 8PM–9PM

SWAP/MEET Zoë and Ron

The gang at *Swap/Meet* enjoys a pair of truly great participants, and the result is a show that proves that you can really do every-thing they say you can do without too much Sturm und Drang. Highlights include some dissection of the male psyche by stylist Bryan LeClerc, and carpenter Jake Kersten waxes poetic about wax finishes for fine furniture.

video diary confession:

"Okay, I'm starting to get a little nervous. It's halfway through Day One, and so far, things have been great. Ron, the homeowner, actually cleaned up his apartment before we got here, and packed up nearly every-thing for us, so the room-clear was quick as anything. Must be an occupa-tional hazard, being in the packing box business! Zoë, as it turns out, is a

very talented artist and has volunteered to create an original piece for Ron. Since he works a lot from home, we're going to focus most of our energy on the home office, making sure it is as organized and comfortable as possible. And since his living room was an absolute disaster, we'll be doing some work in there as well, bringing in a bunch of new furniture, and Curt is building the coolest entertainment center ever known to man. The first coat of painting is actually almost done, and while I hate to jinx myself, this may be the fastest redesign in Swap/Meet *history! But only if I get back to work . . ."*

I'm in deep doo-doo. Only a day into the shoot and already I'm in trouble. Despite the best efforts of both Hillary and Naomi, I never got up the courage to call Ron and clear the air. In part because Gary confessed that when he contacted Ron about participating in the show, he only agreed if I would be the one to redo his apartment, i.e., he wouldn't have to work with me for two days, and would only see me for the reveal and at the party. I could tell that Gary was reluctant to tell me to begin with, only reinforcing for me what must have been the vehemence of Ron's desire to avoid me at all costs. Which wouldn't really bother me so much, except that all day he has been getting more and more interesting, and frankly, attractive.

First, there was the fact of his cleaning and packing up to make our job easier. Considering the state the place was in the night I spent here, it could have been a real disaster, and totally gross and backbreaking for the PA's. He didn't know which rooms we were doing and probably didn't suspect the office would be on the docket. As a result, the room was pretty much intact and full of surprising details. Well-worn books by Anne Lamott and Ursula Hegi, two of my all-time favorite authors, mixed in on the shelves with some interesting first editions, including a copy of

Oscar Wilde's poems with a personal inscription to "T." and signed simply, "Oscar." Pictures everywhere of friends and family, and a couple with the same smiling and attractive girl, who I sort of hate for no good reason.

And what is worse, Zoë is constantly trying to guess about Ron, and everything she says puts him at the totally fabulous and elusively rare end of the man spectrum.

"He seems like a smart guy," she said, when we realized that his bedside table reading included a biography of Alexander Hamilton, the new quirky book by Mil Millington, and WS Merwin's translation of *The Inferno*. And I remembered that he had an easy intelligence in his conversation, even in a bar.

"He must be really fit," she said, when she spotted the set of free weights and treadmill in the small extra bedroom at the back of the apartment. And I remembered the plane of his shoulders, the soft fuzz on the not-so-well-defined pecs, the generous expanse of his arms, and the long legs. Not a great body, built for endurance, not for speed, but not a bad body. A good body to snuggle with, for sure.

"He must be really funny," she said, when we found a large plaque honoring his participation in the Cambridge Footlights, the campus comedy group famous for spawning the gents of Monty Python. When the hell did he go to Cambridge? I wondered and realized that I had never asked him about his education.

Let's recap, for a moment, shall we?

Ron is, by all evidence present, a tall-ish, attractive, Jewish, successful business owner, Ivy-League educated (and I mean where the Ivy was fucking INVENTED), well-read, nice guy who is a great kisser and decent in bed even when drunkish, who tried his damndest to get me to turn a single good blind date into something more. And yes, he did have a little of an edge and a sense of entitlement that could be a problem, but then again he could have just been nervous and overcompensating. And yes, he did make a crude comment at a very bad time that made me feel really shitty, but then again he clearly didn't do it on purpose. This is a generally good guy with some actual potential, who liked me. And I fucked it up.

I'm perturbed by the fact that I now perceive that perhaps I have a personality disorder which made me behave perfunctorily when I should have been persistent, and that my perfidious performance may perversely keep the breech between me and this sort of perfect-ish man, well, permanent.

No wonder Hillary and Naomi were so on my case about him. And now it's too late. I'm done. Zoë is also smart and cute and creative and funny and obviously setting herself up to have a crush on Ron already, and they'll probably fall madly in love and spend long nights cuddling on the gorgeous charcoal mohair sofa I picked out for his living room.

AAARRRRGH!

I need a brownie.

"Really, with the eating, really?" Bob says as he comes to find me to do a segment with Curt out in the carpentry tent. I stop reaching for the thickly frosted brownie that had been calling to me and dutifully start to head outside to the parking lot.

Fucking Bob. I needed that chocolate.

I'm standing outside Ron's apartment door, waiting to do the reveal. Ron has just arrived, and I'm more nervous than I have ever been. I mean, I think the place turned out terrific. His office now looks like the study of a writer, dark wood replicas of heavy antique furniture balanced with some quirky accessories of metal industrial furniture and office accoutrements from the fifties. We've replaced his old laminate shelving with substantial wood floor-to-ceiling library shelving, thanks to Richard, who came in on Day Two and just knocked them out like it was nothing. The living room came out awesome. I upholstered the wall behind the couch in a deep gray flannel, with the lighter gray couch in relief against it; it makes for a dramatic and masculine look.

Zoë painted a large moody abstract canvas in shades of blues and lavenders, almost mimicking that twilight hour just after sunset that some call the violet hour. I found a brushed pewter-finish coffee table with a beveled glass top, and a lovely pair of replica Cambodian rain drums with a beautiful green patina at Cost Plus World Market, which I'm using to replace the old stacks of magazines and newspapers that used to serve as his side tables. Curt's fantastic entertainment center uses heavy industrial pipes and fittings interspersed with dark walnut shelves, and makes for a great statement piece. And instead of side chairs, two oversized ottomans upholstered in a gray suiting material with a lavender pinstripe.

"Hey," Ron says, coming up the stairs with Bob.

"Ron, hi, how are you?" He looks fucking amazing. Damn Jou for being good at his job. His haircut captures that look of being handsomely rumpled without being unkempt. He's wearing a pair of dark jeans that fit him perfectly, a T-shirt from the Beat Kitchen, and a great olive green casual jacket. A pair of sleek Pumas in taupe and brown complete the outfit. Figures. Jou knows about my addiction to Pumas. My collection has reached nearly intervention-worthy proportions. The shoes are Jou's way of saying, "This is the guy, dummy."

"I'm good, still a little sore, but good."

"I know. People who sign up for the show usually think that it isn't really hard work, and that we probably have peons doing the heavy lifting, but not so!" This show runs on its crew, who do work incredibly hard, but we also ask a lot of the participants.

"Yeah, so I found out. But Zoë's place turned out pretty cool, I think; hopefully she'll like it." He seems pretty okay, actually, kind of generically friendly, and certainly no ire in his voice. Maybe I don't need to worry.

"Well, my major concern at the moment is whether you like your place or not." And whether maybe I can get you to like me again in the process?

"I'm sure it'll be great," he says with a grin. "After all, I don't have a cat."

"I'm just never going to live that down." I have to laugh.

"Kids? We're good to go here," Bob calls out, meaning that inside the lighting has been placed as well as the second camera guy.

"Ready?" I ask Ron.

"Yep."

"We're good out here," I say.

"Okay, we're speeding. And, action."

I open the door. As I guide Ron through his new living room and office I explain some of the details of what we did and why. He makes all the right noises, praises everyone's handiwork, and even makes an offhand comment about needing to hire me to come do the rest of the apartment which now, he says, looks a little ragtag compared to his fresh new rooms. I'm sure I blushed idiotically at that. His friends show up, Dave leading the way. He grins at me, and gives me a big hug.

"You mad at me, Lily girl?" he whispers in my ear.

"Why would I be mad?" I say, ever the innocent.

"Absolutely, why would you be?" Dave says. Then he introduces me to the rest of the guys, all of whom seem to like the design. They are a generally attractive and boisterous bunch, comprising a few friends from the University of Chicago Lab School, where Ron went to high school, a couple guys who work for him at the company, and some guys he met in his weekly pickup basketball game.

We finish up the walk-through and get everyone on the bus. The party at Liquid Lounge is already in full swing when we get there, Ashleigh's walk-through having been quicker than mine. Gary grabs Ron and leads him over to do the meet-and-greet segment with Zoë.

"Doesn't she look amazing?" Bryan sidles up beside me and hands me a glass of wine.

"Yeah." She does. Bitch.

"Why the gloomy puss, Puss?"

"Nothing, Bry. She looks fantastic."

I wander over to where Curt has snagged a table. I'm surprised by the level of my disappointment. After all, I was the one who didn't want to pursue something with this guy.

"Hey, princess," Curt greets me. "Good episode, huh? I know the ones with the drama make for better television, but I have to say it was nice to just come in, do good work, and get out."

"Yeah. It makes up for some of the crazier episodes, that's for sure." He's right. A shoot with no insanity is a rare thing indeed, and while some of it can certainly be chalked up to first season learning curve, some of it appears to just be the very nature of filming home improvement television. Weird homeowners, forces of nature, the occasional primer incident . . . all just par for the course in the world of DIY.

"So how come the sad face? Did he hate it?"

"Nope, seems to love it."

"Did he act like a shit because of the history?"

"Nope, he's been great, as if nothing ever happened."

"So? That's all the stuff you were worried about, right? You should be happy." Curt is right. I should be relieved and happy, and grateful that Ron is a more mature person than I am.

"I dunno, Curt. I'm sort of feeling like I blew an opportunity to spend time with a really great guy because I was a little embarrassed about how we got together in the beginning, and because I always assume the worst of guys." I hate getting all introspective, it's maudlin and makes me boring.

"And now you are seeing him over there laughing with Zoë, and you're feeling sorry for yourself, because when he wanted you, he wasn't good enough, but now that he doesn't, you wish he did . . . are you sure its not just about winning? I mean, do you really want this particular guy, or do you just want to know you can get someone like him?"

"Curt, I hate it when you get all fucking smart and analytical on me. Can't we just say that I'm a little blue and not try to figure out why my own idiocy makes me that way?"

"Nope. I mean, maybe with someone else. But if you want to sit at my table and play the Poor Me game, you're going to have to hear the honest opinions. That's the rule."

"You're such a pain in my ass." Curt puts an arm around my shoulders and squeezes.

I look across the room and see Ron and Gary talking together fairly intently. Ron looks over in my direction and then looks back. I decide to be a grown-up and head over to try and talk to Ron.

"I'll be right back," I say to Curt.

"Go get him." Curt winks.

I cross the room and approach Gary and Ron. Gary puts his arm around me and pulls me close to him. "Isn't she the best designer? Ron here was just telling me how much he loves his flat!"

Ron looks a little irritated, but agrees quickly. "Yep. Absolutely, the place looks great."

Gary kisses my temple. "That's my girl!" he says. Ron nods at us.

"If you'll both excuse me, I'm going to check on my friends." Ron leaves quickly, and I know that I'm done for. He's been a good guy, he's played nice for the cameras, he's been a gentleman. But it's clear from the way he looked at me just now, and from the speed with which he hightailed it away from me that he remembers everything that happened and has no intention of forgiving me for it. And I can't blame him. After all, I never even actually apologized. Ron heads over to a group that includes Zoë, Dave, and a couple of other people. Zoë brightens noticeably when Ron shows up, and he stands next to her as he merges into the group.

"Tired, poppet?" Gary says, still squeezing my shoulder.

"Very."

"Shall I fetch you home? We're done here."

I think about this for a minute. I know what he's offering. When we met for drinks after my dinner with Hillary he made pretty clear that he'd like another night like our first. But I was firm with him. That one night, while fun, was a mistake. It derailed our working relationship, and made our friendship much harder to get to.

Lily's Rule #57: Mistakes are a part of life. Feel free to make them with passion and abundance. The repeating of mistakes is beneath the dignity of an intelligent woman and should be avoided at all costs.

Nope. Sleeping with Gary again is off the agenda. Gary seems to sense that my pause is meaningful. He saves me from my head.

"C'mon love, I'll just pop you home so you can rest up. Don't forget, we've still got the season finale to film next week, and I want you in tip-top shape."

I'm grateful for the recognition. "Thanks Gary, that'd be great."

I go over to try one more time to be an adult.

"Hey, Lily!" Zoë says brightly.

"Hey. I'm headed out, I just wanted to come over and say good-bye and that it was a pleasure to work with you."

"You're so sweet! I had a blast." Zoë hugs me.

"Good to see you again, Ron."

He turns to me with an impassive look on his face. "Good to see you, too, thanks again for doing such a great job on my apartment."

I take one more stab. "Well, if you're serious about wanting me to do some other rooms for you, let me know. We're about to go on sabbatical for a bit, and I'd be happy to offer you some ideas. You know, free." It's as close to an apology as I can muster, especially in front of all these people.

"That's a very generous offer," he says.

Gary comes up behind me. "Ready to go, love?"

Ron's face darkens again. "See you later, then," he says coldly.

Dave looks at me a little puzzled. "Bye, Lily."

"Bye, Dave."

Gary and I leave the bar and wait for his car to come from the valet. I feel like shit. And I sure wish I knew why my feelings are so hurt.

episode #12

How Lily Got Her Groove Back

Bravo *Wednesday August 23* 8PM–9PM

SWAP/MEET Webster and Liza

On a special two-hour season finale, the *Swap/Meet* crew takes some up-and-coming students under their wings. Two interior design students take on their first actual real-life jobs designing rooms for each other, under the guidance of Lily Allen and Ashleigh Benning. Then they submit themselves to a fashion makeover by the second- and third-place designers from last season's Project Runway, with a little help from Bryan LeClerc and Jou DuFresne. Highlights include an innovative wall treatment and a wardrobe malfunction.

"Hey, you," Gary whispers in my ear.

Oh, crap. "Hey."

I tried to tell Gary that we shouldn't be together. Unfortunately he took that to mean until after the season wrapped. He seems to think that if it appears that we hooked up during the sabbatical then no one will care if we are together when filming resumes in three weeks. And because I'm a coward, I agreed that we should be chaste as babes until the season finale is done. I figure by then I will have figured out how to end it for good. In the meantime, he's making something of a pest of himself.

"Okay, kids, shall we do the design reveal?" Bob calls out. It's Day Zero, since we need to see the designs and then do whatever shopping and prep is necessary before getting started tomorrow, so we've had to add a day to the shoot to accommodate it. We're in a borrowed classroom at Harrington, and I wander over to a drafting table where a nervous Webster is fussing over his design boards. Richard is giving him a pep talk.

"These are great, man! And you've got the best mentor you could hope for over there!" He winks at me as I approach.

"Don't be nervous, Webster," I say in my most soothing voice. "You're going to show me your boards, we'll talk about what is working and if you need to re-envision anything due to our resource and time constraints. Just present to me as if you were presenting at Harrington."

Webster, a tall geeky-looking fellow, takes a deep breath, while Reg fixes his mike pack. Reg gives Bob the thumbs-up and takes his post.

"We're speeding. And, action," Bob yells.

"So, Webster," Richard starts, "show us what you're thinking for Liza's place."

"Well," Webster begins with a slight tremble in his voice, "well, I thought to begin with, I'd do her bedroom. Since she doesn't have a headboard for her bed, I'd like to create one by making some padded upholstered squares and attaching them to the wall behind the bed. I'd like to reuse the bedstands, but update them by covering them with mirror and silver leaf in an art deco style, which I'd like to repeat on the dresser. She lacks storage, so I'd like Curt to build a chest for the foot of the bed, the top of which will get padding and upholstery so that it can serve as a place to sit as well as storage for bed linens and such. And I'd like to pull up the carpet and refinish the wood floor underneath."

"Sweet!" says Richard. "He did a great job, huh Lily?"

"That looks pretty good, Webster," I start. "Nice color story, good recycling of existing furniture. But the flooring project is just too ambitious for a shoot like this. You've got some detail work in this room that will take a lot of time to do properly. She's got a decent low-pile carpet in a neutral color, and it's in good shape. In terms of priority, that falls way down the list. Now, if it had been some really tragic orange shag, I'd have suggested you do a simple paint treatment instead of the leaf on the furniture, and tackle the floor instead."

"See, that's why she's the genius of the operation," Richard pipes in.

"Well, that's what I want to hear," I say, feeding off of Richard's humor. "Now, let's take a look at the rest of your plan."

A little chuffed by the praise, Webster continues, finding that magic place where you just focus on the work and forget about the cameras. "So for the second room, I want to do the living room. I'm thinking of a Venetian plaster treatment on the walls. I think the lines of her sofa and love seat are good, so I'm just going to slipcover them and add some throw pillows. I'd like Curt to do an entertainment center in MDF, and I found this really funky plastic that I want to cover it in." Webster pulls out a small sheet of a thick plastic in a very funky orange swirl pattern.

"Wow. That's pretty cool stuff, Webster. What do you think, Lily?"

"I think it looks fun. How were you planning on attaching it to the MDF?"

"I was thinking a contact cement?" Webster says.

"Do you think that will work?" Richard asks me.

"It might. My larger concern is more the translucency of the material and the color of the MDF coming through. I think we'll be okay, as long as we get a good primer to white out the MDF and provide a blank canvas and be sure that the adhesive dries clear." Webster looks relieved. I hate to burst his bubble. "But, I think that we are going to want to reconsider the Venetian plaster treatment. It's another time-consuming project that we can't afford."

Webster looks crestfallen.

"But," I continue, "I think I can teach you a glazing process that provides the same sort of depth and texture on the walls that you are looking for, but much quicker."

"Cool," Webster says.

"Hey, what's this over here?" Richard points to a swatch on the board. It is a white material with long loops like ragged chenille.

Webster smiles. "That is the material I want to upholster the chairs in and use for the drapes. It's actually bathmats."

Oy. Bless his heart. He's having what is known quietly on site as an Ashleigh moment. The desire to either upholster something or cover a wall or create a window treatment with a totally inappropriate material.

Not having learned her lesson after the taxidermy debacle, Ashleigh has, during the course of this season, covered the wall of a living room with pages torn out of magazines, made drapes for a bedroom out of fake mink, upholstered a pair of chairs in vinyl place mats, and made a pile of throw pillows out of Crown Royal bags. She used lengths of industrial chain instead of drapes for April's living room, the only feature April kept when she redid her house. I need to let Webster know that he isn't going to do something like that on my watch.

"I understand the desire to think outside the box when it comes to design," I begin, "and using interesting materials in unexpected applications is terrific. But we always have to put function over interest when it comes to designing for someone's home. This material, while an interesting texture and look, is probably difficult for use in upholstery. You can see from this swatch that the long loops would be easy to catch on things if you covered chairs with it, not to mention providing a haven for dust in the window treatment. I think we should take a look around at the fabric store and see if we can find a different option."

"I see what you mean." Webster looks a little sheepish. "Thanks, Lily."

We briefly discuss paint choices and some accessory and lighting details, and then we wrap things up and get ready to head out shopping.

"You're really good," Richard says to me, as everyone is gathering their belongings.

"Thanks. So are you."

"Thanks. I wish I could go shopping with you guys. I have to stay and do the design thing with Ashleigh and Liza."

"Poor baby."

"Hey, I'm meeting Curt over at The Brownstone for a beer later, watch the game, grab a bite. I'm frigging addicted to their macaroni and cheese. You wanna come?"

"Sure. What time?" A night out with the guys will hopefully keep my mind off my boy troubles.

"Seven-ish."

"See you there."

"Later, Gator."

I grab my bag and head out just as Ashleigh is heading in.

"Lily," she says icily.

"Ashleigh," I say, faking enthusiasm. "How are you?"

"Fine, dear. And you?"

"Great. I'm excited about this episode. Should be fun helping a new designer take their first leap."

"Well, I'm glad you're excited. This Liza girl is so tedious, she's called me umpteen times already in the last few days." Webster and Liza were given contact sheets in their prep packet and told that they could call us for advice while they were doing their designs. Webster and I had one brief discussion. I'm sure the same is probably true for Ashleigh, who loves to dramatize everything.

"Well, I'm sure it will be fine once we start filming. I've got to head out to shop with Webster. Have a good shoot, and I'll see you at the wrap party!"

She turns on one Tod's heel and without a word begins checking her BlackBerry.

That Ashleigh. She's a piece of work.

And now, my favorite thing. Shopping. Yum.

"How'd it go today?" Naomi asks me.

We're having one of our rare ice cream confessionals. It's a tradition that started when we found out that Hillary had chicken pox and was going to miss Naomi's big tenth birthday party at the Rainbo Skate Rink. Naomi was upset, and called me, and I came over and we took a quart of ice cream out of the fridge with a couple of spoons and hunkered down in her room to talk. It was the first time she and I had really had serious time together without

Hillary, and we realized that it was good to talk about the stuff that we were confused about without the "resident authority on everything" leading the conversation. So, periodically, maybe once or twice a year, always spontaneous and always with ice cream, we have a good heart-to-heart.

Neither of us has ever told Hillary. Not because we have some desire to keep a secret, or because we think Hillary wouldn't understand, but because it is time that just belongs to us. When we were in high school, we moved the party to Zephyr, mostly due to a waiter named Patrick, upon whom we all had mad crushes, and who would serve us sundaes, named after great old movies, with a wink and a smile. We'd wait until he left the table and make our overtly sexual comments with all the bravado of sixteen-year-olds, consumed by desire for something that frightened us to death.

In grad school, we'd go to Margie's for the nostalgia of it, and order the insane sundae in the huge clamshell, which always made us sick to our stomachs. Now, it's all about pints of ice cream in hand, sitting on my couch, and getting down to business. And if you don't think that you can drink wine with ice cream, you've never tasted a really great muscat paired with Edy's Dreamery Cherry Chip Ba Da Bing. Or a tawny port with Ben & Jerry's New York Super Fudge Chunk.

"It's going okay so far," I answer her, around a mouthful of Häagen Dazs Dulce de Leche. "Frankly, I'm just ready for a break. This whole experience of the last four months has been crazy. I mean, what a roller coaster. I'm just glad we have three weeks before we start filming the new season." Because we are based in Chicago, we have a necessary filming moratorium from December thru April because of the weather. With a thirty-show season, we will be filming nonstop one episode a week from September through Thanksgiving, off for six weeks, then on the road in warmer states from mid-January through March, a two-week break, and then back in Chicago for six weeks. If we get picked up for another season next year, we will start filming right away. The thought is both exhilarating and exhausting, and I exhale deeply, exhibiting my emotion, causing Naomi to exhort me to explain myself.

"I mean, I love doing the show, you know. I really do. And I think with Richard on board and getting our first season under our belts, we could really be terrific. But I still have to figure out the best way to try and manage my life and the show."

Naomi licks her spoon thoughtfully. "Well, what are you having the most trouble with, do you think?"

"Well, after my little tough-love session with you guys, I think I'm managing being a good friend again."

"You're doing very well." She pats my hand condescendingly.

"Fuck you." I take another bite. "I dunno. Things just feel a little off, but I don't want to complain, you know? I mean, it sounds so stupid and 'poor me,' and so much like people who are gabillionaires complaining about how hard it is to manage all that money. I mean get real, right?"

"Honey, just because you have a lot of good things in your life, doesn't mean you don't feel sad sometimes. You're entitled to your feelings. Is this about Ron?"

"I'm not sure. But I do know that my mother has a boyfriend and I don't, and I'm happy as hell for her, and I feel crappy about it. I've had more lovers in the last few months than I've had in the last few years, all of whom are total hotties, including a gen-u-ine movie star, but I've never felt less desirable. You have a great partner, even fucking HILLARY has a boyfriend, and I have a really cool job."

"Why didn't you call Ron before the show filmed?"

"I'm not really sure. I think I just didn't want to put myself out there. I mean, when I act like an ass and get rejected, okay, that's understandable and totally deserved. What's being rejected is my behavior. But if I'm open and vulnerable and then I get rejected, what's being rejected is ME, you know?"

"I know, honey. It's scary out there. Ever think of giving it one last shot?"

"What, with Ron? He made it pretty clear that he wasn't interested in that at the wrap party." The look that was in his eyes is pretty well burned into my brain.

"Sweetheart, you never apologized. You need to call him and say that you are sorry. That you are sorry for treating him like some sort of sex toy who was only attractive to you when you were drunk. That you are sorry for waiting so long to apologize for your ridiculous behavior. That you hope that he can forgive you and get to know you as a person. You need to do it, and if he rejects you, he rejects you. But be honest with him. And give him a chance to be a good guy."

"It's scary."

"I know."

I take a big bite of ice cream, and welcome the pain of the brain freeze.

Naomi laughs at me as my face scrunches up.

"Idiot," she says.

"Fuck you," I say.

Then Naomi makes a gesture with her fingers and tongue that can only be described as disgustingly graphic and totally hilarious. This cracks us both up, and blissfully allows the pressure on me to dissipate for the moment.

video diary confession:

"Okay, it's official. I'm fucking exhausted, and you're just going to have to bleep that out! I thought it was tiring to just get my own design work done, but trying to execute someone else's vision without attempting to make it my own, that is really hard. Webster has been great, and I think he'll be an excellent designer, but as with anyone's first real job outside of the classroom, he's a little hesitant, and is overthinking just a bit. But the rooms are coming together, and I think we'll have a long night tonight, but I genuinely believe Liza will be pleased with our results. In the meantime, I'm going to knuckle down and try and get this entertainment center done. The primer should be dry, so I'm going to stick that damn orange plastic stuff to it before my designer gets angry with me. Bye!"

Deep breath. You can do this. The phone is ringing.

"Hey, this is Ron. I'm not home, but leave me a message and I'll holler back. Beep."

"Um, Ron, this is Lily, Lily Allen. I wanted to call and see how your place is doing, and to find out if you were serious about wanting to maybe have me do another room or something for you. So, um, if you want, give me a call back and let me know. Okay, um, bye."

Shit. That was all wrong. And now I have to have a total *Swingers* moment.

"Hey, this is Ron. I'm not home, but leave me a message and I'll holler back. Beep."

"Hey, it's Lily, again. Ignore that previous message. I'm not calling about your place. I'm calling because I owe you an apology that is so far overdue I think I owe you interest on it. And I want to make it in person, so that you know that it is genuine. So if you are willing, I'd like to take you to dinner whenever your schedule allows and try to make amends. So, call and let me know if that is okay with you. Okay. Bye."

There is a knot in my stomach the size of my head. It isn't helped by the knock on my door.

"Hello, love." Gary kisses me hello.

"Hey. What are you doing here?" I can't believe my doorman let him up without calling. That British accent lets him get away with murder.

"Well, I thought, tomorrow is the wrap party for the season, and then we are free as birds, I thought what difference would one night make?"

"Gary, I . . ." I wish I knew how to tell him that we cannot get involved. My phone rings.

"Hello?"

"Lily, its Ron."

"Hey, that was fast."

"I was on the treadmill when you called, but didn't want to stop so close to the end of my workout."

"It's okay, I'm sort of relieved that you are calling me back at all."

Ron laughs. "I guess that's just the kind of slick bastard I am."

This puts me at ease. "So, about my offer . . ."

"I'll take a free meal. Maybe Sunday night?"

"Perfect. *Japonais*?"

"Aren't you fancy? But if you're buying, I'm there."

Thank goodness. "I'm buying."

"Hey, poppet, where is your church key?" Gary calls out from the kitchen, holding a beer from my fridge.

There is a pause. "Sounds like you have company. I'll let you go," Ron says.

"Um, how about seven? For Sunday?"

"Yeah, sure. I'll meet you there."

"Great. Have a good night, then."

"You, too, Lily."

Gary has placed himself happily on my couch, feet on my coffee table, beer in hand.

I've done one brave thing tonight. Now I have to do another.

"Thanks for being a good sport," I say, picking at my duck, which is delicious, but we ordered so many appetizers that I'm really not hungry anymore.

Ron snags the last piece of sushi. "Hey. It's not that big a deal. I mean, I was pissed. I felt like you had no respect for me at all, but I'm glad to know that you aren't an alcoholic, insane, or mean. And I'm really sorry about making that comment on our blind date. I wish you had called me on it then and there, I'm not really known for being terribly suave, and I really thought I was being funny. But I feel terrible that I made you uncomfortable, and I can sort of see why you might have been leery of me. But what's past is past. Anyone can go through an off time, we just obviously met inconveniently."

"I don't know. If you ask Hillary and Naomi, I sabotaged myself with you on purpose."

"Why would you do that?" he asks, chewing.

"Because I'm an idiot? They think I have a fear of relationships. The better a guy is, the more actual potential he has, the more likely I am to run like the wind in the other direction." Okay, that sounded a little more flattering than I had intended. But he doesn't pause.

"I know what you mean. I did that for a long time. You know, trust-fund baby, party boy, dated the girls with the longest legs and the fewest brain cells. Then I fell hard for someone who turned out to be in it for the potential financial security."

"Ouch."

"You're not kidding. I found out because my dad bought her off." He smiles ironically.

"You mean like in the movies? You're not good enough for my boy, how much for you to go away?"

"Sort of like that. Anyway, that sort of put things in perspective for me. I used some of my money to buy a small packaging company that was going out of business, and so far, we're making a go of it. I stopped showing off the fruits of my grandfather's labor and make a practice of living only on what I'm earning with my business. And I started looking for girls with a little more substance."

"Wow. That's really impressive. I wish I had a clearer sense of what my problem is. I also sort of wish I had a trust fund!" I wink at him. He laughs. "Can I ask you something?"

"Sure."

"Our first date, you said something about Dave owing you fifty dollars. What was that about?"

"Dave had been trying to fix me up for years. I'd always call the girls, but then find some reason to not actually go out with them. When he gave me your number he bet me fifty dollars I'd never have the balls to follow through and take you on a date."

Have I mentioned that I am a total moron? "What made you actually ask me out?"

"You could complete a sentence. You seemed like you weren't terribly needy. You made me laugh. It was just the right time for me to let go of some of my bullshit."

"Very clearheaded."

"Years of therapy, m'dear. I'm very in tune with myself." He pauses. "But you seem to have figured it out, right? I mean, your relationship is going well."

Relationship? "My what?"

"Your relationship. I know you aren't supposed to talk about it, but it's okay. Gary told me at the wrap party."

Shit. "What exactly did Gary tell you?"

"That you guys were together. That you were keeping it on the down-low because of the work thing. By the way, you should tell him that he shouldn't use the phrase 'on the down-low.' He sounds like an idiot saying that with that accent."

I laugh. "That's what Curt calls him, the Britiot. And we are not together."

"But I heard him at your apartment the other night."

"So you did. Right before I explained to him in no uncertain terms that we are not, nor were not, nor would ever be, together." I take a deep breath. "Look, I had a brief fling with Gary which was a mistake of enormous proportions. I'm sure that's not much of a surprise to you, since you've done nothing but be a witness to my stupidity since the day we met. But in that weird 'only in the movies' kind of way, it just reinforced that he is not what I want, either in general or specifically."

"So what do you want?" He reaches over to pour more sake in my glass.

"I wish I knew. I know I want marriage, but I don't know if I want children. I know I want someone I trust, someone to be with, but I also know that I want my independence. I seem to know more about what I don't want than what I do want, and I feel like what I want most is another chance with you, but you scare the crap out of me."

"I scare the crap out of you? Not exactly a ringing endorsement of my charms." He raises one eyebrow in a sardonic gesture that makes him even more attractive.

"Do you have any idea how many times I've met you? Probably once a year since I was twelve. You are the guy I've never been able to get. The guy I've had crushes on nearly every time I've ever had a crush. You're always attractive, very smart, very sweet, and never, not once in my life have you ever been interested in me. I've watched you with the pretty girls my whole life, the girls with the great bodies, the A-list girls. And you've always been happy to borrow my homework, or ask my advice, or hang out and watch a movie, even sleep with me if you're drunk enough, bored enough, horny enough, or curious enough.

"But you've never wanted to actually date me. I know that sounds weird. But you're never the guy I get, you're usually the guy that pushes me into the arms of the guy I settle for. The night we spent together, that was familiar territory for me, up to and including ending up feeling like I had made a bad decision to sleep with you so soon.

"When you tried to actually take it to the next step, I panicked. How could I trust you when you have been disappointing me my whole life? Even when I know it isn't actually you, but what you represent to me from my past. I wanted to just run away completely. But I was still a moth to the flame. I can't ever help wanting 'that guy,' so when you came home with me that second night, and then left, it hurt my feelings.

"I thought you couldn't even stay attracted to me for an entire evening. I know I acted like an ass, and none of this is any excuse, and I should probably get some of that there therapy you like so much. I do really like you, and I would love an opportunity to start over with you, but if you're willing to give me that chance,

you have to know that it is really, really a terrifying place for me."
Well, now I've said it.

"Wow." Ron takes a sip of sake. "That was very *Chasing Amy*."

I look at him. He's grinning.

"Schmuck."

He starts to laugh.

"It's not funny! Those are my deepest darkest fears I'm divulging here, mister!" But I'm giggling, too; it was a little, as Bryan would say, *dramatical*.

"I know. It's what makes it so cute."

"You think I'm cute?"

"I think you're insane. And maddening. In a really cute way."
He gets up. "I'll be right back."

He walks away. I take a deep breath. Where the fuck did all that stuff COME FROM, anyway? "I've met you my whole life and you never want me . . ." Who talks like that? He'd be insane not to bolt.

The waiter comes over. "Miss, I'm supposed to tell you that the bill has been taken care of by a fan, and if you'd like to follow me, he'd like to meet you."

Wow. Talk about a perk of being on TV. This dinner was going to cost me a fortune.

"Can you please let my dining companion know when he returns that I will be right back."

"Of course, miss. This way, please."

I follow him through the restaurant to the back bar. I see Ron sitting at a table. He stands up.

"Hi. My name is Ron Schwartz. I'm a big fan of the show, and I just wanted to meet you." What a goofball.

"Hi, Ron. I'm Lily. Thank you for dinner, that was unnecessary, but I'm very grateful."

"It was my pleasure. I was hoping you might join me for a drink?" He gestures to the seat beside him. I look at it and sit. Ron looks me in the eyes. "You know, it's funny, but I feel as if we have met before."

"Nope. I'd remember." He leans forward and kisses my cheek. "Well, then," he says. "I'm glad to meet you."

Lily's Rule #1: Second chances at the really best things in life are rare and extraordinary. Treat them like the little miracles they are.

I lean forward and kiss his cheek. "I'm glad to meet you, too."

where Are They Now?

I've just left the studio, where I was filming my bits for the end-of-season "clip show," a two-hour special with all the highlights of our first glorious season, intercut with some blooper footage, some revisits to old rooms and participants, and interviews with the cast and crew. Hard to be nostalgic about things that are all less than a year old, but it was sort of cool to see which rooms stayed the way we had done them, which had been totally refurbished, and to check in and see what the participants were up to. Especially since everyone else in my life has been up to their own adventures.

Samuel and Birdie are expecting twins in late winter, timed to not interfere with the baseball season.

Mom and Jacob have settled into a quiet routine. He now helps her babysit the cousins as a major part of their social life.

Paul bounced back from his small miscalculation on the intervention show and went on to produce a series that has already been nominated for several awards for documentary programming.

Curt bumped into Zoë (from the Ron episode) having break-fast at Manny's Deli about a month after the shoot and ended up staying for lunch. They've begun talking about moving in to-gether.

Naomi and Alice moved in together, with Hillary's blessing, and seem to be doing very well.

Hillary and Charlie made it through three whole months of dating exclusively before she found enough little quirks about him to make her bail. But Naomi and I have hopes that she is tak-ing baby steps toward being able to sustain a relationship. In the meantime, Chandler is back on Shabbas Goy duty.

Bryan and Jou continue to go to therapy and threaten to break up every fourth session or so. They also now have a second show they have signed on to do for TLC called *Fashion 101*, which will start filming during the *Swap/Meet* winter break.

Ashleigh continues to be a raving bitch, much to the delight of fans and the distress of those of us who have to work with her. *Time Out Chicago* did a feature article on the two of us and dressed us like the Wicked Witch of the West and Glinda for the photo shoot.

Jake got poached by another show and was replaced by a really cool woman named Billie, whom we all love, and who blissfully doesn't try to hit on me.

My dad announced his remarriage to a woman named Julie, who is a golf pro at his club in Florida. She's only seven years older than I am. We haven't met, but if it's her influence that is making my dad actually take the initiative to call me once a week or so, she can't be that bad.

Gary got over me in about thirty seconds, turning his atten-tion to a pharmaceutical rep he met while in his doctor's waiting room. She is frosty, but they seem well suited.

After a three-week break, much of it spent hanging out with Ron, we got the new season under way. It's been going very well, with some really fun episodes, but I'll be ready for those six weeks off we have coming up.

Ron turned out to not be any of those guys I accused him of being, but instead, is just himself. And I like him very much. And he likes me. I'm almost done redecorating his apartment. And he's almost done remodeling me. Who'd have thought that the interior design I needed was THAT interior?

Holy Boyfriend, Batman!

Or as Bob would say, "Really, with the happiness, really?"

Really.

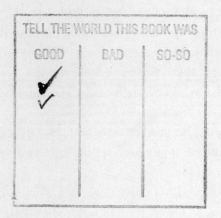